For my amazing godsons, Matthew, Andrew and George.
You've all grown to be wonderful young men and I'm so proud of each and every one of you.
Each one of you is in charge of writing your own life story.
Make sure you write a good one... always be happy and don't let anyone else hold the pen!! xx

1

I'd always promised myself that revenge would be sweet, that it would give me closure and that once I'd taken someone from him, someone he loved, I'd consider myself his equal.

Yet tonight I stand here, knowing how close my moment is. It's a feeling that makes me both excited and anxious with a trepidation that's almost too much — my whole body feels as though it's turned into a huge mixing pot of emotions, all whirling around together, as a million questions form in my mind. Questions I'll never be able to answer.

I stare into the night and imagine the ghost of my young, beautiful sister. She floats before me, gives me a sad, painful yet hopeful smile, with eyes that are now dull and distant. They no longer sparkle, and I watch the vision that circumnavigates my mind as she tries to speak to me — but sadly, I can't hear her. Not any more. Her laugh was lost forever. Her voice a distant memory. And once again, my heart shatters into a million pieces as a sob rises to my throat and, angrily, I swipe at my tears, wish for the years we should have had, for the life that was stolen from us all and with an anger that threatens to erupt from my throat by way of a scream, I try to calm myself, knowing that right here, right now I'm *about to get my revenge and, once I have, our beautiful sister will finally be laid to rest – exactly twenty years to the day after she was murdered.*

Stepping behind the old, rusty fire escape, I use it as a camouflage, pull my jacket tightly around me and give a shudder as I try to get warm but feel the frost bite angrily at my cheeks. I have no choice but to bide my time, to wait impatiently, and like a child I begin to play a game with myself, laugh as the breath leaves my lips, fogging the air with an ephemeral white cloud, one that barely has the chance to dissipate before the next warm breath is released again. I watch it plume from my mouth and disappear into darkness. The chill makes me think of snow, and I roll my eyes towards the powder-grey sky in an attempt to look for the stars, and just for a second, I realise that a strange numbness has clouded my mind, and nothing feels real. It's as though my brain hasn't engaged, hasn't admitted what I'm about to do and with angst my heart constricts like it's held in a vice. My breathing suddenly becomes laboured. Bile burns my throat, and I take several deep inward breaths until the nausea stops and, in its place, I feel a constant internal trembling that refuses to stop.

Concentrating, I try to focus. I think back to the hours, the days, the years I spent studying what he'd done. The people I had no choice but to get close to, the forced friendships, relationships and the enemies I made along the way. Each one a necessary part of the jigsaw, one I've been slotting together for half of my life, learning just a little bit more with each new acquaintance I made. All the time wishing I could fully understand his reasons, or motives. I studied them and him and the calculated way he'd killed each of the women, how he'd arranged them, placed a red silk scarf around their necks, always tied to the left, and then, as a final act of control, the way he'd placed a small chess piece within the folds of the material. Each piece ranging from a pawn to a queen, depending on how valuable he'd thought the kill had been.

His murders had become a regular event. An apparent surge of power that had given him an adrenaline buzz like no other, until the day he made an obvious mistake. A murder that hadn't gone to plan. One that hadn't happened quite the way he'd wanted it to. And in his annoyance, he'd taken my sister's body, and dumped her in an unmarked grave, a place where she'd been cruelly lost to us forever, and I wonder what it was that went wrong, why he couldn't leave her to be found, like he had the others. And what chess piece he'd decided to award her in his final act of power.

Glancing down at my watch, I note the time, the date. The fact that tomorrow, like he does every year, he'll demand an outing. A search of another area. Another day of him pointing to spots, laughing as the dig begins, only to shake his head, and with amusement, he'll point to another area, another spot where the body of my sister might or might not be. And every year, I watch from a distance, wait, and hope that this year will be the year he takes us to her grave, gives us closure for what he did. Rather than leaving her cold and alone where no one can visit, leave her flowers, or whisper a prayer.

Looking up, I take in a deep breath. Try to remember what I need to do. How I need to be. What I need to emulate. When he hears the news, he just has to know it's a sign. He must know I've copied his ways and that she was taken by way of revenge, and repeatedly I go over the steps, one by one, all the time worrying that I'll make mistakes and even though I've killed before, I wonder what will happen if I'm caught. When I'm caught. Which prison I'll be locked in. The thought of small places, locked doors, gates or restrictions of any kind terrifies me and, while I can, I take in huge gulps of cold, sharp air, allow it to hit the back of my throat as the breeze blows down the ginnel to hit me in the face and, while hovering behind the fire escape, I take a moment to free my mind, to look up at the rusty structure, at the way it twists around itself, with metal footplates that are far too old and weak, and casually I lean against it, feel it move and creak beneath my weight.

Hearing a noise, I look to my left, to a door in the wall. It's a door that leads to the village shop. A shop I used to go in and I wonder if old Mr

Wilson still owns it and how he will feel when he finds out that a body has been found, murdered in his alley, and with a wry sense of amusement, I try to imagine him on the local news in the morning, standing in the shop's doorway, with its dirty, unkempt windows, wishing he'd swept the causeway, or created a window display that looked warm and inviting, rather than the way it has always looked with piled-up boxes all standing on top of each other, like a warehouse that sells everything for less than a pound.

Moving my hand to my pocket, I momentarily lose my concentration. Allow my fingers to rub against the pliable texture of the red silk scarf, the smooth ivory of the solid chess piece. A bishop. A stalwart piece for the one woman who stood by him. She'd always remained tall and steadfast to the end, and I laugh at the irony, look up to the sky and realise that my mother would approve of my actions. Finally, she'll get the justice she deserved for the daughter she lost. She's no longer here to see it but as I stare into the cloudless sky, I can still imagine her pale, drawn face, the way she used to rock back and forth in her armchair, or pace up and down the hallway. She'd waited patiently for hours. Then for months that turned into years, hoping her daughter would come home, and with every single second, her heart would break just a little bit more. The happy, vibrant mother I'd once known had quickly disappeared into herself. To a place where every birthday and Christmas was pushed into the background. A place where nothing mattered. Not until my sister was found. And in the end, she sat, broken, withdrawn, without any wish to live or function, in a world where she'd felt it wrong to smile, to be happy or to show that she'd moved on, just in case the world thought that she didn't care. And in her final days, the days when she wished and prayed for death to take her, her whole life had been centred around watching the television, reading newspapers and scouring the internet, searching for clues. She'd been trying to prove that somehow, somewhere, my young, beautiful sister might still be alive. Until eventually, when it no longer seemed feasible, she simply prayed that she'd live from one anniversary to the next, for that day when, once a year, he'd walk free. A day when she'd watch the news with a strange intensity, watching the way he made a huge pretence of looking for her. All the time knowing that the day he found her, the day he gave her back to us, would be the last time he'd ever be allowed any kind of freedom outside of the prison walls.

The sound of a door slamming across the road brings me back to reality and I look up. Study her, the woman I've made it my business to know. She's all legs and stilettos. Her bright copper hair falling casually onto her shoulders, where a Bardot-style top is worn, to reveal a long, pale, slender neck. They're clothes made for someone much younger than she is and, impatiently, I take a step forward and force myself to wait and watch as she places the long leather strap of her handbag over her head, twists it to lie flat across the thin, tight-fitting clothes that would be more suited to a warm summer evening, rather than the chill of winter.

Suddenly, I begin to laugh, an internal giggle that threatens to explode, as I realise how worried she is about losing the bag, about it being taken from her. When in reality, she's about to lose so much more. She just doesn't know it – not yet.

Taking a single deep breath inward, I hold it. I'm almost too terrified to breathe. To move. To do anything that would give me away. Then, swiftly, I pull the scarf from my pocket, twist it around my gloved hands and watch as she foolishly and unknowingly strides towards me...

2

Watching stealthily over the top of her monitor, Lexi Jakes tapped her pen against her teeth, rolled her eyes towards the clock and began counting the seconds, in the hope that the time would pass quickly, that the news she'd been expecting for every minute of that day wouldn't happen. And that, for once, she'd be able leave the office completely unscathed by the past.

Anxiously, she listened to the buzz of the office; every sound infiltrated her mind as she subconsciously listened for any change, any sound that was different to the norm. Which was close to impossible in an office that was never quiet. There was a persistent murmur of voices, of excitement, of men's shoes as they moved heavily across wooden floors, while papers were shuffled, phones rang and reporters shouted between themselves as they constantly threw information from one desk to another.

Surreptitiously, she cast her gaze across the long rows of bench desks, watched the flurry of activity, the way that every desk was covered in files, pens and Post-it notes – all of which were being moved around at speed, like a giant game of dominoes with each of the players trying to take his move at the same time as his opponent. But this wasn't a game; this was real life. It was a place where investigations, features and columns were written. A room full of desks where random stories or articles were picked up, tossed down, approved and dismissed, all in a split second. And more so, it was a place where other people's devastation satisfied the morbid curiosity of others and sold the newspapers of tomorrow.

'I don't want good news,' Simon, the chief, had often said. 'Good news doesn't sell papers. Readers, they have a sick sense of curiosity that simply isn't quelled by a nice little story, so get out there – find me some bad news.'

Picking up her mobile, Lexi began to scroll. She was looking for any mention of her father's name, of the barbaric way he'd killed one woman after the other. Every year, on the date of his last murder, she fully expected to see his name flash up in the news and, as always, she found herself shocked and emotional by everything she read. Yet today, for the first time in twenty years, there was nothing. Which was odd. And strangely, she felt unusually discomfited by its absence. Without thinking, she pulled her chair closer to her desk, flicked through the pages of her diary, checked that she had the right date. Then, through squinted eyes that were almost too afraid to look, she saw the telltale star, the number twenty that she'd scrawled in the margin, took note of the way she'd angrily circled it in red. It was something she'd done for as long as she could remember, an annual reminder of what he'd done. Of how many women he'd killed. The families who still didn't have all the answers and the fact that it was twenty years since the worst day of her life, when she'd watched her father hauled out of her childhood home by a barrage of armed police, who'd all thundered through their house like a hundred elephants, stampeding past her all at once, in the same two minutes.

Desperately, Lexi tried to dissipate the image. Tried to remember what life had been like before that day. What it had been like to have a daddy, rather than the person everyone either hated or described as 'that serial killer', for a father. She rolled her eyes away from her monitor, tried to think of the daddy who'd simply smiled at her, been kind to her and praised her for doing the tiniest, most insignificant thing, and for the first six short years of her life, that's what he'd done. He'd been there, he'd looked after her. And then, as though he'd never existed, he was gone, taken away from her, and locked up like a caged, angry animal with the whole world hating him for what he'd done. A moment in time that had left her with constant flashbacks, visions of him being dragged away, screaming, his face all contorted, and how as they'd dragged him past the room, he'd clung painfully to the door jamb with his eyes fixed on hers.

'Alex, you be a good girl for your mummy and... and don't forget, your daddy loves you. He'll always love you...' he'd shouted arrogantly as, finally, his fingers were prised free, and he was dragged out of the house, leaving her to watch as the police had pushed him unceremoniously into the waiting vehicle.

At the time, she hadn't understood what was really happening or why they were taking him away and, fearfully, she'd stared into his eyes, momentarily begged for the truth, for answers to the questions she couldn't bear to ask. Little did she know that the only time she'd see him after that day would be the once a year, when, without exception, he'd appear on the local news and there'd be pictures of his face spread all over the television, or the internet, for all the world to repeatedly judge and jeer over.

Which was why today, on the twentieth anniversary of his twentieth kill, she'd fully expected the press to mention him, to make a big effort, to talk about what he'd done, the women he'd killed, concentrating as they normally did on Melissa Jameson, the one woman whose body had never been found – but, unusually, there was nothing.

Hearing a last-minute flood of phone calls vibrate through the office, it became more than obvious that the final sprint to the finish line had begun. That within the next hour or two, the paper would go to print and for the few hours that followed, a sense of achievement would circulate the office. It was always a time of informal celebration that happened just once a week, before everyone sprung into action and the planning of the next week's edition would begin.

Glancing at her column, she read and reread the article she'd written. She knew that something was missing but couldn't work out what. Gave a half-smile at the headline, 'Million Pound House Draw!' It was a prize draw like no other and for the price of a pound, a luxury house could be won. It was her job to create a hard-hitting campaign. Her job to ensure it sold tickets. For the fourth time that hour, she rearranged the photographs, chose an internal one with soft amber lighting that seeped warmly from the image. 'That's the one,' she whispered as she flicked through all the other pictures, admiring them.

Rolling her eyes enviously towards the desks opposite, she watched the investigative journalists, the way they worked, answered phones, and knew that if anything new came in, it would land on their desks first. They'd get the tip-off. And initially, it looked as though they were winding things up, leaning back in their chairs, watching the clock. But then Lexi noticed a shift in their mood. It was as though someone had plugged them in, and they began to scurry around at speed, with an enthusiasm that bounced between them. And, with interest, she sat forward in her chair, felt the nervous adrenaline surge through her until it filled her mind. With her hands pressed tightly together, she steepled her fingers, held her breath and watched as one reporter after the other took on a new and excited look. And even to an outsider, to someone who couldn't read the signs, it would have been more than obvious that something new had come in – and she watched as a tidal wave of emotion surged through them all.

'I'm just waiting for some more detail,' Simon yelled out, holding a phone to his ear, a finger in the air. Immediately, he furrowed his brow and dropped his gaze. The tension that crossed his face became palpable. His normally pink, flustered face had turned ashen, grey, and a hand went to his scalp, where he clenched his fist angrily.

'Come on, boss, what is it?' one of the younger, more impatient reporters shouted as two others hushed him, and another held a hand up, palm out, desperate to hear what was happening.

'It's Johnny. He's been sitting on the story all day... just waiting for a name...' Simon announced. Then he stopped, sighed, looked up excitedly, and with eyes as big as saucers, he caught her gaze.

'There's no good news.' Lexi played the words over and over in her mind as nervously she took in a deep breath, heard the office fall into silence. It was a room now heavy with anticipation. All reporters had turned at once. All were waiting for Simon to put the phone down, for the news to break.

Nodding and with his lips pressed tightly together, he threw his phone at the desk. 'Jesus Christ.' He brought his hands up, waved them around. 'OK, folks. This is big. We've got a copycat. One body, but without a doubt he's emulating the strangler Peter Graves. Even down to the red silk scarf and the random chess piece that was left at the scene.' He paused, pulled his black-framed glasses from his face, threw them at the desk to join the phone. 'We're still waiting for a name. Police have got it shrouded in bloody secrecy and Johnny – well, he's just sitting there hoping they'll release it in the next few minutes.' He paused, swallowed. 'Get ready, folks. If the story comes in, it'll take the cover and it's gonna need editing and proofreading. Everyone else... let's start shuffling things around. Drop a few articles back – make me some space.'

As she heard the word 'copycat', Lexi felt the floor move beneath her. Her fingernails sank into the edge of her desk, her fingers went white with the pressure, her breathing became erratic and the walls began to close in around her. It was a claustrophobic reaction, in an office where she was the only woman, surrounded by at least twenty-five men. The need to move became overwhelming. The need to leave the room, to make an escape, suddenly essential. Her eyes darted from desk to desk and even though every part of her wanted to walk out of the room, she couldn't stand, couldn't move. Knew that to run would cause them all to talk, and a hundred different comments would be fired around the office, all at once. Comments she didn't want or need to hear.

'Red scarf – why red? Don't they sell other colours?'

'Leaving a chess piece seems a bit odd, don't you think? Wonder what he left? A pawn, or a queen... Peter Graves was quite fond of pawns, wasn't he?'

'Psychopath... there's only one place for men like that; he should have been thrown down a hole and shot.'

The words infiltrated her mind with the force of a hurricane, making her stare anxiously at her desk, and, determined not to show any emotion, she kept her eyes fixed on the two identical monitors. Watched as the screens flashed intermittently, her inbox jumped repeatedly in one corner. One story after the other, dropping in at speed.

'Peter Graves...' She whispered the words in a daze, bit down on her lip, then closed her eyes as tightly as she could, saw the father she remembered. He'd been the very same daddy who'd tucked her into bed each night, before disappearing into the darkness to viciously kill someone else's daughter. 'How could he have done that?'

At the time, she'd been young, shielded from the truth, and had found herself piecing snippets of information together, watching the late-night news during the long nights while her mother had been working and when she'd been left in the house alone. Eventually, she'd come to realise exactly who her daddy was, and what he'd done. It was probably where her inquisitive nature had begun, the lead-up to her becoming a journalist. And now, even though she was submerged in this world, she dreaded the sound of his name. Cringed at any mention of him in the news, in the headlines or, like this, associated with another killer.

With the room spinning around her, she pressed her fingers to her ears, tried to block out the endless noise, the constant mentions of his name. Each time she heard it, it was like a long-lost memory coming back to haunt her, to poke her in the ribs, or to stab at her repeatedly, like the point of a blade pressing against her skin, each time a little harder, a little deeper until she could imagine it penetrating her lungs, until eventually she could barely breathe, paralysing her just a little bit more.

'You chose this industry. You wanted to be close to the news and... you knew his name would appear,' she mouthed, 'and it's only an article, just like the rest.' She shrank back in her chair, knew that this wasn't like the rest and wished wholeheartedly for the floor to open, for a giant hole to swallow her, and she began taking deep inward breaths, while all the time trying to convince herself that all was OK.

Suddenly, she wished she were home. She wanted nothing more than to be curled up in Nate's strong, loving arms with both their daughter, Isla, and their new kitten, Agatha, cuddled up between them. It was an image she held in her mind, until she furrowed her brow, thought of Nate, of the way he'd changed, the way he was acting differently, more secretive. Which shouldn't be a problem, not after all the secrets she'd kept from him. But for some reason, it was. She was scared for the future, for the way life could turn out and, desperately, she picked up her mobile, flicked the screen, fixed her gaze on her screen saver, on the picture of both Nate and Isla. Sighing, she took in the mischievous smile that crossed his face, the way they looked at one another, their noses touching, and Isla's tiny two-year-old hands clasped to each side of Nate's face with her lips puckered in a loving daddy's-girl gesture.

Blowing out a long, deep breath, she pulled the keyboard towards her, tried to focus and, with her fingers poised, she tentatively clicked on her mouse, went to open Johnny's article that was now flashing repeatedly in the corner of every screen in the building.

Urgent Comms. Cover Story – Copycat murder in picturesque Yorkshire Village.

With her heartbeat pounding audibly in her ears, Lexi noticed the room go silent. A telltale sign that everyone else had clicked on the article too and, without hesitation, she opened the attachment, needed to know what it said, sat as far away from the monitor as she could and, with her arms wrapped around herself in a hug, she rocked herself back and forth as she began to read.

Scarborough Police have released the name of the woman found murdered in Hunmanby village during the early hours of Monday 9 December 2021 as being Jessica Graves, long-standing and devoted wife of renowned serial killer Peter Graves.

Confused, Lexi jumped to her feet. Shook her head repeatedly, stared at the name, read it over and over again. Felt sure she'd read it wrong. Then, with an overwhelming surge of emotion, she reached unsteadily for the chair, felt it slide from beneath her and, with an agonising thud, she landed heavily on the solid oak floor, heard a long, dramatic sob expel itself from somewhere within her and closed her eyes as the embarrassment sprung to them in the form of hot, scalding tears.

'Sorry, I...' She began to claw at the furniture. 'I'm fine. Sorry. I just...' Jumping up, she held a hand to her chest, concentrated on the continuous, violent booming of her heart, forced herself to stare at the screen and, with her lunch threatening to expel itself, she sat back down, inched her chair as far away from the monitor as she could get and awkwardly felt it bump noisily into the wall behind her.

With a hand to each side of her face, she pressed them as tightly as she could against her cheeks. 'It can't be you... It just can't be...' she whispered, felt the tears swim in front of her eyes as she stared at the woman's face on the screen, the distant memory of the mother she'd been and, slowly, she shook her head, closed her eyes and prayed that, once she opened them, the picture would have faded... that the woman looking back at her would be someone else's mother.

3

Stepping out of the office and into the vast communal corridor of the Georgian office block, Lexi suddenly felt alone, vulnerable, fearful, and she peered anxiously over the balustrade and into the hallway below as a keen icy draft of wind blew upwards. With one hand on the oak banister, smooth with years of use, she crouched down to sit on one of the stone steps, took a moment to listen, to breathe.

With tentative fingers she began to trace the shape of twisted metal balusters, and, needing something to occupy her mind, she admired their shape and craftmanship. Noticed how each one had individually been cast with just enough space between them that she could see the corridor below, the second flight of steps and the jet-black panelled door that led to the pavement.

Listening cautiously, Lexi fully expected the solid oak door to be open, for someone to be standing there, looking up at her from below, waiting for her with a red silk scarf in their hands and, with a nervous expectation, she stared at the door, waited until it eventually swung open, and the sound of a woman chatting loudly on her phone echoed through the air, leaving the wooden door to bang loudly behind her. Closing her eyes, Lexi listened to the voice, heard it slowly diminish and then it was as though it were never there, as it disappeared down one of the long, distant corridors below.

With her nerves already on edge, every sound, every movement, felt exaggerated. After reading the rest of the article, Lexi's mind had begun twisting and turning with never-ending questions. Each one flying past her, like tangents spinning past at speed. And with her arms protectively wrapped around her knees, she tried to comprehend what had just happened. Her birth mother was dead. Someone had cruelly taken her life in the very same way her father had killed others on so many occasions before, and no amount of wishing, or wanting, would bring her back. While biting down on her lip, she tried to decide if she'd want her back, if she'd have even wanted to see her and, more so, if she were wrong to feel or think in that way. She hadn't seen her for almost twenty years, not since she'd been a very young child and, even then, she couldn't ever remember a time when she'd asked for her, cried for her, or really wanted to see her. Not even after she'd become a mother herself, which was a thought that saddened her to the core. Especially when she thought of her own daughter, couldn't imagine a single day without Isla, and it hurt her deep inside to know how easily her own mother had walked away, given her up, hadn't challenged the courts to get her back. Deep down, she tried to imagine walking past her mother in the street, wondered whether she'd have recognised her and what she'd have said to her if she had. With a bitter ache that seeped out from her core, she wondered how much her own mother had thought of her over the years and whether or not she'd ever regretted what she'd done.

Slowly, Lexi brought herself back to the present. She wiped her eyes on the back of her hand, rummaged in her bag for a tissue, desperately wanted to close her eyes, but couldn't. Not for more than a second. The fear was too great. The danger too real. Over and over, she imagined that red silk scarf, that chess piece. The way it had been left twisted within the folds of the scarf and the fact that it had only been a bishop, not a queen... It was a thought that caused a continuous hum to take over her thoughts, like the engine of a car, one that was going much too fast, and, with the metaphoric turn of the car's wheel, another question would arise and the only conclusion she'd been able to come to was that the killer still had his sights firmly set on someone else – that there was a target he considered more worthy of the queen. And if this were a revenge attack, like most of the news channels were saying, the only two people left that Peter Graves might actually care about were either herself or Isla. It was a thought that made her mind race with fear; an image of Isla sprung to her mind. 'He's never met her, he doesn't know she exists,' she whispered as the bile burned her throat. Anxiety spun around her mind. 'No one knows who she is.' She blurted the words out loud, purposely twisted her hand around the baluster, counted to ten, tried to control her breathing. *Don't forget. No one can hurt you. Not here, not now. They don't know who you are. You have a new life, a new identity. A new name. You're safe.* They were the words she'd been told as a child, words she'd believed and, without doubt, she'd quickly become Lexi Jakes, daughter of Maggie and Stanley Jakes. Her old identity, Alexandra Graves, had died with her past and just a few chosen people knew who she really was, that she'd been the daughter of a serial killer, of Peter Graves. And those few people were people she trusted, people she'd grown up with.

Rolling her eyes, she looked up at the skylight, a pitched gable design that, during the day, allowed light to flood the hallway. Yet tonight, not even a star could be seen. The glass was shrouded in an unusual darkness, where clouds filled the sky and rain fell in torrents with a sound so loud it almost felt hypnotic. Slowly, she took the steps through the coldness of the hallway and towards the ground floor, where dust and discarded rubbish had blown in from the pavement outside.

Standing in the shelter of the doorway and looking out at Whitby Harbour, Lexi realised that the rain was coming down much faster than she'd thought and even though she'd feigned illness to leave work early, the surrounding darkness made it feel so much later than it actually was and, for once, she wished for the streets to be full. For the crowds of tourists to be walking up and down, all with their bags of chips in hand, laughing as the seagulls swooped in search of a dinner. The town normally had a crowd so thick it was easy to become lost within it. Yet tonight, the weather had driven everyone indoors. The streets that surrounded the harbour were almost bare of pedestrians, all apart from the odd one or two who ran past with umbrellas held close to their bodies, their faces hidden, making each one dark, mysterious and threatening.

Running with her bag held closely to her, Lexi made her way along the rough pavements towards Whitby Swing Bridge, and cursed that she'd chosen her annual parking pass by cost rather than locality. It had been a decision that now left her with a long walk to the other side of town, up the 199 stone steps and along a long, dark, dimly lit path that led past the abbey. A walk she had to do every single day after work, no matter how late she finished.

Think how fit you'll get, she'd thought on the day she'd bought the pass. *Think how good your ass will look when you've climbed those steps a few times a week*. But that had been one day in the summer. A day when walking, running up and down the steps and seeing all the tourists had been more like fun. Not on a day like today, when she'd left her brolly neatly stowed in her glovebox, along with her gloves and emergency sweets. 'Some days, Lex, you make terrible decisions, don't you?' she chastised herself, while continuously searching the way ahead, looking back over her shoulder, making sure she was still alone.

Running across the bridge, she pulled her coat tightly around her. Then, stealthily, she took a left on to Church Street, where the shops were brightly lit, music came from within and windows were full of brightly coloured Christmas decorations, lights, Santas and nostalgia by the bucketload. It was a sight that made her think of home, of how excited Isla would be on Christmas morning. Especially if Lexi could put the past behind her, put a tree up in the house and make it special, just for once. This year, she was determined to enjoy it, to make it into a happy time rather than a memory she'd rather forget. This year, they would have a real family Christmas, just the three of them together for four whole days.

While still making her way through the streets, she thought of Nate, and of how he'd been acting. Of how many extra hours he'd worked. The stress he'd been under. 'It's a big job, worth a lot of money,' he'd constantly told her. But she could see the worry in his eyes, knew that it was a job that could easily go wrong, right up to when the site shut down, and, until the job was done, he couldn't stop, couldn't relax. Lexi was determined that this year, once he'd left the job behind for the Christmas period, they were going to spend every moment together and get their relationship back on track, just as she wanted – as a family.

'Hey, Lexi, you want a cuppa? I'll put the kettle on,' her friend Abigail shouted from the doorway of the tea rooms. 'It's been an age since we sat down for a chat.' She stood with the door open, mop in hand and, for a split second, Lexi pondered the thought, saw the welcoming lights beyond, the smell of fresh baking seeping out from the kitchens within.

'Not tonight, Abby,' Lexi shouted. 'I need to get dry, take a shower. Promised myself a night in front of the fire and, the way I feel, the sooner I get there the better.' Giving a hurried wave, Lexi felt the surge of water run down her collar, knew that if she'd jumped in the sea she couldn't have got much wetter, then cringed as she looked up the 199 steps, saw water cascading towards her in torrents, a mini waterfall that was fast threatening to turn into Niagara Falls as the rain spilled over the edges and onto the path below.

Wiping the water from her eyes, she looked over her shoulder at a narrow, empty street. Couldn't decide whether she should make a dash for the car, climb the slippery stone steps or go back to the tea rooms, to where Abigail would make her a welcoming pot of tea, break out the biscuits and fold her coat round the radiator in the hope it would dry. At least then she could sit and wait for the rain to stop, and she would normally have done so, but the storm in her mind continued to brew and, for her, getting home was the only viable option.

'You OK, love?' A man's voice came from behind her, making her jump. Her skin bristled and she turned to the street that just a few seconds ago had been empty, saw the man running towards her. He was approaching at speed, his head down, umbrella up. 'I'm going up there. You know, if you want to share?' He kindly held the umbrella out, smiled, offered her the shelter then raised his gaze to look up at the steps. 'Wow, that's coming down fast.' He stood by her side, much closer than she'd have liked, his eyes following the stream of water that not only gushed towards them but also over the step edges, making the journey up look just a little more than hazardous. 'I tend to climb these steps every day, but I've never seen it this bad before, have you?' he asked in an obvious attempt at making conversation. A conversation Lexi didn't want or need and, resenting the intrusion, she nervously took a step back, checked the road behind him and allowed her eyes to dart from one shop doorway to the other. Tried to think of a reason, any reason to go inside.

'I'm fine but thank you.' She paused, did her best to stay polite while fearfully pulling her hands out of her pockets. 'I do appreciate the offer... but...' Nervously, she took another step to one side, curled her fists as she did. Hoping he'd walk on past, she waited. When he didn't move, she looked him up and down, then pushed her way past, began to climb the steps one at a time. Each step was slippery, treacherous, yet with the determination of a mountain climber, she held on to the metal rail as tightly as she could, felt herself tremble as ice-cold water tumbled up and over her shoes.

'Seriously, get under the brolly. I really don't mind.' The man's voice came from beside her. He matched her step for step; once again he was so close that Lexi stopped in her tracks to stare angrily at the floor.

'I said I was fine,' she snapped. Nervously, she looked over her shoulder, wished she'd waited for one of her work colleagues, felt sure that one of them would have eventually been heading this way. But in her haste to leave and to be alone with her thoughts, she'd simply run from the office, knowing that if she walked with someone, she'd have to chat to them, explain her sudden mystery illness and, knowing how inquisitive journalists were, she'd have to answer so many more questions than she'd have liked. Besides, they'd have wanted to go over and over the new developments, dissect the story and, unbeknown to any one of them, they'd have openly chatted to her about how someone had emulated her father's murders... how this time, they'd killed her mother and of how the police had described it as a possible act of revenge, potentially the first of many. A thought she really didn't want to consider.

Taking a step back downwards, Lexi weighed up her options. Watched through the shadows as the man pressed his lips tightly together in what looked like a sly and menacing smile, before once again holding the umbrella towards her. 'Hate to see a beautiful young woman getting drenched. Especially round here, the land of Dracula.' He pointed upwards. 'Plus, it's pretty dark up there at this time of year – you wouldn't want to be by yourself, now, would you?'

'Look,' she snapped, 'I don't need a damn babysitter and before you ask again, I'm quite happy getting drenched.' She stood her ground, lifted her hands, held them up defensively in front of her, gripped her car keys tightly, allowing just one of them to poke out between her knuckles. 'Now if you don't mind, I'd like to get to the top of these steps. Alone.' Glaring, she saw the look on his face, the way his mouth dropped down at the sides, his bottom lip protruding like that of a sensitive child. Then he fixed his jaw and set off towards the car park.

4

I stand, hidden by a noticeboard at the entrance of the church of St Mary the Virgin. And, knowing that you will, I wait for you to run past, before moving forward to stand behind one of the stone pillars, where I know I'm shielded from your view.

I watch you climb into what you think is the safety of your car, and I laugh as I take a step forward. Slowly, I make my way between the other vehicles until I'm just inches away from your passenger-side door. Laughing, I dare myself to touch it, to put my fingers on the handle, to open it, for you to know I'm here. But instead, I watch over your shoulder, see the look on your face as you sit there, wiping the rain from your face while over-revving the engine. And suddenly I smile, realise how easily you could become my next victim.

Stepping backwards and into the shadows, I pick up my phone, search for news and feel a surge of adrenaline as the press release appears. It's the headline I've been waiting for and, jubilantly, I congratulate myself with a twisted smile, knowing that I did everything right. That the press has linked my killing with his, and that my efforts, my years of planning didn't go to waste, and with a hand pressed tightly over my mouth, I imagine him being told. Of the words they use. Of that moment *when he realises that she's finally been taken from him, just as he took my sister from me.*

Fixing my eyes on your car, on your number plate, I wonder if you have any idea that you're on my list and, mentally, I make a note to tell you why, to let you know what your daddy did. Whom he killed, and how it affected my life and how on that very day I lost everyone. Nothing was ever the same; my mother changed. It was as though someone had flicked a light switch within her. She never looked at me or my younger sibling the same, and I presume she was scared that we too could be taken. But that didn't explain the way she withdrew, faded into herself and, year by year, how her mind disappeared to a place where my sister still lived, a place where she still hugged and loved all of her children in equal measure, rather than having just enough love and energy for the daughter she'd lost.

Hovering in one corner of the car park, I realise how many times I've stood here, watching you. I've paid attention to where you park, and I've concluded that you always park within two or three spaces of where you are today. An act that tells me you always arrive early, while the car park's still quite empty. Which makes you a creature of habit. Someone who likes continuity. Someone who's cleverly hidden themselves from the world for so many years; you've learned how to blend in without being noticed.

And even though you think you're invisible, it wasn't hard to find you. Everyone has a past, people they've trusted with their secrets, and you, you think you've hidden your past, erased it from history. But to do that you'd have to delete everyone you've ever spoken to, trusted and cared about. And even though you've put the past behind you, moved on with your life, others haven't.

I nod decisively as your tail lights drive away from me. I no longer hold my hand to my mouth or supress my laughter. Now, I allow myself to laugh out loud, a full-on hysterical outburst. One that sees me holding my sides and looking up at the sky as the wind blows my hair and the rain lands heavily on my face. I stand there waiting, hoping you'll come back, but knowing you won't and, in my frustration, I begin planning your murder. The anticipation and build-up will be just as much fun as killing you and I take pleasure in the fact that, once again, I'll cause him pain, I'll take away someone he loves, until he can no longer sleep, no longer think. He'll be all alone and wondering who will be taken next, how long it will be before someone comes for him. And with these thoughts spinning through his mind, while locked inside, there will be nothing he can do about it but wait.

Turning, I head along the path and towards the slippery stone steps that lead back into the town. For a moment, I stand at the top of the cliff and look at the sea, at the waves that roll dramatically towards the harbour gates. Each one thundering forward to crash against the harbour wall. And I wonder if you should die here, on a night like tonight, a night when your body would be dragged out into the depths of the sea. It's a thought I like and I decide that the sea should play a part, but not this sea, not here. Having a death with no body is wrong; they have to know I took your life. And with a half-smile, I suddenly realise what I need to do, where the killing should happen. It's the perfect place. A place I know you'll run to. A place where you'll think you're safe, when, ironically, it's the one place where killing you will be more than easy.

5

Slamming the door behind her, Lexi flicked on the hallway light, immediately tapped the alarm code into the system and, as though in slow motion, turned to systematically check and recheck each of the deadlocks in turn, before stepping towards the stairs and slumping against the oak balustrade, where she slid down the wooden structure to land in a heap on the bottom step with her shoulders dropping forward.

With a sigh of relief, she kicked off her rain-soaked shoes, dropped her coat onto the step behind her and ran a cold hand through the copper tendrils of her wet shoulder-length hair.

Sitting there, a relentless internal shuddering began. It shook every inch of her body with a force so powerful, she wrapped her own arms around her knees to calm herself. She couldn't move and stared into space, until her gaze landed on her handbag that she'd simply abandoned by the door, the most recent letter she'd written to her mother, now wet from the rain, poking out from within. It was a letter she always wrote, one a year, which was carried around in her handbag before she resigned herself to the fact that, like all the others, it would never be posted.

'I... I'd written to you. I... I was going to find you. I was going to tell you how much I'd needed you after he was gone, after he'd been arrested. How I'd wished for you to be there and how often I'd walked through that dark, cold house, looking for you, for a mother who was never there, a mother who chose to leave me home alone.' She squeezed her eyes together for a moment, felt the tears burn her cheeks. 'Do you know how that made me feel... how cruel that was?' Swallowing down the tears, she rocked back and forth, felt nothing but the cold, and the fear. 'And now I have questions – questions I need to ask, questions I should have asked twenty years ago but couldn't and you... you were the only one who could have given me all the answers.' Angrily, she picked up the bag, pulled the letter from inside and, while using the wall for support, she held the envelope between her fingers, stared at the name and address that was clearly printed on the front. The letter inside was a list of questions that would never be asked. Answers that would never be given.

Instinctively, she folded the letter, pushed it into her pocket, hid it from view and, with purpose, she crawled up the stairs, while all the time rolling her fingers, twisting them painfully together until they formed tight, unyielding fists. Her first line of defence. The only way she knew how to prepare herself for a battle she couldn't see, couldn't win and didn't understand.

Every part of her ached for a woman she used to know, for the caring, loving mother she should have had. And now she had no idea how she should act, or even how she should feel and, automatically, she went into her bedroom, kneeled beside the divan, pulled open the drawer in its side. Digging through the layers of jumpers, she carefully moved one after the other until her fingers felt the edge of a box. A small box, just six inches across. A box filled with letters. Ones she'd written to her mother. Each one had the same questions. All asked year after year, repeatedly.

'Why, why didn't you love me? Why didn't you protect me? Why didn't you save me from what was to come? It was cruel, the way you left me alone in that house, night after night. Yet still you did it.' Whispering, she dragged the letter from her pocket, ran a shaking finger across the envelope, and even though it was still damp from the rain, she placed it on the floor and tipped out the others beside it.

She'd written twenty in total. One every year since he was arrested, since she'd been six years old, something her foster mother, Maggie, had suggested. 'It's a way of venting your anger, my lovely. A way of saying all the things you can't bring yourself to voice,' Maggie had said with a hand on her heart. And even though Lexi had begun writing that very same day, ironically, none of the letters had ever been posted; all had been kept, stored in the tin. All waiting for a day when she felt strong enough to post them, in the knowledge that the moment she did, she'd have exposed who she was now and where she was living, and, more so, it would have given Jessica Graves, the woman she'd once called Mum, the opportunity to come back into her life, to hurt and neglect her – all over again.

As she closed the box, the knowledge hit her that she'd never write another and as she pushed the tin back into its hiding place, scalding-hot tears began to fill her eyes and, with a determination she didn't know she had, she bit down on her lip, took slow, deep breaths, and stopped them from falling.

Standing up, Lexi checked her watch, pulled the dark blue voile to one side and, inquisitively, she looked through the window and beyond the trees that lined the street, wishing and hoping for Isla to be climbing out of the car, holding tightly to Nate's hand and skipping beside him as they walked towards their home, where she'd be safe and away from a cruel world that Lexi hoped her daughter would never have a reason to learn about.

'Hey, Agatha.' Her fingers lovingly reached out to stroke the smoky-grey kitten who'd suddenly appeared in the room and sauntered across the bed towards where Lexi stood by the window. Rubbing against Lexi's hand, she gave off a low, gentle purr of welcome as she flopped onto her side, her paws outstretched, clawing repeatedly at the air, vying for attention. It was a sight that made Lexi smile. A small act of love that gave her just a little hope for the future. 'Did you have a good day? I bet you did, didn't you?' she asked as she gently swept her hand from head to tail. 'Where's Nate? Eh? He's late, isn't he?' She smiled as the questions fell from her mouth. It wasn't often she beat him home, and, after taking another look through the window, she wished he were here.

Giving an involuntary shudder, Lexi lifted a hand to her hair, felt the wetness beneath, felt momentarily thankful for the peace, for being alone. She knew she needed the time to compose herself, to hide the happenings of the day deep within her, and had every intention of taking that promised shower, of warming herself up, before the house was once again filled with noise and laughter. Laughter she'd have no choice but to join in with, especially if she wanted to continue the façade, to hide who she really was, even from those closest to her.

As she began to undress, Lexi smiled at the way Agatha followed her around the room, jumped on and off the bed, prowled protectively back and forth, giving her the occasional suspicious glance as though waiting for her to do something wrong.

'What's up with you today?' Looking around the room, she tried to work out why Agatha was pacing, rather than taking the opportunity to curl up in her favourite place on Isla's pillow. Dismissively, she shook her head, once again checked the time, and skimmed a comforting hand over the kitten's coat, before removing the rest of her clothes and dropping them in a pile at the bottom of the bed. Agatha immediately made a valiant effort of pouncing on the discarded underwear, followed by the abrupt realisation that the clothes held no interest whatsoever and, with an incensed thrust of her tail high up and into the air, she gave Lexi a look of indignant disgust, before ambling out of the door and down the stairs in search of something more interesting to entertain her.

Walking from bedroom to bathroom, Lexi pulled open the shower door, turned on the water and waited for it to warm. Then with an audible moan of satisfaction she stepped under its flow, allowed it to hit her directly in the face and for just a few seconds, she held her breath and closed her eyes. While turning in and out of the spray, she ran her hands almost seductively through her hair, massaged the almond oil shampoo into her scalp. Once finished, she stood with rivulets of water running over her shoulders and down her back, all the time hoping that somehow the heat would rinse away the stress and trauma of the day and that, once she stepped out of the shower, her life would have returned to normal, and her mother would still be alive and in a position to read all of the letters and answer every one of her questions.

With her hair wrapped in a towel and her body draped in a long satin dressing gown, Lexi padded down the stairs and into the kitchen. With the acrid taste of bile still in her mouth, she reached for the fridge and looked inside, squinted as its light illuminated the dark room behind her.

'OK, so, we have wine, eggs and olives. Tremendous.' Annoyed with herself for not remembering to call at the shops, a job she'd been supposed to do on the way home, she lifted the jar down from the top shelf, sniffed at the contents and pulled a face. 'OK, maybe not the olives, which leaves the eggs and the wine. Unless there's something in the freezer.' Opening the door, she peered in, spotted the box of fish fingers, knew they were Isla's favourites. Along with the sliced bread, she quickly dragged them from within and laid them out on the side. Then, without further thought, she pulled the wine from the fridge, tipped the remnants into a glass, realised how little was left and shook the bottle in disgust. 'How did that get so empty?' she whispered as she took a moment to take in the deep aroma of both apricot and lemons, before quickly knocking back the few millimetres of clear white fluid in one.

With her eyes resting on the kettle, she considered boiling it, allowed her fingers to hover over the switch, felt her mind accelerate and, with unsteady legs, she shook her head, made her way through the house and straight to the settee, where exhaustion took over and she sat back. She listened to the sound of the clock ticking in the hallway and, with her eyes fixed on the front door, she watched it, waited for it to open, hoped that Nate would walk in, her baby girl close behind him.

Feeling her breathing slow, Lexi curled her body into a tight ball, wrapped her arms tightly around herself in a hug and took slow, calming breaths as her eyes began to close in a feeling that was both pleasant and overwhelming all at once.

6

'Hey, what's going on?' Nate's Irish lilt disturbed her sleep. His words drifted through her mind, made her turn and gravitate towards him. Reaching out, she grabbed at his hand. Felt a sense of relief as the soft, warm pressure of his lips pressed against her forehead, and she smiled seductively as her hand went out to touch his face, but grasped at the air and recoiled quickly as she heard his footsteps retreat towards the kitchen.

'Jesus, Lex. You didn't go drinking a whole bottle again, now, did you?'

Hearing the annoyance in his voice, the way he tutted loudly and then the sound of the glass bottle rattling to the bottom of the recycling bin filled her with dread. Sitting forward, she held a hand to her chest, where her dressing gown had splayed open and, quickly, she pulled at the material, readjusted the belt.

Dragging the damp towel from her hair, she rubbed at her scalp. Wished she'd taken the time to dry it properly. 'Nate. There was just a drop left in the bottle, honest. I was tired, I... I... didn't feel too well.' She didn't know how to explain and the events of the day came rushing back, the pain, the disorientation, and grief hit her like a tidal wave all over again, and she found herself gasping, pulling air into her lungs, closing her eyes and silently chastising herself for having slept at a time when she should have been composing herself, getting herself ready to talk about her day, and preparing herself so she'd be able to answer any question without emotion, as though talking about someone else's mother. Someone else's pain.

'Where... where's Isla?' She peeled open an eye, then the other to see a pair of boots stamp towards her, where they stood in the doorway, still covered in mud. Scowling, she manoeuvred her body, waited for Nate to make a further comment as he pulled off his hi-vis bomber jacket and threw it on the floor right next to the door. 'Nate... where is she?' Without comment, she watched the boots disappear back towards the kitchen, tried to work out what he was doing, heard nothing but the ticking of the hallway clock, an unnatural silence causing another wave of panic to heave itself through her. 'Isla, Isla? Come to Mummy.'

'She isn't here,' he finally answered. 'She's at me ma's, was having a good time baking some mince pies and stuff, so I let them be. Ma says she'll keep her for the night, give her a bath and put her to bed.'

Sitting up, Lexi twisted. She could hear water running, the kettle being filled, the way Nate angrily slammed it down on the side, switched it on.

'You need some coffee.' It was a statement rather than a question and Lexi felt herself cringe inwardly as Nate appeared back in the doorway, leaned against the jamb. 'Me ma's got the house all Christmassy. Isla loves it and I thought her staying there would give us a chance to make this place a bit like Christmas too – you know, get the presents down from the loft and wrap them while she isn't here. At least then we could put them back up there for a bit and it won't be such a rush in the last few days.' He looked her up and down, then moodily arched his eyebrow. 'But, by the looks of you, it's probably a good job she's not here, 'cause you... you don't look fit for anything. You should probably take yourself up to your bed.' He perched on the edge of the settee, stared out of the dark, rain-battered window, contemplated his words. 'Lex, the drinking. Do you want to tell me what that's all about? 'Cause, well, I'd say it's becoming a bit of a habit, don't you think?' He was referring to the past couple of nights, when on both occasions the anxiety of knowing the date, and the fact that her father would no doubt be in the news at some point, had caused one glass to turn into two. Each one emptied much faster than normal.

Rolling her eyes, she stared beyond him, concentrated on the architrave, noticed a cobweb that hung precariously across the corner of the room, threatening to drop. 'It was about that much, Nate.' She held her fingers together to show the amount. 'There was barely an inch left in the bottle. I've had a hell of a day and I was just tired, that's all.' She paused, didn't have a clue how she'd begin to tell him what had happened, what relevance it had to her, or to her family. The whole conversation of who she really was, who her family had been, was a conversation they'd never had and, feeling ashamed of her past, it had been one she'd never wanted to share. The longer she'd left it, the more difficult it had become. As far as Nate was concerned, she'd grown up on Lindisfarne, a tiny island only connected to the mainland for a few hours a day. It had been a place she'd loved, a place where she'd found a new life, a new iden-tity, and she hadn't felt the need to tell Nate anything different, or to give him all the sordid details of who her real family had been. It had been a lie that had become her reality and by the time she found out she was pregnant, by the time she and Nate became seri-ous, it was easier not to fill him in on the fact that she was the daughter of a serial killer and that for the rest of their lives, on the same date of every year, her father would be splashed across every newspaper in England.

Inching herself up on the settee, she once again saw him stride away, only to return a few seconds later with two mugs in hand. The smell of steaming hot coffee drifted towards her.

'Oh my God, what did you do?' Watching him place the mug onto the coffee table, she grabbed at his hand, noticed the small but deep gash, the dried, crusted blood. 'That looks nasty.'

'It's nothing, I had a bit of an accident – down on the site, slipped with a chisel.' Quickly, he pulled his hand from her grasp, rubbed it down his jeans. 'I was trying to finish the job, went a bit too fast.' He twisted his face in a half-smile. 'It was my own fault.'

Still feeling a little woozy from sleep, Lexi gazed lovingly into his eyes, and lifted a hand to pull him slowly, seductively towards her to feel the roughness of his unshaven chin against her face and the coarse touch of his hand as his fingers twisted with hers. In need of the intimacy, she lifted her fingers, brought them down to rest on the back of his neck and, with anticipation, she felt his breath against her cheek and, eagerly, she parted her lips, pulled him closer, caught the strong scent of his aftershave – an unusual deep, musky smell that drifted past her to set her senses on fire. Momentarily, his lips touched hers, before slowly pulling away.

'Lex, you...' With a look of indecision, of sadness, Nate took a step back, dropped heavily to sit on the footstool and lifted the coffee mug to his lips, to replace her kiss with a long slurp of strong black coffee. 'You know it's Christmas in a couple of weeks, don't you?' He stood up, slouched his shoulders, made a move to leave the room. 'I mean, we have a two-year-old in the house and we haven't even put up a tree.' He shook his head. 'All the other houses have one, and I know you've always said that you don't much like Christmas, but she doesn't know that, and she deserves one, Lex.

And this year, there's no excuses. We need to put the tree up, tell her Santa Claus is coming and make things nice.'

Jumping up, Lexi pushed herself back into his arms, held him close. Felt him respond, and his arms tighten around her. 'Nate... I'm sorry, you're right... we'll get the tree down, we'll make it all pretty.' She closed her eyes, remembered the Christmas after her father had been arrested. The way she'd been left at home, all alone, to stare aimlessly out of her bedroom window. She'd watched others putting up trees, fairy lights and baubles. Given half-smiles at the fake snow they'd painted on windows, the 'Stop here' signs they'd put out for Santa, the food she'd watched them eat. Then she'd sat in the darkness, alone, waiting for her mother to return, not knowing if and when she would. Whether she'd bring food with her. Or whether once again she'd go to sleep cold and hungry and wondering what she'd done that was so wrong, to be left alone at Christmas.

Looking up longingly into Nate's eyes, she wondered if it were the right time to tell him about her past, about her memories, about her reasons for hating Christmas, how life had been for her and how she'd ended up living on the island in Maggie's care. But most of all, she wondered if she should tell him that the woman who'd be all over the front page of tomorrow's newspapers was the woman she used to call Mummy. 'I...' The thought of telling him terrified her; the words refused to fall from her mouth and instead she lifted her mouth to his and teased him with her tongue. Waited until he began to respond.

Pressing her back against the door jamb with his body forced tightly against hers, she took pleasure in the way his mouth seared a path down her neck, and with slow, gentle, rhythmic movements how his hands moved over her body until, finally, he reached the edge of the satin dressing gown, which he moved to one side and continued to move his mouth, his tongue, his teeth, along her shoulder blade, making her moan with desire. 'Jesus, Lexi.' Suddenly, his mouth recaptured hers, his fingers traced the curve of her spine, moved downwards. Then he stopped. Searched her eyes with his, and with laboured breaths, he placed a hand between them both, sighed, stepped away. 'I could really use a shower. I'm...' He lifted an arm, pretended to sniff at his armpit and nodded in affirmation. 'Yep, I don't smell so good, and my hands are covered in crap, so...' Purposely, he turned his back, kept his eyes averted, leaned over to stroke a purring Agatha, who'd suddenly begun to coil herself around his ankle. 'Let me go get cleaned up. Then... then we need to get that tree down and sort those presents out. Before our daughter turns into a mountain climber and ends up in the loft, searching for the damn things herself.'

'Nate, she's just two...' Feeling herself flush, Lexi moodily pulled her dressing gown back around herself and retied the belt as she realised that Nate had made an excuse; he hadn't gone through with the lovemaking for the second time that week. Picking up her coffee, she flopped back into the settee. She needed time to think. As she drank her coffee, she took time to glance around the room. It was a room they'd both loved, decorated and furnished together. They'd made love in it repeatedly, especially in the early days of moving in. But now it was a room surrounded by stacking boxes, each one full to the brim with far too many toys for one two-year-old girl to play with and – with even more hidden in the loft, all waiting to be opened during a Christmas-morning frenzy – she knew she needed to get rid of the old and broken, before new ones arrived. She inched forward in her seat and contemplated the task, while still seething that Nate had walked away at a time when she'd needed his love and touch the most.

'Nate. Can we go and get Isla?' she suddenly asked. 'It wouldn't take us long.' She stared into the depths of the coffee cup, felt the need to hold her daughter, to tuck her into bed, to curl her body protectively around hers as she slept, to know she was safe. 'I really want her here with me tonight and...' The words caught in her throat. She couldn't bring herself to tell him why she needed to bring Isla home or why she felt overwhelmed by emotion. 'If we can go and get her, I'll get the presents down the minute she's asleep. I'll wrap them all, put the tree up and then, when she gets up in the morning, we'll play Christmas carols, let her see how magical it can be.' She gave him a half-smile. 'That'd be nice, wouldn't it?'

'Don't be daft. We don't need to go and get her. She was happy enough at me ma's. They'd made enough cake to feed the five thousand and by the looks of our Isla, she was planning on eating most of it. She's probably wired on sugar by now and besides, Lex, I'm knackered, I've been at work all day and I could really do with a bite to eat.' He rubbed his stomach for effect, turned and looked towards the kitchen. 'But I'm guessing the fridge is empty, otherwise you'd have started something cooking, wouldn't you?'

Seeing the look of disappointment on his face, she glanced at her phone. Thought about the fish fingers and bread she'd taken out of the freezer to defrost, decided it would be easier to phone one of the many takeaways, and eat while listening to the music, wrapping presents and putting up the tree. It was an image she wished she could love, an image of how life in a normal household should be.

'Nate, what's that aftershave you're wearing?' The words fell from her mouth with a sudden realisation that she'd smelled that scent before but not on Nate and, irritably, she pushed the coffee mug as far away from herself as she could, took a deep breath in. She watched as he purposely took a step further away. 'You don't normally wear aftershave for work.' She spoke without thinking, knew he'd never worn it before, not on a building site and certainly not where all the men were covered in dust, grime and whatever weather was being thrown at them during the day.

Sighing, Nate pulled his phone out of his jeans pocket, and as though trying to appease her, he began to tap at the screen. 'I'll message Ma, tell her not to put Isla to bed, although' – he turned his hand to look at his watch – 'it's already past seven. She could be asleep already.'

'I thought you said she was making pies?' Shaking her head, her gaze landed on the clock. Tried to work out how long it would have taken Nate to get home. 'It's only a few minutes' drive and... you said your mum was going to be giving her a bath. Not even Superwoman could have done all that in the time you took to get home.'

Shrugging, he glanced up the stairs. 'As I said, I'm gonna take a shower.' Watching him, she saw his hand go to his jeans, to pull at his crotch, and his obvious discomfort. Then once again, his fingers tapped furiously at the phone, then after a final swipe, he threw the mobile onto the stairs, where he sat, pulled at his laces, kicked off his boots, his thick woollen socks and wiggled his bare, rain-soaked toes in the air. 'Oh, that feels good, so it does. Almost as good as sex.' Laughing at his own joke, he hesitated before moving towards her and dropping another kiss on her forehead.

Pondering his words, Lexi realised that not only had he ignored her question about the aftershave, he'd also used an analogy about sex, just a few minutes after he'd embarrassingly halted their lovemaking.

'Nate,' Lexi shouted, 'did you say you'd let your mum know we're collecting Isla, or should I do it?' Climbing up from the settee, she padded to the bottom of the stairs, picked up the mobile, waved it around in the air, and went to follow him up the stairs but halted as she heard the shower, Nate's voice bellowing out in song. Undecidedly, she flopped down on the step, decided to call his mum herself, tapped in the passcode, felt the unusual vibration and saw the words *try again* appear on the screen.

Quickly, she went through all other passcodes she thought he might use. Nothing worked. Confused, she stared at the screen, couldn't understand why he'd change his number, not without telling her and, angrily, she threw it back down on the step. She felt the need to drag fresh air into her lungs and, with only one place she could go while barely dressed, she snatched open the back door, allowed it to slam behind her.

Leaning against the brick wall of the extension, Lexi began to compose herself. One thing too many had happened in one day and she looked up at the sky where the earlier clouds had now dissipated. The stars shone back at her, and a tear dropped down her cheek. The night sky was a sight she normally loved, one that reminded her of life back on the island, where with the minimal use of street lighting, the sky had always looked brighter, and she fondly thought of the nights she'd sat cuddled up to Maggie. Sometimes in the garden, other times on the beach, where they'd both shared a blanket and watched the sunset, each trying to pick out more asterisms than the other.

Looking up at the bathroom window, Lexi saw it open, the steam rush out. A clear sign that Nate had got out of the shower and was towelling himself dry. Closing her eyes, she felt her world spin on its axis and for what seemed like the hundredth time that day, she felt the need to put her poker face back in order. Her life as a journalist made her naturally inquisitive; she didn't like not knowing the answers, especially if she thought someone had something to hide and, to her, changing your passcode meant exactly that.

Struggling with her emotions, Lexi took in a deep breath, felt the cold, moist air hit the back of her throat. It was the promise of more rain to come, and she looked up to see dark, moody and unforgiving clouds. The weather in the east of England was a perpetual cycle of good and bad, just like her mood. But tonight, being alone was good. It gave her time to compose her thoughts.

Walking across the grass and stepping from stone to stone, Lexi made her way through the long, narrow garden, past the apple tree now bare of leaves, the holly bush that desperately needed taming, and the palm tree that would have looked just a little more at home in the Caribbean. They were all trees that had been here long before she had, each one a stalwart to the garden, rustling with the breeze, making her stand and listen to every sound, every noise until she came to stand beneath the giant acer. It stood at the very bottom of the garden, on the boundary between theirs and the house next door's. Leaning against its trunk, she thoughtfully looked back at the house, the place she called home.

Sighing, she wondered how she could turn her hatred of Christmas around. How she could try and remember all the good Christmases she'd had with Maggie, rather than the one that haunted her; after all, it had been just one Christmas of many. But one Christmas when she'd been left alone, without a tree, a gift, or any kind of celebration. It had been a life she'd never wanted Isla to know about, to be a part of, and she certainly hadn't wanted her to know or understand the misery she'd once felt. Yet today, everything had changed. For just a moment the world had stopped spinning, and Lexi had realised just how precious life was, how good her life on the island had been, and how her anonymity had been both her best friend and worst enemy. But now she had to make a decision. She had to decide what to do next, whether or not she should tell Nate who she really was. Who both her mother and father were. And how, after twenty years of waiting, someone had taken it upon themselves to take revenge for what her father had done. Trembling, she wondered if she should tell him how she feared for her life, how she feared for both him, and for Isla. Of how her father had killed twenty women, all with families and friends. And of how now, the one that had killed her mother might want to kill her too.

Strolling slowly back to the house, she knew what she had to do, knew what secrets she needed to keep. After opening the door, she carefully closed it behind her, tiptoed through the kitchen and into the hall, where she stood at the bottom of the stairs, and with her head tipped to one side, she listened to the movement above, to the sound of drawers opening and closing. Then with her focus on his phone, she positioned it back in the exact place where he'd thrown it moments before.

7

Pushing the mountain of stuffed teddy bears to one side, Lexi squeezed herself into the small space she'd managed to create between her daughter and the wall. It was a place where she could just about lie down, curl her body around Isla's and breathe in the scent of baby shampoo, talcum powder and mint toothpaste. Counting the blessings she held tightly in her arms, she felt happy in the knowledge that her little girl was home, where she was safe, and where, for now, no one could hurt her.

Fixing one eye on the door, Lexi listened to the noises that came from below, to where the smell of cooking drifted up the stairs along with the annoying sound of Nate's mobile, which seemed to bleep constantly. Someone was messaging him, and she could imagine him picking it up, tapping the screen, then dropping the device back down on the counter between bursts of song as he most probably danced around the kitchen to his favourite playlist.

The sound of him singing would have normally made her smile, especially as she remembered a night similar to this one. A night just a few months after Isla had been born, when she'd gone down to find him standing in the kitchen doorway, a wooden spoon in his hand, totally naked, apart from a small and frilly apron that he'd tied around his waist, along with a tea towel that he'd wrapped around his head like a makeshift bandana. 'If you want the chilli,' he'd sung, 'you've got to kiss the cook...' Closing her eyes, she could see the look on his face, the humour in his gaze and his arousal that had suddenly become more than apparent beneath the apron.

'No... not really.' The singing stopped and Nate's voice, barely a whisper, drifted up the stairs. 'She's in the bedroom, with Isla. Give me a minute.'

Puzzled, Lexi pushed herself up, ran her fingers across her baby's cheek, moved a soft curl of hair away from her face and leaned forward to kiss her on the forehead. Then, inquisitively, she moved across the room to stand in the doorway, heard the kitchen door click to a close, Nate's whispers disappearing behind it. The sound of his voice was now muffled, could barely be heard, and again she shook her head. The fact that Nate was answering his phone at all was a small miracle. He normally hated technology, left his phone constantly on silent. His very own way of rebelling. 'It's like being tagged,' he'd said in the past. 'Wherever you are, whatever you're doing. The stupid thing goes off and you've got no damn choice but to answer it. Well... I don't like it.' His thought process, along with the fact that Nate managed to break more screens than anyone else she knew, meant he did everything he could to forget his phone, to leave it behind, each time making excuses for why he hadn't taken it with him. Yet unusually, tonight, he'd become eager to communicate, and once again Lexi's mind went to the passcode. Along with the calls, changing the number was out of character. She was sure he'd been wearing a new aftershave and for the second time that week he'd walked away from their lovemaking.

Shaking her head, she tried to validate his reasons. He was tired. Busy at work. On a tight deadline. The job had to be finished by Christmas; the building site had to be emptied and secured for the holidays. Knuckle-rubbing her eyes, she took a deep breath in, smiled as Agatha ran up the stairs and curled herself around her ankles. Being just a kitten, she craved attention and Lexi happily kneeled beside her, ran a hand across her fur, watched as she leaned in, purred, closed her eyes, arched her back. 'You need a little love too, don't you?' Lexi whispered as she glanced back into Isla's room, saw the perfect shape of her baby safely curled up under the duvet.

Walking to the window, she checked the locks and even though she felt relief that the house was secure, that no one could get in, she couldn't stop the overwhelming fear deep within her, the terror of how easily someone could hurt her or Isla, just because of who her father had been. Yet, even with that probable threat hanging over her, she had so much to be thankful for, so many things in her life had been good. Until, of course, Nate had begun acting differently. He'd distanced himself from her, making it impossible to ignore the fact that their perfect life wasn't as perfect as she'd always made out and something didn't feel right. She just didn't know what.

Sitting on the edge of the bed, she began playing the past few days over and over, allowed her journalistic mind to work overtime, knew she couldn't and wouldn't settle until she'd worked it all out. The one thing she did know as a journalist was to bide her time, to ask questions at exactly the right time, to make sure that, whatever answer was given, she had the perfect retort.

Making her way into the bedroom, she stripped off the clothes she'd worn to go and collect Isla, pulled on a pair of comfy pyjamas, sat down on the bed and ran a brush through her hair. Catching her reflection in the mirror, she stared at the woman she'd become, the illusion she'd created from the girl she'd once been. She'd been a child lost and alone, taken away to grow up on the island, hidden from the world, away from all the evil, and protected by the incoming tides. By tomorrow, that hidden identity could quite easily become exposed to the world and for a second, she thought of Simon, of her colleagues, of how they'd react when they saw her photograph splashed across the nationals, along with pictures of her birth mother, her father and all of his victims. Their pictures and lives would be laid out for the world to see, to read and, once again, to judge and dissect.

She tried to think back, to the way life had been on the island. She'd liked the anonymity, the way Maggie had surrounded her with love and the fact that she'd felt so loved; she'd been the only child on the island who hadn't wanted to go to boarding school. It was something all the children did. At nine years old, once schooling was too difficult to maintain on the island, they were all sent to Longridge Towers. It had been a move Lexi had resisted. Moving and making new friends had been the last thing on her mind, and instead, she'd spent a lot of hours sitting alone, reading books and listening to music.

Determinedly, Lexi gritted her teeth. She knew what could be coming, how the press would hound her and how life would never be simple again. She blew out through puffed-up cheeks; she needed someone to talk to. Needed someone who understood her. Tried to decide if Nate was the right person to get her through this, to get them all through this. He was, after all, the one person who barely knew her at all and she could feel the barriers automatically begin to stack themselves around her like a giant Tetris game, each block dropping into place at a hundred miles an hour.

Holding tightly to the bed, she felt her mind spin with anticipation, knew that once the wall was up, once the barriers were erected, they wouldn't be breached. It had been a coping mechanism she'd learned over the years, a way of protecting herself from hurt, a way of keeping bad people out. It was a wall she thought she'd built against her mum, but her murder had affected her more than she liked, and her gaze shot to the stairs, to where she could still hear Nate's muffled voice on the phone below and, hurriedly, she made her way along the landing, stood on the top step, tried to listen.

'Sure,' he whispered, 'make sure you're not late...' The words were a simple statement, meant nothing. And Lexi prayed that he'd say more, something positive she could hold on to, something that proved Nate loved her or that whatever he was up to, it wasn't anything bad. More than anything, she wanted to know he'd be there for her, no matter what that future held.

Climbing back onto Isla's bed, Lexi gave a contented smile, and for a moment she pulled her baby in close, felt the need to ensure Isla stayed inside the wall, protected within her very own boundary while she simply stroked her daughter's hair and watched the way she curled her body tightly against her like a baby limpet, with lips all pursed like a rosebud waiting to bloom. Feeling a rush of love, Lexi stared at Isla's face, the shape of her eyes, her nose. Desperately, she tried to see Nate within her, felt the doubt creep in as thoughts of her last visit to the island prodded at her mind like a long, spindly, accusing finger. Picking up her phone, she flicked through her photographs, found the last one she had of Harry, the one Maggie had unknowingly sent her. *Look who's back on the island*, she'd written, alongside a picture of a smiling Harry. It had been taken in the summer, outside the pub, with him practically lying across the top of one of the wooden picnic tables, his wetsuit unzipped to the waist, his bare chest exposed, his hair unkempt and wet from the sea.

'It was unfinished business,' she whispered, 'that was all. Just something we needed to get out of our system. It didn't mean anything. Did it?'

It was true. She'd seen it as a way of closing the door on the past. Of putting her and all her secrets far behind her. After all, he was one of the few people who knew her, who knew who she really was and what her father had done. Every one of her dirty secrets. But now, almost three years later, she found herself staring at his picture, holding it beside her daughter's face, and looked cautiously between the two. Then, determinedly, she flicked back to the picture of Nate, focused, wouldn't allow herself to believe that Isla was anyone's but his.

'Lex, are you coming down? Chilli's almost ready,' Nate's voice whispered as he hesitated outside the door before continuing along the hallway, where she heard the bathroom door open and close. She heard the sounds as the toilet flushed, the tap ran and the towel was dropped unceremoniously on the side of the bath, just as normal.

Closing her eyes, she tried to remember a time when she'd last felt this uneasy, this unsure, or paranoid about everyone around her. Early evening was normally a time that she looked forward to the most, a time when she was home from the stress of work, a time when she and Nate had historically talked about the fun parts of their day while drinking wine, listening to music and sharing a moment. Yet right now, she couldn't help but feel alone. Nate was keeping secrets from her, hiding things. It was a side of him she didn't like, and she didn't want to sit with him, not with so many uneasy thoughts flying around in her mind. She took the easy option, decided it was easier to stay curled up in bed and pretend to be asleep, rather than go down and ask all the difficult questions, ones she wasn't sure he'd want to answer.

Angrily, she rubbed her eyes, bit down on her lip. 'Lexi Jakes... Alexandra Graves...' she growled under her breath. 'Whatever the hell you're called. You're a hypocrite. An absolute bloody hypocrite.' Breathing in, she held back the tears. 'You have secrets, far too many bloody secrets.' She paused. 'So many more than he'll ever have.' She knew she'd hidden things from him, important things,

things that affected both her life and his, and realistically she knew she had no right to judge, no right at all, and as she rolled her eyes towards the door and puffed up her cheeks and blew out, she saw him walk along the hallway before heading down the stairs.

'I'll dish it up, shall I?' she heard him say, but instead of answering, she picked up her phone from where she'd dropped it on the bedside cabinet and flicked through the numbers. Came to the one for Maggie, wished that Stanley was still alive. She wanted to see him, wanted to feel his arms envelop her in a hug. With a mixing pot of emotions, she stared at the names. *Maggie and Stanley Home.* She still hadn't edited it, hadn't been able to bring herself to remove his name, and knew that between them, they'd have known what to do. And now, with Maggie alone on the island, she wondered whether she should call or not.

While allowing her finger to hover above the call button, she felt her heart constrict, but couldn't press the button. The moment she did, she knew she'd want to be back on the island, in that cottage, where she'd always felt safe, secure and loved. Not that she didn't feel love here. With Isla, she always felt loved and needed. But here, she was the protector; it was part of being a mum, a parent, one who did all they could to keep their offspring safe. Which was normally very easy. Isla had no filter. She either loved or hated you, a feeling that could change with the wind, and with her only being two and a half, she had no problem in showing her feelings. Right now, Isla's love was for her mummy. Lexi had taken great delight in how excited she'd been when they'd turned up at Nate's mum's house to take her home, how she'd run and jumped into her arms and how she'd happily dropped fairy kisses all over her mouth and face.

It had been a fun, sobering moment. A joy to be back with her daughter, until the events of the day had swamped her thoughts and, without being noticed, she'd left Nate to chat to his mother, made her way into the hall, kneeled on the floor with Isla's coat held tightly in her hands, where she'd lifted it to her face and breathed in deeply. Once again, she could see her mother's face, the red silk scarf, imagined it being wrapped tightly around Isla's neck just as it had been around her mother's.

Was it really revenge? Will it happen again? Who will be next?

Closing her eyes, she could feel her mind racing forward, visualising all the bad things that could happen, all the ways she could stop them. Had to stop them. And for a moment, she'd held her breath, hoped the feeling would pass, knew it wouldn't, and counted slowly until, finally, she pulled a breath into her body as the acrid taste of bile rose in her throat.

'Nate, come on, we need to go,' she remembered saying as she'd dashed to the door, and, while still holding Isla's coat tightly in her arms, she'd run down the path to the side of the car, where she quickly spat the bile out of her mouth, hoped that no one had seen, and felt relieved as the bright yellow lights of the car had flashed and Isla had run down the path towards her.

8

After lying awake for most of the night and punching her pillow more times than she could remember, Lexi eventually got up and walked along the hallway to stand in the entrance of Isla's room. With the night light beside her bed still switched on, Lexi watched her daughter sleep, and felt her heart constrict when Isla opened sleepy eyes and gave one of her biggest, most innocent smiles before once again snuggling into her pillow and falling back into a deep, natural sleep.

Giving an involuntary shiver, she wondered what the day would bring. How she'd cope and whether today would be the day she'd have no choice but to explain to Nate who she really was, trust him with her secrets and see how he'd react when she told him that someone was most probably going to try and kill her or their daughter, possibly both. It was like a death sentence hanging over her, and for a split second she thought of her father, of how he'd have felt all those years before, knowing he'd never taste freedom again, that once they'd locked that prison cell he'd never be free. And even though he'd done that to himself, she wondered if this was what it felt like. Would she ever be free of this feeling, the deep-seated anxiety? Shaking her head, she made her way down the stairs, couldn't understand how or where she'd begin to explain, how she'd tell Nate that the last three years of his life had been a complete lie, and that in reality he had no idea who she was, who they were, how their lives would end up.

Padding slowly around the kitchen, she felt the need for just a little normality. Flicking on the kettle, she made some coffee. Then, with her mug in hand and her laptop on her knee, she sank into the warmth of the pillow-backed settee, pulled her big woollen blanket around her knees and began scrolling through the endless pages of news, just about all of which were talking about Jessica Graves, about her brutal death and of how similar her murder had been to the ones her husband had committed some twenty years before. Each article questioned the killer's motive, whether it was a revenge killing or not, and if it were, why now? Why had Jessica Graves suddenly had to pay for what he'd done?

Taking in a deep breath, Lexi's mind went from her mother back to Nate. It was more than obvious that he was up to something but right now wasn't the time to think about it. Right now she had to focus on what was most important, on the fact that she could be in serious danger and that, just by association, so could Isla. As a reporter, she'd learned how to step back, how to read between the lines and how to take nothing at face value. Not unless it could be proven. And even if she could have proved it, what difference would it make to her tonight? Tonight, she had no intention of confronting Nate, or of making her situation worse than it already was. Today he wasn't her biggest enemy or the person she feared the most. And even though she knew it made her come across as weak, she really didn't care. Bringing Isla home had been more important than anything. And keeping her safe was imperative. Even if that meant she'd lost the opportunity of being alone with Nate. Of having the perfect chance to speak to him, but thoughts of Isla and holding her close had taken over her mind, and the thoughts of doing so had been the only thing that had managed to slow down the constant spiral of never-ending questions, accusations and self-doubt that had dominated her thoughts for every minute of the previous night.

Sitting back, she pushed the mystery phone call and random texter to the back of her mind. Hoped that Nate would mention them himself, tell her that it had been one of the lads from the site who'd changed his passcode, played a practical joke. It was what they did. The moment they all got together, ten grown men suddenly turned into two-year-olds, each one playing jokes on the other – a daily occurrence that had begun in kindergarten, continued through school and hadn't stopped, not even in adulthood. Their whole day was a series of tricks, where the banter became sillier, their reactions more and more dangerous.

Pressing her lips tightly together in a satisfied pout, she stood up and went to the kitchen, where her laundry basket still sat, full of clean clothes all waiting to be ironed, and with her stomach clenched with nerves, she began sorting through the clothes. The anticipation of the day ahead was already too much. Talk in the office would all be about the copycat. About how he'd murdered. Why he'd murdered. All the gruesome details. Whether and when they thought he'd strike again. It was a conversation she didn't really want to be a part of and the idea of debating who might be his next victim would be one conversation too many. After all, Jessica Graves had been murdered by someone emulating Lexi's father – which continually brought her back to the same question about revenge... would her mother be the only victim?

With a huge sob, Lexi made her way back to the settee, grabbed her laptop and once again scrolled through the news, with a hundred thoughts that now prodded painfully at her mind. Someone somewhere had to know who had done this. There had to be a clue; there had to be something that would alert her to who it had been. Didn't they always say that the villain returns to the scene, appears somewhere in the middle of the action to gloat in the aftermath of what they'd done? Would her mother's killer do the same?

After what felt like an hour, she looked away from the screen, felt the need to distract herself and glanced at Isla's toy mountain that needed sorting. Hastily, she began organising them, placing all of Isla's favourite toys into one pile, all the ones she didn't like or play with into another. After less than half an hour of sorting, she stood back and nodded. 'You get to stay. The rest get to go,' she said with a satisfied yawn, and began to head towards the kitchen but stopped at the bottom of the stairs, listening.

'No, Daddy, no tickles...' Isla's voice giggled with delight and, hypnotised by the sound, Lexi took the steps one by one and stood in her bedroom doorway to see Nate sitting up against his pillows and Isla straddled across him, her hands rhythmically clapping against his, until as quickly as he could, Nate reached around her, poked and tickled her, watched her squirm, and then continued the game.

'Hey, look who it is. It's your mummy,' he whispered as he leaned forward, buried his face in her soft golden curls and blew a loud, vibrating raspberry on her neck.

'Ahh, don't... Mummy, tell him...' Making herself more comfortable, Isla wiggled on the spot. Grabbed at her daddy's hands, held them in place. 'Like this.' Slowly, she once again clapped her hands against his. 'Clap, again...'

Moving forward, Lexi dropped her dressing gown to the floor, slipped into the bed beside them, felt the need to hold her family close, to enjoy the moment. 'I see you have some company,' she whispered to Nate, whose eyes never once left those of his daughter, the look of love on his face more than clear to see.

'Well, I just kind of turned over and there she was. My very own little bedbug.' Again, his fingers tickled a giggling Isla, who writhed on the spot and, with mischief on her face, she fell into the space between them, curled herself into a ball, tucked her head under her daddy's chin and placed a thumb firmly in her mouth.

Staring, Lexi framed the picture of them both in her mind. Felt suddenly aware that everything was about to change, that once the news was broadcast, her secret was likely to come out and Nate would find out who she really was, resent her for not having told him sooner. Slowly, she ran a hand down Nate's bare chest, felt the solid muscle beneath her fingers, felt almost afraid to touch him as the memories filled her mind and the tears sprung to her eyes.

'Hey, what's wrong?' He lifted a hand to her chin, placed a soft, gentle kiss on her lips.

'Oh, I'm fine,' she lied. 'I was just thinking how beautiful this is, all of us together, happy.' The words tumbled from her mouth. 'I... I love you both so much.' Choking back the words, Lexi jumped from the bed. She didn't want him to see her cry, didn't want to go through the explanation, not yet. She grabbed at her dressing gown. 'Are you ready for some breakfast? I'll make some, shall I?' She tried to smile but turned away to hide her tears.

Wriggling free of her daddy's arms, Isla set off down the hall-way. 'Come on, Mummy, I want breakfast, and Agafa...' she shouted as she ran, 'Agafa, come get breakfast.'

Laughing, Lexi kneeled back on the bed, leaned into Nate, who quickly pulled her towards him. His lips grazed her forehead; she felt the strength in his arms as he wrapped them around her. 'You were up a bit early, weren't you? I turned over, expecting you to be there, but you were gone. I wondered what was wrong?'

'Oh, nothing.' Lexi continued the lie. 'I couldn't sleep, made a start on sorting Isla's toys out. There's a huge pile you could take to the charity shop. She never plays with them and, to be honest, I doubt she'd even miss them and we... we have to make room for the

Christmas tree.' She prised herself out of his arms, went to follow her daughter down the hallway. Looked down the stairs where she could hear Isla rattling the box of kitten treats, her normal morning routine of feeding the cat before she'd eat breakfast herself. 'Did you see Agatha?'

Shaking his head, Nate leaned back against his pillows, linked his hands behind his head. Smiled. 'I'll get up in a minute. Look for her. She's probably fast asleep on someone's bed.' He raised an eyebrow as Isla ran into the room, noisily shaking the box of treats.

'Ag... Agafa, come on. Treats.' Looking around the room, her bottom lip protruded, her eyes filled with tears and she turned to Lexi with a hopeful glance. 'Mummy, where's Agafa? Why didn't she come?'

9

Surreptitiously, I make my way up one side of the tree-lined road and down the other. It's a road I've walked along so many times. A place where I've been to watch you and, as normal, I inquisitively stare through the illuminated windows of all the houses, where even though it's still early in December, Christmas trees stand in most of the windows, all covered in baubles of every imaginable colour and bright twinkling lights that sparkle in the early-morning darkness.

Each house is a two- or three-storey Victorian terrace with symmetrical brick and stone sash windows, brightly painted front doors, pretty tiles that line the porch and a small concrete kerb in front of each of the bays, the only indication from the outside that there is a room below and a place where the old coal chutes of years gone past used to be, now replaced by small and impractical windows.

Each newly trimmed-up house is a sight that fills me with joy; the celebrations are a sign of things to come. Yet still, I understand the pain and the suffering some of us feel when, once again, we feel lost and alone, with no wish to face the outside world. An unrealistic façade, when a huge proportion of the population just wish for it to be over, wish they didn't have to put on the constant smiles, or the pretence of having fun.

Yet now, even with a daughter of your own, you still block it out and disregard Christmas in every way you can and I've noticed, as you did last year, you wait until the very last moment before you acknowledge it's happening at all, and I shake my head, wonder why – because unlike my sister, who still rots somewhere in the ground... you... you still have everything to live for. You still have your life, your perfect existence, your well-paid job, a house that most people would die for and a little girl who's still so full of so many dreams and wishes that you could tell her just about anything and right now, right at this moment in her life, she'd believe every single word.

While staring thoughtfully at one of the houses a few doors from yours, I see the front door burst open and, instinctively, I duck behind a low wall, keep my gaze lowered and pretend to mess with my shoe. Through the corner of my eye, I see a man walking towards me, and as he passes, I hear him shout a cheery goodbye. I can't help but notice the two identical little girls, both around three or four years old. They're bouncing up and down on the doorstep, in unison, alongside a scruffy Old English sheepdog who sits obediently, and I feel myself supressing the laughter as I realise that the whole scene looks like one from Peter Pan. *A scene where the children suddenly hold hands, float upwards and into the sky, disappearing to a place where children don't grow old and, longingly, I think of my own older sister and of the few years we had together as children, and of how now as adults there are moments we should have shared, and years that should still be ahead of us.*

Taking in a deep breath, I feel the venom fill my veins and I struggle to compose myself and, while staring into your house, I watch you through the bay window, the way you're frantically running around, lifting cushions, and tossing them up and into the air. Then, looking up, you put your hands on your hips, allow your shoulders to slump in what looks like an act of despair and glance wistfully out of the window. Your eyes land straight on me, making me slink backwards until I'm standing to the side of a tree looking back at you, in a bare window that's completely void of Christmas cheer, and it suddenly occurs to me that the sight makes me happy. After what your father did to my family, you don't deserve any pleasure. Your life shouldn't have any decadence at all and even though I understand that Christmas was taken away from you too, that all of the memories of the years gone past have blurred your vision and how each year the thought of the constant jovialities fills you with dread, I can't help but blame you – just for being a part of him.

Pulling my coat firmly around my shoulders, I wait until you disappear from view, look back along the road, then slip through the gate, into the drive and make my way across your driveway, to stand beside your car. You've left the wheels on an angle, perfect for slashing, and I laugh as I crouch down and sit on the cold stone drive, lean against the tyres in an act of defiance. Looking at my watch, I calculate that within the hour you'll leave for work and, while considering my options, I hear a soft, gentle purring. It suddenly comes from beneath your car. It's unexpected, but surprisingly I feel myself smile as I notice the smoky-grey kitten that emerges to rub itself against my hand. It's vying for attention, and as gently as I can, I run a hand down its back, feel it arch against me, then smile as it confidently climbs onto my knee and paws at my chest. Unusually, I realise that it's the first time I've seen it outside, and while holding it in my arms, I pull it in close, take pleasure in the way it purrs.

Rebelliously, I watch you through the windows. 'She's looking for you,' I whisper to the kitten. 'She doesn't know where you are, does she?' I realise how easily I could take everything away, how in the blink of an eye she could lose so much, and I laugh, knowing how many times I've thought of this moment, of doing something so evil, so unbelievably cruel that you'd realise just how close I've been and how much power I truly have.

10

After giving Isla her breakfast and waving Nate off to work, Lexi locked the doors and began to methodically search the house, room by room. She knew it was odd that Agatha was missing, that she hadn't appeared the minute Isla had rattled the treats box, and even stranger that they'd managed to get through breakfast without her running into the kitchen to sit beneath Isla's chair, waiting for the small pieces of buttered toast to hit the floor.

Feeling a sense of unease, Lexi crept between rooms, cautiously peered under beds, inside the washing basket, behind curtains and radiators. Tried to think of every single place where a tiny kitten could have become trapped, and even searched through toys she'd piled up earlier in the hope the kitten had climbed into a box.

'Agatha, here, Agatha, where are you?' She sang the words as she checked each room in turn, moved each box, looked inside. 'Come on, Agatha, make a noise, let me know where you are.'

While moving the bedside units to one side and tossing the duvets, Lexi watched Isla's panic as she simply ran from room to room, rattling the biscuit box, looking dismayed.

'Where... where did she go?' She lifted her tiny shoulders in a shrug, her bottom lip wobbled, and Lexi began trying to think of excuses she could give, reasons why the kitten may have disappeared. Running down the stairs, she quickly opened the back door, looked outside. 'Agatha, come on...' Retracing her steps from the night before, she remembered going outside, walking the path to the acer, looking up at the stars. She couldn't remember whether Agatha followed her out or not. It was rare she ever left the house, something Lexi had never encouraged her to do, and if she were totally honest, she much preferred the idea of a house cat, rather than one that brought back half-dead mice for breakfast.

Making her way from garden to the kitchen, she stood with her hands on hips, looked at the clock, and, feeling that she had no alternative, she reached for her mobile and phoned the office. 'Simon, I'm so sorry, I'm gonna be late. It's our kitten, she's gone missing, Isla's completely distraught and I'm terrified the kitten's gone and got herself trapped somewhere and can't get out.' She paused, looked down the hallway, made sure Isla wasn't listening. 'And if I don't find her... well, you know.' While thinking about her options, she heard Simon throwing instructions around the office. 'In fact, can I ask a favour? After yesterday, I still don't feel too well... and I wondered... if I could throw in a last-minute holiday? I've got a few days left over. Ones I'm supposed to use before Christmas, and under the circumstances...'

When Simon agreed, she sighed, dropped the phone, and felt a surge of relief that she could stay at home. Deep inside, she felt almost terrified of leaving the house and, surreptitiously, she made her way around the house, checked the doors, the locks, realised that the last place she wanted to be today was at work, listening to the gossip. The idea of parking her car and walking through the dark streets of Whitby alone was much too much, especially when she didn't know whether her mother's killer would come for her next and, with sadness in her eyes, she turned to watch Isla as she tossed cushions up in the air, innocently looking for a missing kitten, totally oblivious to the vicious world that was happening outside. It was a world where people hurt others. Killed others and caused shock waves and fear within communities. But more so, this time the shock waves were once again rippling through her home, her life, her family.

Picking up her laptop, she saw the notifications mounting up. Felt her anxiety levels soar. Her stomach lurched, and once again she quickly began to scan the news. Opening each article as slowly as she could, she saw her mother's face appear before her on the screen and, while shaking inside, she found herself tipping her head to one side, studying the profile. It was only now that she realised how much older her mother looked. Yet still she had that look in her eye, that same twisted smile that crossed her sly, evil face. It was a look that made Lexi cringe and move back from the screen. A look she didn't want to see, or to remember.

Scanning the screen, Lexi picked out the last of the stories she wanted to read. Went through each reporter's theory in turn, felt her stomach twist as they speculated about the lead-up to her mother's death. The way her father had murdered his victims, and how some twenty years before, his six-year-old daughter, Alexandra Graves, had mysteriously disappeared from the public eye, following a reporting embargo that had shielded her from the press. Some thought that she too had been buried on the moors, and that her father must have killed her too. When, in reality, she'd been locked in a small, dirty bedroom by her mother, with just a mattress in the corner to sleep on. A quilt with holes in had been her only warmth, and for a split second, the memories infiltrated her mind. She could see the reflection of herself in a mirror, a small, helpless child cruelly abandoned for days upon days. Dirty. Hungry. Left to look after herself with no heating, or food.

A sudden knock on the door broke through her thoughts. 'Amazon delivery.'

'OK, OK. Just leave it on the doorstep.' Nervously, Lexi peered through the window, caught hold of Isla as she sped towards the door, ushered her back to the toys and wondered what the delivery might be as the driver waved the small package around in the air before placing it on the step.

With the voile pulled across the window, Lexi watched the delivery driver, who stood on his tiptoes and anxiously peered down the side of the house. His hand was waving around frantically, pointing with urgency. 'No problem, darling, but there's a hell of a commotion coming from your wheelie bin. Doesn't sound right to me and... well... it sounds like something's trying to get out.'

'Agatha.' Without a second thought, she threw the front door open. Saw the man immediately retreat to a position further down the path, his hand held above his head in a friendly wave, making Lexi sigh with relief as she watched him disappear through the gate.

'Something isn't happy about being in there,' he shouted over his shoulder. 'And if I were you, I'd stand well back when you open that lid 'cause if it's a rat, it'll be jumping right over your shoulder.' As he turned on his heel, Lexi saw his shoulders jiggle up and down in amusement, and with one eye on where Isla still played with her toys just inside the doorway, she cautiously cocked her head to one side, listened intently to the unusual soft shuffling that could be heard inside the bin. Fearfully, Lexi thought about his words, considered the fact that a rat could have got inside and thought about ignoring it, going back in the house, and leaving it for Nate to deal with. But then, a gentle yowl filled her ears. A sad, pathetic yowl that could only be one thing.

'Agatha...' she whispered, and took a step closer to the bin, threw the lid open, and froze. She wanted to scoop the kitten up, hold her in her arms, but couldn't and, with her breath accelerating, she heard a scream leave her lips as she took in the sight of Agatha, the red silk scarf that was tied in a bow and wrapped tightly around her neck.

11

With her foot balanced on the accelerator, Lexi forced herself to breathe, slowed the car angrily at the traffic lights and revved the engine until they turned from amber to green. Turning the car as quickly as she could, she headed out of town and automatically aimed for the A171 towards Middlesbrough.

With her heart banging in her chest, she drove at speed. She constantly checked the roads around her and consciously paid attention to every car that followed. Every driver. Mentally made a note of how they looked, the way they acted. On more than one occasion, she purposely sped up, or slowed down until they passed, all the time trying to decide whether they'd been remotely interested in her or her car. And with her mind on high alert, she took in the carnage that surrounded her. The piles of clothes, toys, practically everything she owned, and then in the middle of it all sat Isla, strapped into her car seat, with Agatha's basket buckled in tightly beside her.

While trying to calm her mind, she purposely took slow, deliberate breaths. Thought of the moments after she'd found Agatha, the hurried, hysterical phone call to the police, the response she'd had.

'I'll get an incident team out to you within the next twenty-four hours. In the meantime, keep the scarf in a sealed plastic bag. Don't let anyone else touch it.' The police officer had responded in a professional yet unemotional way. It was probably the hundredth call she'd taken that morning, each one a matter of urgency to the caller. Each call another job they had to deal with, with an over-stretched workforce.

'I don't think you understand. The killer was at my house. Outside my front door. What if... what if they come back?' Lexi had whimpered. 'What if they try to kill me, my daughter? She's here. She's just two years old; how the hell am I supposed to protect her?'

'Miss Jakes. Is your life in any immediate danger?'

Lexi had glanced at the locked front door. The way Isla sang softly as she played with her toys, the coffee that stood on the side table, still steaming in the mug. 'Er, no... I...'

'OK, that's good.' She had paused. 'Now. Make sure you lock the doors and if anyone comes to the house, ask for identification before you open the door, and if anything changes, if you feel in any danger, phone back immediately using 999 and we'll get someone straight to you. In the meantime, is there anyone you could call, someone you trust? Could you ask them to come and sit with you? Try and think of somewhere safe you could go. Maybe there's a friend, or relation you could stay with?'

Every emotion had sped through her, the words 'somewhere safe' sticking in her mind. Every instinct had told her to run for safety, to go back to the island. Every part of her had screamed out loud with an overwhelming need to keep her daughter safe, and with the responder's voice ringing loud and clear in her mind, she knew what she had to do, that the only place she'd ever felt truly safe had been the island of Lindisfarne, where twice a day the sea pulled in, creating a natural impenetrable barrier from the world outside.

Automatically, she had dropped into a routine she'd mentally practised for years. Had run around the house and grabbed all the essentials. Clothes from both her and Isla's wardrobes. Isla's favourite toys. Toiletries from the bathroom. All of which were thrown into bags and dropped into the laundry basket, on top of the clean, unironed clothes she'd folded earlier.

In the ten short seconds that followed the phone call, her whole world had collapsed around her; her deepest, darkest fear hit her with force. Someone knew who she was. Where she lived. Whose daughter she used to be – still was. Someone had been within two feet of her own front door. Of where Isla had been playing. And that someone had made it very clear they'd wanted her to know they'd been there, and that no one was going to protect her, apart from herself. Which meant that she had to protect Isla too. With adrenaline coursing through her veins, every imaginable thought had driven her on. Were they coming after her? Was she next? Would she be made to pay for what her father had done? Had the scarf been a warning or a threat? Each scenario had the same ending. Each vision had burst explosively through her mind and brought her back to protecting Isla and, with terror clouding her mind, she could imagine the eyes of her beautiful, trusting child, the way they looked at her, just wanting and deserving to be loved. The mere thought that someone could or would hurt her had broken Lexi's heart in two and she'd had no intention of waiting for it to happen, or for them to even consider taking their revenge.

'Mummy, I'm not dressed.' Isla yelled her obvious displeasure from her car seat, where she sat surrounded by a pile of teddy bears, toys and an unamused-looking Agatha, who, after her morning's ordeal, had curled up in one corner of her pet carrier with one eye open, pretending to sleep.

'I know, honey, Mummy's sorry, but we had to leave so quickly. There wasn't time, was there?' She swallowed the acrid taste of acid back down her throat. Felt the burn. Wished she'd had more time to prepare. More time to plan. But hadn't. And now, in a confused and anxious state, she kicked herself for not having grab bags already packed. Especially after the day before, and after her mother had been killed, having to run should have been at the forefront of her mind and, angrily, she felt the tears begin to fall uncontrollably down her face, until she had no choice but to pull into a lay-by and take a moment to compose her thoughts.

Ensuring all the doors were still locked, Lexi wiped her eyes, turned in her seat, smiled at Isla and began pulling toys out of the washing basket. 'I'll tell you what, baby girl, let's get you dressed right now.' She paused, lifted the bags out of the washing basket and paused as she spotted a sweater, one of Nate's. Then, determinedly, she pulled it to one side, rummaged deeper until she got to Isla's small pile of miniature clothes.

'Here you go, there are some leggings, and here's a T-shirt. How's that?' Unclipping her daughter from the child seat, Lexi pulled her into her arms, hugged her close, then with a forced smile on her face she pulled at her pyjamas, hooked them up and over her head and began to replace them with the clean but unironed clothes. 'That'll do for now, won't it?' She nodded eagerly, hoped Isla would agree, watched as she immediately climbed into the back of the car, peered at Agatha, then inquisitively picked up the small cardboard box. The delivery that had arrived just before Lexi's whole world had spun on its axis.

'What is it?'

'I don't know, baby. I think it's something your daddy must have ordered.' Lexi turned it over and over in her hands and furrowed her brow. She couldn't remember putting it in the car, didn't know how it had got to travel with them and, miserably, she read her own name on the address label. Felt a sob rise to her throat. It was the last delivery she'd ever receive at that address. Without a doubt, she knew she'd never go back. Not to that house. Not even if she wanted to. And she felt both angry and sad, all at once. Without thought, she pulled at the parcel, tore back the connecting tape – saw the small plastic chess set fall from within.

'What the hell...' Frantically, she tossed the pack up and down as though it were burning her hands. It was as though she was too afraid to touch it, felt her mind rotate with questions, couldn't understand why Nate would order the game.

Angrily and without thought, she picked up her mobile. Dialled Nate's number and, unsurprisingly, heard it go to his voicemail. Found herself throwing the phone at the passenger seat, and with her lips pressed tightly together in anger, she began helping Isla back into her seat, just as the phone pinged and Nate's ringtone filled the car with music.

'Lex... I just saw the missed calls. All fourteen of them. What's wrong? Is Isla OK?' His voice came over the speakers. It was a call she'd wanted but dreaded, and right now she trusted no one, not even Nate. Everyone around her could be dangerous. Everyone could want her dead, including him.

And now, with her eyes fixed on the chess set, she wondered how much he knew, whether he'd somehow worked out who she really was. Was this his way of punishing her? Had he purposely tried to scare her?

'Nate, I needed you, but... but like always, you didn't answer.' She grabbed at the phone, took it off speakerphone so that Isla couldn't hear, and felt her throat constrict as the words left her mouth. Barely able to speak, she held back the tears. 'I've asked you... so many times to keep your phone on.' She paused, sniffed. 'I've asked you to answer. But you never do. You just can't do it... not even for me, can you?' The anger, fear and frustration suddenly burst from deep within her, and with the memory of him answering it to his friends the night before, her mind began to turn somersaults as she went over what had happened. What he'd been doing that morning. Where he'd been. He'd been looking for Agatha too. He'd searched the house alongside her. The garden. Yet strangely and even though Agatha had still been missing, he'd left for work early. So much earlier than normal and right before the chess set had arrived. She stared at the handset, realised how little they actually talked. How their lives had been built on the initial lust, the way they'd fallen into bed and, just a couple of months later, how they'd learned of the pregnancy, quickly bought a house, moved in together. Initially, she'd felt his resentment of being forced into a relationship that had started out as a bit of fun, a few nights out, a torrid affair that had turned into something neither of them had set out to achieve. Although, after Isla had been born, she couldn't have asked for a better father for her daughter. Without a doubt, Nate loved Isla. But what about her? Right now, she needed someone to talk to. Someone she could trust with all her heart. Someone who could help her. The question was, could Nate be that person?

'Nate, where are you?' Swallowing hard, she heard him pause, listened to the sounds of the phone, the lack of building-site noise. 'Are you at the site?'

'Course I am – I mean, come on, Lex, where else would I be?'

Nothing felt right. Suspicion took over her thoughts as she heard a chime in the background, similar to the one her clock made in the hallway. 'Are you at home?'

'Lex, don't be so daft, you're paranoid. Now, are you going to tell me what's happening, what all the missed calls were about?'

Taking a moment, she closed her eyes. Went back to that morning. Someone had been outside their front door. What she couldn't understand was how he'd missed them. How he'd walked right past without seeing them. After all, whoever had put Agatha in the bin would have had to gain her trust and take the time to tie a neat bow around a wriggling kitten's neck, which would have been almost impossible. Unless, of course, she already knew and trusted you. Which begged the question: even if Nate hadn't seen anyone lurking around, how the hell had he missed the noise that Agatha had been making?

'Nate... I can't do this right now.' She glanced in the rear-view mirror at Isla, who'd settled down in her chair, her eyes drooping heavily. Even though she was probably too young to understand, having this conversation in front of her wasn't fair. Besides, as always, Lexi couldn't think of the words, didn't know what to say, how to explain. 'Isla is listening, and... I'll call you later.'

'Don't you dare. Lex. Don't you dare put the phone down.'

'I have to go.'

'Lex, talk to me. Tell me what the hell is going on. You are acting all weird. Have you been drinking again? 'Cause if you have and you're driving with my daughter in the car, I swear to God...'

'Why the hell did you buy a chess set?' The words fell from her mouth to interrupt his flow and, with Isla almost asleep, she realised that her words had been much louder and sharper than she'd intended.

'What?'

'Why the hell did you buy a chess set?' She held her breath, didn't really want to hear the answer.

'Lex, seriously, are you pissed? 'Cause I've got no idea what the hell you're talking about.' He paused. 'You hate chess.'

'I know and yet, still, we took a delivery of a chess set only this morning, right before I found Agatha in the dustbin.' She held the phone away from her ear, wiped the tears from her eyes. Omitted to mention the red silk scarf.

'What – the hell – how the hell did she get in the damn bin?'

'That's the question, Nate.' She paused, swallowed. 'She was scared, terrified in fact.' She closed her eyes for a beat. 'And what I can't understand is how you didn't hear her when you left for work, because she was yowling so damned loud it's a wonder the neighbours didn't hear her.'

At the other end of the phone, she heard Nate physically sigh. He always had a way of going quiet when under fire. Didn't like any kind of conflict; in fact, his totally relaxed attitude to life, along with his come-to-bed eyes, had possibly been the exact things that had attracted her the most. But today, she didn't like it. He seemed much too calm, and by way of self-protection she could imagine her brick wall once again begin to erect itself. This time it went up at speed, so quickly she couldn't stop it. Closing her eyes, she could hear his words, couldn't allow them to penetrate her mind.

'Lex, what's wrong? 'Cause it seems to me that you're looking for an argument.' His voice was now sharp, abrupt. 'So, come on, what will it be, a five-minute or ten-minute argument? 'Cause I'd kind of like to know how bad this is before I get home.'

It was the sentence that normally made her smile. Especially when she knew she was in the wrong and arguing for the sake of it. In fact, it was quite often the one sentence he'd come out with that would normally make her laugh. But today was different. Today, his words had no effect at all and without another word she glared at the phone, flicked it off. Saw his name disappear. Then she switched off the power, threw the phone on the passenger seat, started the engine and glanced through the rear-view mirror at Isla, who now slept peacefully, completely oblivious to what had just happened.

12

Leaving the A171, Lexi joined the A19 and automatically headed north. It was a route she'd taken at least a hundred times before and as she saw signs for the A1, she felt a huge sigh of relief leave her body. Her shoulders began to relax. The pressure that had built up in her mind had begun to subdue, and a calmness filled her as she headed for her childhood home, the one and only place she'd ever felt truly safe.

With tired eyes, she glanced in the rear-view mirror, felt thankful that Isla had slept for most of the past hour, a time when her anxiety had been at its worst, yet now as she neared the island, the deep-seated nausea began to pass, which was surprising as she'd munched her way through half a tube of stale-tasting Pringles that had been lying around in the car for much longer than she could remember.

Indicating right at the Lindisfarne Inn, Lexi puffed up her cheeks, blew out, could almost feel the intensity of the island as she got closer and closer. After crossing the train lines, she leaned into the twists and turns of the road, sat up as high as she could in her seat, until excitedly she rounded the last corner, looked for the causeway, and disappointedly she was met with a view of the incoming tide. Waves rolled unceremoniously to lap over the edge of the causeway with a growing intensity. Angrily, she simply stared at the island. It was almost within her grasp and, for a moment, she tried to work out how deep the water would be, whether she could risk the crossing.

'Damn it,' she cursed, punched the steering wheel, heard the horn blast and through her rear-view mirror she saw Isla jump out of her deep, peaceful sleep, a look of panic on her face. 'Oh, honey, Mummy's sorry. It was just the car; it made a horrid noise, didn't it?' Pulling the handbrake on, Lexi had no choice but to park. To wait. If it had been the summer and she'd been alone without any luggage or weight in the car, she'd have considered the risk, but with the water so cold, the car so heavy and having Isla with her, trying to beat the tide would be a foolish thing to do, a thing that the tourists often did and failed.

Slumping back in her seat, Lexi thought of all the times she'd seen them take the risk. The way they'd thought the water shallow enough to drive through and how they'd got it disastrously wrong, which had meant the coastguard would be called out and by the time they got there, the occupants of the car would be standing on the car's roof, with waves lapping around their ankles, the car ruined and towed away by the tide, or left so full of the sea it had to be recovered by tow trucks later.

Checking her watch, she turned in her seat to see Isla comically tipping her head from side to side; she was looking her teddy bear straight in the eye, chatting away, with Agatha watching suspiciously from within her cage.

'It's OK. Mummy said sorry for making the noise,' Isla said in broken baby words with her tiny, high-pitched voice that had a soft lilt of Nate's Irish tone, nodding enthusiastically. It was a sound that suddenly made Lexi's heart constrict and she looked at where her phone lay beside her. It was still switched off and she wondered how many times Nate might have tried to call her back. Whether he'd even worked out that she'd gone, left forever with little or no intention of ever going back. His whole idea of a family Christmas, of a tree, turkey and trimmings, had disappeared in a single morning, along with all the presents that were still up in the loft, waiting to be wrapped and, without warning, another heart-wrenching sob left Lexi's throat. The presents had been the last thing on her mind and now she wondered what she'd do and how she'd give her baby girl a Christmas at all. But after finding Agatha wrapped in the scarf, she'd known that someone out there had known where she lived, where her child lived, that the scarf had been a warning and, in her terror to keep them both alive, all thoughts of Christmas had been a million miles from her mind.

Picking up the phone, she allowed her finger to hover over the on button, then threw it back on the seat. She couldn't bear to ask the questions, could hear the constant accusations that came from within her, didn't want to consider them. Closing her eyes, she could see Nate's face, his smile, the passion they'd shared. Had it been enough? Should they have had more of a connection, more trust between them? She'd had his child, hadn't she? She should have been able to tell him everything. Her worries. Her fears. Who her father was, and what he'd done. But for some reason, she hadn't. She'd kept her past and her identity from him.

With one eye on the chess set, she felt doubt move slowly through her thoughts. If he had bought the chess set, if he had meant to upset her, punish her in some way, then maybe she deserved that, but the thought that he could do anything to Isla was unbearable, yet still he'd done it. Or... had he? But if he hadn't bought it, who had? She tried to find the answers but couldn't. Wondered if she was looking for them far too closely.

Sitting back, she tried to relax against her seat, stared at the incoming sea, ran a hand through her hair. In her panic that morning, she hadn't even brushed it and she quickly began digging around in the glovebox, her handbag and then through the large grey holdall that was dragged through from the back footwell. Pulling out a make-up bag and hairbrush, she began to tidy herself up, stared back at herself through the rear-view mirror.

'You'll have to do,' she whispered. Then, slowly but determinedly, she turned the car back in the direction of The Barn, pulled into its car park and felt grateful for the restaurant's refuge. She took in the large stone and wood-built building that served the best coffee around, and suddenly, she felt herself relax. No one could possibly know where she was, not unless they'd followed her, which she was sure that no one had, but suspiciously she looked at each car, most of which had just arrived in the car park, something that always happened the moment the causeway closed. The Barn was both a restaurant and a coffee shop. The perfect vantage point where the island could easily be seen. A place where they could wait for the causeway to open, and most of the people that had parked were doing exactly the same as she was – simply waiting to go to the island.

'Mummy, I'm hungry.' Isla dropped her teddy, held out her arms, looked down at the seat belt and waited until Lexi unclipped it.

'You're a big girl now, it's about time you learned to open this yourself.' Lexi smiled, watched as Isla tried to press the oversized button with her tiny little finger, pulled a face, then shook her head, gave a pleading smile and waited.

'It's easy, look. Press here,' Lexi said as she pointed to the button, unclipped the belt and then lovingly ran a hand over her daughter's cheek, held it there protectively. 'You're such a good girl, aren't you?' She held her gaze, smiled. 'Now, this place does the best chippies ever, or...' She tried to remember the menu. 'I think they do maccy cheese? Do you think you'd like some of that?' Watching as Isla nodded to the idea of her favourite food, Lexi grabbed at a coat from the wash basket and gave a longing look at the island, now mysteriously surrounded by the sea and mist. So close, yet just out of reach.

'Do you see, Isla? That's Holy Island.' She paused, waited for Isla to climb onto her knee. 'This is where Maggie lives. You remember Maggie coming to visit us, don't you?' Lexi allowed herself a moment's recollection. Remembered the pleasure she'd taken in Maggie's visit, the way she'd nervously tidied the house, arranged the guest room and the way Isla had immediately warmed to her, followed her around and insisted on being with her for the duration of the visit.

Isla nodded enthusiastically, held out her arms for her coat. 'Will Maggie feed Agafa? She's hungry.' Lexi peered over the top of Isla's head at the kitten, who'd woken up, stretched, and was now clawing impatiently at the cage door.

Puckering her lips at her daughter, she smiled as Isla responded immediately, wrapped her arms around her neck, cuddled in. Breathing in, Lexi closed her eyes, held on to the moment. Realised how much both Isla and the kitten depended on her, needed her. Isla was far too small, and Agatha had been far too pampered as a house cat to hunt for herself. Neither could survive without her and she had every intention of looking after them both. By taking them to the island, she was hiding them from the world, just as she'd been hidden as a child. It was all she could think to do, because whoever had killed her mother was very probably out to kill her too.

13

I can't describe the anger I feel as I stand here with the easterly wind blowing relentlessly over the top of the dunes. It's cutting through me, chilling me to the bone, making me wish I'd killed you in the car park, while I had the chance. After all, by killing you then, you'd have saved me the journey of coming here, of reinstating my life on the island. And even though not everyone is pleased that I keep returning and blending into island life, I'm slowly making my existence here just a little more believable. And although I never wished for it to happen, some days I even feel as though I belong.

Looking at my watch, my anger grows. I made my intentions very clear – I was at your house, right outside your front door – and I'd have thought that a threat like that would have sent you racing for the car. Certainly, in plenty of time to make the crossing. But maybe I got it wrong. Maybe you won't run back to the island as I'd thought and even if you are, it doesn't look like you made the crossing.

Thoughtfully, I'm standing on the edge of the water, poking the toe of my boot in and out of the sea. Just the thought of the water makes me shudder as one cold wave after the other rolls towards me. Each one faster, crueller and colder than the one before as they bounce up and over the pebble beach. It's a sign that the tide is coming in, that the sea is about to completely surround the island and that, once it does, everyone on it will be isolated from the mainland – for at least five hours.

Pulling my coat tightly around me, I zip it up, kick out at the grass, at the tufts that stick up along the edge of the paths and I make my way off the beach and through the sand dunes, all the time climbing until I reach the highest point near The Snook. From my vantage point, I keep my eyes on the water and for just a few seconds I wonder what it would be like to walk back to the beach and straight into the ice-cold sea until it covers me completely. I stand and consider the option while all the time knowing how unpredictable the water can be. How the tides can change. And that to accidentally fall into the water, even for a few seconds, at this time of year could cause the body to go into shock and kill the strongest of swimmers and, with a morbid fascination, I wonder what it would be like to watch you drown. Whether you'd fight to survive. Whether you'd simply sink deeper and deeper, until you dropped beneath the surface and disappeared to a place where no one would find you.

For a moment, I stare at the water, at the ripples caused by the tide, imagine it happening, then smile with delight as a small grey seal pops its head up and out of the sea; the image of you is lost. And instead, I take pleasure in the animal. It's swimming a little way from the island and spins around like a comical periscope, until it stares directly at me. And suddenly, I find myself looking into a pair of coal-black eyes that are wide and sparkling with moisture. It's one of the most beautiful creatures I've ever seen, and I watch it until it dives below the surface, disappears below waves. They're waves that are growing more intense by the minute, and I think it's gone. Then, magically, it pops back up, as though playing a game of hide-and-seek, all by itself, while constantly looking for food that's been brought in on the tide.

As the seal finally disappears, I use my vantage point, stand on my tiptoes, get a view of the causeway. It snakes out towards the land, disappearing below the waves, only for a small part of it to emerge again beside a hut that stands out of the sea on stilts, and I feel the anger bubbling within me, feeling furious that you didn't come and, with a feeling of desperation that stays with me, I just hope that I did enough. After all, it's what you do, you always do. You run towards the island in times of distress, and away from it the moment you get too comfortable.

Strangely, I should be grateful for your late arrival: it gives me more time to plan, and even though I feel a bitter disappointment that you didn't make the crossing, I'll bide my time, get settled back in, make a few acquaintances, and wait for the tide to recede.

Smiling, I feel the adrenaline within me. I've waited so long for this moment. It feels almost painful. It's now twenty years since I saw your face on the news, a similar age to myself at the time, a similar child in so many ways. And even though your face had been blurred out, I could still see how pale, thin and haunted you were. Just by the way you hung on to the adult's hand, your face turned pathetically upwards. You acted your role well as you were led past the cameras. Everyone knew you were guilty, just by association. You carry his blood, which means you must be evil too and, in my mind's eye, I've imagined your face every day since. Tried to visualise your life. What you were doing. How happy you were and where you'll be when I finally take my revenge. The only bonus I didn't expect is that you have a daughter. Imagine my surprise when I heard this news of her birth and how stupid you'll feel when you realise that, by trying to protect her, you fled away from danger – only to run directly towards it. Your life is about to end – you just don't know it yet, and once the tide comes in, you'll be trapped on the island... with no means of escape.

14

It was almost two o'clock in the afternoon, five hours after she'd arrived in Northumberland, before Lexi drove through the thick, misty sea fret and, with the island emerging before her, drove slowly along the causeway. Storm Arwen had caused a lot of damage to the road, and she swerved in and out, making sure her car missed the potholes and small sections of road that had been completely washed away. Workmen were quickly trying to repair the damage, and she found herself staring inquisitively at the diggers, lorries and contractors who moved back in to do their work as the sea went out. With a satisfied wave, she took pleasure in the way the causeway twisted around the island and with each twist or turn in the road, it revealed just a little more of the island at a time, like a long, winding snake. Each bend in the road made her smile grow wider, her heart boom with a little more rhythm. It was a welcome feeling after what felt like a whole day of it beating rapidly, making her feel as though she'd been running at speed, unable to stop, or to take a break, even if she'd wanted to.

Looking across the island, she glanced at The Snook and the many sand dunes that formed the landscape of the nature reserve, imagined the long rocky beach she'd always loved, which stood right at the other side, currently out of sight, but in her mind, she could imagine every stone, every rock precariously balanced on top of the other. A tradition created by the tourists, where the stones were originally stacked by way of navigation, yet now it happened because one tourist copied the other, seeing the stones and creating a pile of their own.

Slowing the car, Lexi stared at the intricate pathways leading through the dunes, paths she'd walked so many times before, each one leading to the coast, carefully winding its way around the island's edge, until like everything else on the island it eventually reaches the castle. Everything about the island made her smile. Each part gave her a significant memory, and the further into the island she drove, the more she felt her breathing return to normal, her shoulders relax, her anxiety subside.

Looking across at her phone again, she felt a deep-seated sadness. Now she'd had time to think about it logically, she knew that Nate couldn't be responsible for tying the silk scarf around Agatha, or for scaring her half to death. There was no possible reason for him to do that. If Nate had known who she was, who her father had been, her mother's murder would have given him the perfect opportunity to bring the subject up, to start the discussion she'd been avoiding for years.

With one hand on the steering wheel, she turned the phone over and over with her other. She felt a surge of guilt and realised that when he got home, the house would be empty, and his life would never be the same.

Taking in a deep breath, she tried to clear her mind. Continually looked out to sea, imagined the chess set falling into her lap, relived the fear she'd felt. Had it been a coincidence? But if so, why? Why had the chess set turned up the morning after her mother's death? Why had Agatha been tied with a red silk scarf? Someone had been close enough to do that and most probably the same person who'd sent the chess set. Yet still, her mind ran over the conversation she'd had with Nate. She could still hear the shocked sound of his voice. Which all led to a bigger, more sinister question. If Nate hadn't ordered the chess set, who had?

There were so many unanswered questions. And now, she regretted having hidden so much of her life from so many people. People like Nate, his family, people she used to love. Correction – still loved. In trying to keep her anonymity, she'd lost just about every person she'd ever cared about. Every time someone got close, she'd run away, started again. For the whole of her life, she'd been too afraid to allow anyone to love her, just in case they left her too, abandoned her just like both her mother and father had.

'Hey, don't go back to sleep. We're nearly there,' she whispered excitedly to Isla, whose eyes once again drooped heavily in her car seat. 'We're gonna see Maggie. You love Maggie, don't you?' It was true, Isla had always gravitated towards Maggie. During every visit she'd always clung to her like a baby limpet. Followed her around, talked to her repeatedly. 'And when we get there, one of the first things we need to do is get Agatha out of her basket.' She paused, looked through the rear-view mirror at Isla, who at the mention of Maggie's name had now sat up as high as she could in her car seat, peering eagerly out of the window. 'Agatha's been in there a long time now, hasn't she?' She pressed her lips tightly together, hoped Isla wouldn't take it upon herself to let the kitten out. Thought about how, at The Barn, they'd done just that and how difficult it had been to catch her again and the resistance she'd shown at being placed back in the cage.

'Oh look, Isla, there's the big car park,' she gasped. 'Wow, it's already getting full and there's a coach. I didn't expect that today. The island is going to be busy.' With a furrowed brow, she wondered why there were so many visitors. It was still early in

December, too early for the solstice, but that didn't stop the young at heart turning up for the beach barbecues, or the music and dancing that often happened by the lime kilns. And even though the winter weather could be cruel, most would brave the elements to balance their rock towers on the beach, or simply sit on the grass to take in the sea, and the stars. It was a festival that used to happen on just one date a year. Yet now, it went on for weeks. A celebration so good, the visitors wanted to recreate it whenever they came, and even though it was frowned upon by the authorities, it was a festival the island didn't seem to mind; after all, the visitors brought revenue to the islanders. But so many people on the island so late always made her worry as to whether the causeway would be open long enough for them all to leave – before the night drew in and once again the sea cut them off.

Inching forward in her seat, Lexi negotiated the narrow lane, the square. Headed for the Manor House Hotel and pulled in through the gates, into the car park, manoeuvred her car past the ice-cream board and across the gravel towards the sheds, where she stopped to stare at the priory. It stood menacingly to her right, surrounded by the remaining sea fret, giving it a mysterious and eerie feeling that sent a series of shivers travelling along her spine. Both the priory and the castle had been a view she'd grown up with. Her childhood playground. A place where she'd spent hours and hours, ignoring the world, pretending that life on the mainland didn't exist.

Taking a deep inward breath, she looked over her shoulder, gazed at the hotel. It was a building she'd seen for almost all of her life, standing just across from Maggie's home, and a place she'd always loved, especially when the tourists had arrived. The bar was normally full to bursting, the atmosphere bouncing with fun and laughter. Yet now, she wondered how full it would be, and for once, she wished to have the island to herself, a moment to reminisce over old times and memories past.

With a slight hesitation, she climbed out of the car, gasped as a strong, easterly breeze whipped her hair around her face like a blindfold, temporarily covering her eyes and restricting her view. Holding on to the car door with one hand, she used the other to move her hair just in time to see Maggie's rotund frame hurtling towards her.

'Oh my God, I saw you drive past, I just knew you'd park in here.' She paused, looked Lexi up and down. 'Let me look at you.' A pair of strong, sturdy hands gripped Lexi's shoulders before she felt herself surrounded in a bear hug. It was a hug she willingly fell into. Felt the relief fall from her body as she took a deep breath in, took in the same unmistakable scent she'd loved as a child, felt herself smile as Maggie repeatedly kissed her on the cheek.

'Mwah, mwah, mwah, mwah... I've missed you so much and thank God you came, now... let me check you're OK.' Maggie furrowed her brow, stared into her eyes and slowly shook her head with a knowing look. 'You're home now. It's over. You're safe.'

'Oh, Maggie. Am I... am I safe? What if – what if the killer follows me? What if he knows where I am?' She realised that she could have been followed, and if she had, she'd have brought the killer to the island. The thought made her legs go weak, her fear palpable, and she reached for the car, held on to the door.

'OK. I've got you. That's right, lean on the car.' Maggie held on to her arm. 'You've had a hell of day, my girl, haven't you?' She gave her one of her deep, empathetic looks. It was a look that Lexi could immediately read. And without too many words or questions, she knew that Maggie would understand what she'd gone through and, best of all, she'd know the best way to make her feel better. It was something she'd always done, surrounding those she loved with a protective cloak, shielding them from the rest of the world. It was something Lexi had seen so many times before and always done in a way that left her and the other foster children cocooned with a love that lasted a lifetime.

'Why was I different?' Lexi had once asked. 'Why did I stay, when all the others came and went?'

'Oh, that's a simple one to answer.' Maggie had touched a hand to her heart, brushed the hair away from Lexi's face and kissed her on the cheek. 'You, my girl. You got me here.' She'd paused, looked thoughtful. 'The others, they all had homes to go back to, all of them apart from you and Harry and neither of you had anyone else, and to let either of you leave, it would have broken my heart.' The words had been heartfelt and, as other children arrived, Lexi had carefully watched as Maggie had pulled them all into the safety of the house, made each one of them welcome. Lexi tried to remember if she'd ever really said thank you, if she'd ever told this amazing woman how much she appreciated everything she'd ever done for her. Knew she had to make it a priority to do so.

'Now then, come on. Let's get this little girl out of the car, take you both to the cottage.' She paused, smiled. 'Isla's never been to my house, have you, and I... I have some sausages in the oven, some fresh crusty bread.' She pulled the car door open, unclipped Isla from her chair and pulled her into a familiar hold that the child happily fell into.

With her eyes still closed, Lexi remembered the first time she'd met Maggie as a terrified six-year-old. It had been a day when she'd arrived on the island in the care of a social worker. She'd felt so unsure of what was happening, of the future, of where she'd end up. Yet within minutes of arriving, Maggie had settled herself on the floor beside her; she'd leaned back against the settee, and casually plucked what Lexi had thought to be a random book from the bookcase. Turning the pages, she'd begun to read. Just a few pages at first, with all the best voices. Until she'd lain the book down on her lap, tipped her head to one side and whispered, 'Do you know what, I'm so tired, but I do love this story and... well, I'd really like to hear what happens next.' There had been a pause, a soft, gentle smile, followed by a nudge. 'And I was wondering. Seeing as you're such a big girl, I thought that maybe you'd like to finish the story for me? And if it's OK with you?' She had patted the worn leather sofa. 'I thought we might we sit up here, together, on the settee.' She'd thumbed the book. 'It's a bit comfier than the floor, and if you like, I could make us some lovely hot chocolate.' She'd paused, bit down on her lip thoughtfully. 'I think I have a bag of those marshmallow things in the cupboard; we could sprinkle them on top, wait for them to melt and then drink it while we finish the story.'

Sitting forward, Lexi had tried to work out who she could trust. If she could trust. Wasn't sure. She remembered taking her time to study the woman. To look at her eyes. At how gentle they were. And then at how soft her hands looked, and how nervously she'd played with the apron strings that had been tied around her waist in a bow.

'What if I don't know the words?' Lexi had finally replied, her eyes fixed firmly on the settee. 'I don't know all my words yet.'

'Well...' Maggie had responded. 'That dictionary, it is a big book to learn, isn't it? And to be honest, I'd have been surprised if you'd known all the words in it, because I don't know them all yet either and I'm a lot older than you are.' She'd laughed. 'But if we read the story together, I could always help you. And if you come across a word that you're not sure of, we could try and work it out. And if we're still a bit stuck...' Again, she'd paused, turned to the bookshelf, pulled another book towards her. Waved it around in the air. 'We could look it up in this big old dictionary.'

It was an act she saw Maggie do with other children. An act she perfected over the years that followed and it worked especially well if the children were scared, needed time to blend, or simply to understand how much love Maggie had to give. It was a love that was theirs for the taking, so long as they wanted to take it. And now, here Maggie was, with Isla in her arms, loving her and taking care of her in that very same way.

'I didn't know where else to go,' Lexi suddenly whispered. She didn't want Isla to hear, held back the tears. 'Whoever it was. They knew where I lived, they were right by my door. Just feet from where Isla was playing.' A sob left her throat. 'What if...' She pointed to Isla, who'd now wriggled out of Maggie's arms and was busy pulling her teddies out of the car. 'What if Isla had gone outside, what if...' Her voice trailed off as the tears began to fall. 'Especially after... you did see the news, didn't you?' She couldn't say the words, knew that Maggie would understand.

'Well, she didn't go outside and you're here now. You're safe.' Maggie's warm, gentle voice surrounded her. 'Besides, where else would you go? This is your home. And without a doubt' – once again, Maggie's arms surrounded her with love – 'this is exactly where you should be. You can leave the car here. It's safer than parking it on the road or leaving it in the main car park; at least then we can keep an eye on who is around it.' She took in a deep breath, peered over Lexi's shoulder to where Isla was pushing her teddies into a rucksack. 'Now, we should go back to the cottage.'

'Maggie... Agafa, she needs to come too,' Isla whispered; she pulled on Maggie's skirt, stood on her tiptoes, pointed to the kitten. 'She wants to come out.'

'Well then, we'd better take her home, hadn't we?' Maggie's smile lit up her face as she reached into the car and pulled out the basket. 'Do you know what, when you've eaten up your sausages, I have some blueberry muffins that you might like.' She paused, winked. 'They came out of the oven about half an hour ago, and I bet they'll be just about ready to eat.' Giving Lexi a questioning look, she saw the way Lexi gazed at the hotel, waited. 'So, why don't me and you go and take a look at what's cooking, while Mummy has a few minutes to say hello to her friends?'

Shaking her head quickly, Lexi took Isla's hand in hers. 'No, it's fine. I...' She looked down at her daughter, felt that invisible thread holding them together. Felt almost terrified to leave her and took slow, deep breaths before looking up and catching Maggie's eye. 'I've been so scared...' she whispered. 'So frightened to let her out of my sight...' She paused, swallowed. 'They were right there. Right outside my door and I'd never forgive myself. Not ever, if...'

Maggie's arm immediately went around her shoulders and she nodded thoughtfully before speaking. 'And you know that I'd die before I'd allow anyone to hurt her, don't you?' She stepped forward, pointed to the cottage across the road. 'And that house. It's been a safe house for years. A lot of children have been brought here, all as scared and vulnerable as you were.' Again, she paused, lifted a hand to Lexi's cheek, followed it with a kiss. 'I promise you. No harm came to any of them, not ever. Not on my watch.'

Looking wistfully at the hotel, Lexi tried to peer in through the window. Desperately wanted to step inside, just to be somewhere familiar, somewhere that held the memories, a place where she knew Harry would be.

'Go on...' Maggie leaned forward, and as though reading her mind, she tapped her gently on the shoulder. 'Why don't you pop inside? He only got back this morning.' She stared deep into Lexi's eyes, smiled. 'I told him you were coming. He's dying to see you.'

15

Walking into the dimly lit bar, Lexi nervously slid herself onto one of the bench seats. Picked up the menu and pretended to read. It was a menu she'd helped create during the time she'd worked there. Yet today, it looked new, fresh, somehow different and she used the cardboard as a screen to hide behind, while looking around – surreptitiously taking in all the familiar faces, along with one or two new ones.

Realising that a good percentage of the people who were sitting in the bar had been coming to the Manor House for several years, she tried to relax. Noticed how they congregated in corners, kicked off their shoes, made the most of the comfortable settees, with views of both the priory and the castle through the windows, and the soft music that played in the background.

The more obvious newcomers sat huddled up together. Munched on their freshly served food, chatted in hushed tones and nervously tried to control the dogs who sat hungrily waiting for the leftovers. All apart from one group of young adults, who sat in a small group, had a pile of rucksacks by their feet, drank beers and cider like they were going out of fashion. An air of excitement surrounded them, and Lexi eavesdropped on their conversation, knew they'd come over for a party on the beach, a night of camping down by the old lime kilns, a place where camping was strictly forbidden.

Suspiciously, Lexi moved her gaze from one group to the other. And even though there were one or two new people on the island, it was the man who sat at the bar that kept drawing her attention. He was young, late twenties with dark hair, and unshaven. He seemed to pivot on his stool, anxiously stare over the top of his pint, and Lexi rolled her eyes from side to side, tried to work out who he was watching, where his gaze had landed, whether he was alone, and with an anxious feeling inside, she thought of Isla, wished she hadn't left her to go with Maggie, began to stand up and inch her way towards the door in the hope she could escape, run to Maggie's, lock the door.

'Well, well, well, look who finally rolled in.' Harry's voice boomed across the bar. He'd been pouring a pint, stood it on the chrome serving tray in front of the man, flashed her a warm but pensive smile. 'I almost didn't believe her when Maggie said you'd called...' He stood back with his hands on his hips and playfully he pushed his tongue firmly in his cheek. 'Yet here you are, back on the island, looking all grown-up.'

Feeling the colour rise to her cheeks, and with one eye constantly watching the man, Lexi wafted the menu around in the air, used it as a fan. Then, with a determined effort, she stood up, copied his stance. 'All grown-up indeed. It isn't that long since I last saw you.' She thought back to the last time she'd been on the island, the intimacy they'd shared and, feeling terrified she'd been falling in love with him, the way she'd run from the island, cruelly left him behind, a typical Dear John letter left on the pillow. Smiling, she nervously pressed her lips together. Wondered whether she should have stayed on the island, allowed the relationship to develop, see where it had really been heading and given him the chance. 'You're looking good, Harry.' She poked him in the ribs. 'Couldn't you have got all ugly or fat or something during the past three years?' She took a quick step backwards, looked him up and down with appreciation, then fell into his arms, took comfort in his hold, held on for a little too long. 'It's good to be home, Harry,' she whispered, kissed him on the cheek. 'Who's the guy?' She looked over his shoulder at the empty bar seat, the half-pint that stood abandoned on the bar. Spinning around on the spot, she felt confused, was sure he hadn't walked past her, and tipped her head to one side, looked through the door, towards the resident stairs. 'Is he staying here?'

'Yeah, he's a resident. Room nine. Think he said he was an author, working on his next novel. Why, were you planning on going over and chatting him up?' He laughed, raised his eyebrows in question.

'Don't be daft, he just looked a bit overly inquisitive. I didn't like it.' Even though Harry had explained who he was, she felt the internal angst once again build inside her. She tried to focus on her breathing, on what Harry was saying.

'Maggie said you were bringing Isla with you.' He gave her a cheeky grin, looked over at the table where she'd been sitting, his eyes searching for the child. 'Where is she... I...'

'Where do you think she is?' She pointed through the window. 'I kind of thought it a good idea to lock her in the car. I told her to be good and stay quiet.' Seeing the look of horror on Harry's face, she couldn't stop herself from laughing. 'Oh Harry, you should know better. Maggie's already whisked her off to the cottage, along with our kitten and half the teddy bears in the north-east. Apparently, she's making her famous sausage sandwiches, followed by blueberry muffins that miraculously just seem to have come out of the oven.' Lexi glanced through the window, then gasped. 'Actually...

you're about to meet Isla right now.' She watched Maggie walk past the window, a very vocal Isla trotting along beside her, noticed the way Harry tipped his head to one side, stared as Isla ran into the bar, stopped, and cautiously studied the room, until she spotted her mummy and ran to her with a bright smile to light up her face.

'Apparently, we needed some crisps,' Maggie announced. 'The green and blue packets that we have at the cottage are not the right ones and only the ones in a red packet will do.' Smiling, Maggie waved and acknowledged various customers as she marched through the bar, Then, with one hand on her hip, she leaned on the bar, waited for Shelly, one of the regular barmaids, to dig through a large box of crisps until a packet of plain crisps was found.

'Crisps, hey. I thought you were having sausages?' Lexi asked as Isla wrapped herself like a limpet around her leg. A pair of sharp, pointy fingers gripped her skin like a vice. 'You don't even like crisps.' She ruffled the two-year-old's hair. 'Anyhow, you don't need to hide.' She wriggled out of Isla's clutch, held out her arms and lifted her up. 'Do you think you could say hello to Harry?'

With Isla snuggled tightly in her arms, Lexi watched as she peeked at everyone in the bar, except for Harry. Which wasn't surprising, as the only man Isla had ever really been around was Nate. And although Harry was more than loveable, and larger than life, he was very different in both looks and personality and it suddenly occurred to Lexi just how much of a showman Harry had always been. He was the young man with the unruly blonde hair, the one who'd always entertained the crowd with his jokes or his songs. Growing up, he'd been the tall, scrawny kid who made everyone laugh, but now he caught people's attention for a very different reason, especially the women who circulated around him, listening to his every word.

'Come on, Isla,' Lexi continued, 'say hello to Harry... he's... well, he's kind of your uncle.' She paused, thought for a moment. 'That's right. He's your uncle Harry; you've never had an uncle before, have you?' She gave him a half-smile, caught his eye, saw him nod pensively, and with a yearning she didn't know she had, she thought about their teenage years, the years they'd lived together at Maggie's as 'temporary' siblings. It had been a time when both had needed the other, a time when confidences had been shared, and a time when in every other life they'd have been childhood sweethearts – yet that line hadn't been crossed, not until they'd been much older. And now, Lexi wondered if that line should never have been crossed at all. Wanted to kick herself for having been so weak, so vulnerable at the time. And slowly, she took a breath in, knew that leaving the island had been the right thing to do. After all, if she hadn't gone when she did, she'd have never met Nate, she wouldn't have become a journalist and Isla... she held tightly to her daughter, wondered if she'd have ever been born at all.

'I guess I can go with being an uncle...' Pressing his lips tightly together, Lexi sensed his unease, saw the hurt in his eyes, the way he avoided her gaze. 'I could be good at being an uncle, ask anyone.' He tried to laugh, spun around as Maggie's hand landed lovingly on his shoulder, and tapped him on the cheek as she held his gaze, gave him a motherly look.

'Right, we'll be off,' Maggie said. 'I've got the cottage all warm and cosy. No doubt we'll get back and Agatha will have eaten all the muffins. She really doesn't like the cage, quite the escapologist she is, and up to now she's climbed up everything including the Christmas tree.' She paused, passed Isla the bag of crisps. Held a finger to her lips, pretending to share a secret.

Suddenly looking nervous following Maggie's departure, Harry stepped from foot to foot, looked down at the floor, struggled with the words and, eventually, he pointed to the bar.

'Lex... I've got to ask, is she...?'

'Harry, don't,' Lexi cut in. 'Just, don't.' She felt the floor move beneath her feet, the air leave the room, and the need to sit down suddenly became more than overwhelming, until she felt Harry's arm slide unexpectedly around her, guiding her to the empty seat that stood by the bar.

'Look, do you want a coffee, or something... you know, stronger?' He pointed to the jars, to the different strengths of bean. 'You kind of look like you need it. I could make you an Irish coffee, or I have a bottle of that gin you like.'

'Hey.' Thankful of the change of subject, she slapped him playfully on the arm. 'How the hell would you know what gin I prefer?' She looked at the coffee machine. Thought of all the days she'd worked here, battled with the buttons. The way she'd cursed it at both breakfast and dinner, hated it with a passion, yet somehow, she'd always got it to work, and served the coffee with a smile. And just as she had so many times in the past, she ran a finger across the oak bar, stopped when she reached the edge of the machine. Closed her eyes. Made a wish.

'I should get going.' She looked through the window, where the rain had begun to lash against the glass. 'I can't expect Maggie to look after both Isla and Agatha, can I? Especially if Agatha has taken to climbing the Christmas tree. Besides, it's forever since I saw her and... well, I have a huge urge to hug her so much, tell her how much I appreciate her.' She paused, knew he was staring at her, felt the colour once again rise to her cheeks.

'Lex,' he asked nervously, 'are you coming down the beach tonight?' He walked past her, sidestepped a golden Labrador, and quickly ran a hand lovingly over its head as he passed. It was a simple yet caring action. One that was very typical of Harry, where everything he did was followed by a smile, a cheeky comment, or a knowing look shared between himself and one of the punters.

'The beach, why the hell would I want to do that?'

''Cause there's gonna be a party. A few of us are going down there, making a few fire baskets, having a barbecue, you know the drill in December, Lex. It's what we do.'

She shook her head, closed her eyes. Remembered the last time she and Harry had sat on the beach in the darkness, the promises they'd made, ones she'd quickly broken. She breathed in slowly. Felt the angst growing inside, the way it rose from her toes, stopped at her throat, squeezed and constricted like a scarf tightening around it. Swallowing, she shook her head, thought of Isla, of protecting her, flashed a look through the window and to where Maggie's quaint cottage stood, beyond the hotel gates. 'I need to take care of Isla. It's been a big day for her, and I can't expect Maggie to look after her, it wouldn't be fair.'

Harry stopped in his tracks, leaned against the bar. Turned. 'Why don't you bring her with you. I... well, you know I'd love to see her,' he said hopefully. 'You know, get to know her a little and eventually, you never know, she might even like me.'

Rolling her eyes, she shook her head. 'For God's sake, Harry. Have you seen the weather?' She pointed to the window. 'You'd be off your trolley to drag a two-year-old down to the beach in the middle of the night. It'll most probably be cold, dark and chucking it down.'

Running a hand through his hair, he turned, caught her gaze, raised an inquisitive eyebrow. 'Lex, sun sets at just four o'clock; it's hardly the middle of the night, is it? And the weather will dry up, I checked.' He waved his phone around in the air. 'And as for Maggie, she'll be loving every minute of having Isla to herself, and you just know it.' He walked out of the bar and into the carpeted reception, looked over his shoulder, waited for her to follow and momentarily leaned back against the oak balustrade of the staircase, before turning towards her. Smiling, he looked her up and down. Then, with the energy of a bodybuilder, he stepped forward, picked her up, spun her around. 'Lex.' He stared into her eyes. 'I'm so glad you're here and... Argh,' he growled. 'Come on. Come down to the beach with me tonight.' He held her gaze, lifted a hand to her face. 'I've missed you... and I still have no idea what went wrong, why you left?'

Feeling the stress of the past two days catch up, Lexi avoided his eyes, laid her head against his shoulder, felt his arms tighten around her. 'Harry. I...'

'Shh...' he whispered, allowed his lips to graze her forehead. 'Do you know what, don't, don't tell me, I... I don't need to know. You're... you're back now...'

Lexi could see him struggle with the words, the pain he'd obviously felt, the abandonment he'd have had to go through, felt the guilt tear through her. He'd been the last person in the world she'd ever wanted to hurt, or to leave behind. The one person she'd been too afraid to love. And, ironically, she felt the security within his arms that she'd failed to find there before, couldn't imagine letting go. And now, three years after she'd run from him, she tried to understand why she'd ever left, knew deep down it had been the right thing to do. That staying would have made it worse, more painful that it had been.

'I'm so sorry.' She didn't know what else to say. Watched a young waitress walk past with plates full of food, her eyes wide with interest, a wry smile crossing her face.

'Hey, it's fine,' he said. 'You had your reasons.'

Shaking her head, she turned in his arms. Looked through the door and into the bar. 'No, Harry, it isn't fine.' At the time she'd known she had her reasons, but now she felt the guilt, knew how much hurt they'd both been through since that day. Wondered if it had been worth it. Her whole life had changed so much because of that decision. It had gone from being a slow, almost calm existence of daily life on the island to one that was like an unpredictable nightmare, with twists and turns she'd have never imagined. Struggling with her emotions, she tried to decide whether all she'd ever needed had been right here, on the island – she just hadn't known it.

Puffing up her cheeks and blowing out with frustration, she moved away, tried to think of a way to change the subject, searched the walls, the pictures, the map of the island. 'So, the beach tonight, who's going...' Her words were swallowed in a gush of air as the front door flew open, and a tall, familiar-looking woman rushed in.

'Hey, baby, surprise... it's so good to be home. Did you miss me? Did you? Did you?' Her voice was shrill, more than excited. Her arms immediately launching themselves around his neck, her mouth possessively landing on his, where it lingered lovingly. She was all coats and bags; her perfectly coifed, long copper hair floated effortlessly around her shoulders, making Lexi look at the door to see if the rain had stopped, or whether the woman had been followed in by a butler with an oversized umbrella.

Waiting for the passionate embrace to end, Lexi looked her up and down, took a step back, felt shocked by how similar they looked, from the colour of their hair to the shape of their bodies. Both tall, slim, with generous bosoms and long copper hair. The only thing that stood them apart was that everything about this woman screamed money, from the expensive boots to the wheelie case she dragged in behind her. Whereas Lexi lived more in the moment, spent her life in jeans and hoodies, had always lived on a budget, with any spare money being spent on Isla.

Moving slowly backwards and with the blood draining from her veins, she closed her eyes, held on to the balustrade, wanted the floor to swallow her whole. She should have realised that Harry would have a girlfriend. That life here on the island had moved on and that she couldn't simply walk back in, expect everything to be the same and take her place as though she'd never left. But then, shocked at the thought, she shook her head, knew that starting again with Harry hadn't been an option, not on her part. After all, she loved Nate, thought of how he'd be feeling, knew she had to call him.

Lifting both hands up as though in submission, Harry prised the woman from him. Took a step behind reception. Gave Lexi an apologetic smile. 'I... I... wow, I didn't know you were coming back today. It's good to see you.'

'Well,' she said, 'listen at you acting all formal.' She reached forward, patted him lovingly on the cheek, turned and seemed to notice Lexi for the first time. 'Oh, I'm so sorry. I didn't know you had company.' She looked Lexi up and down, furrowed her brow. 'It's Lexi, isn't it? I think we've met before.' She pointed into the bar. 'When I first came to the island, I used to work a couple of nights in the bar and weekends at the castle.' She winked at Harry. 'And of course, my Harry, well... he speaks of you often,' she said possessively.

Lexi smiled at the woman, could slightly recollect the face, the strong-smelling perfume. But something was different, and with a furrowed brow, she tried to remember the colour her hair had been, felt sure she'd lost a lot of weight, and although she had a more than distinctive look, Lexi felt sure she'd have remembered more about her, especially her name.

She casually looked Lexi up and down, held out a hand. 'You remember me, don't you? I'm Becca. We met the last time you were here.' She laughed. 'I met Harry not long after you left and, well, the rest is history; we've been together ever since. Haven't we, babes?' Dropping off her coat, Becca moved towards Harry. Leaned in, her fingers affectionately twisting a piece of his hair as her eyes searched his with a promise of what was to come. 'In fact, why are you working? I thought it was your day off?' She pushed out a lip, rolled her eyes. 'I wanted to surprise you. I've missed you and you know I wanted to spend some time with you.' She lifted both of her eyebrows seductively. 'How about we go get acquainted?'

Picking up the bag in one hand and the wheelie case in the other, Harry gave Lexi an apologetic smile, stacked one on top of the other, began to walk towards the back door. 'I wasn't supposed to be working. Only just got back myself, managed to slip across the causeway, right before the tide came in and... well, Maggie commandeered me the moment I landed, said she wanted to get the cottage ready for Lexi arriving. She still works two nights a week, so I offered to help her out. Took a shift.' He kept one eye on the bar as he spoke, took an obvious step away from Becca, who'd continued to drape herself across him. 'And tomorrow,' he continued, 'I'm doing a shift on the lifeboat, on the mainland. So I hope you packed warm clothes, 'cause tonight, come rain or shine, we're off down to the beach to have some fun.'

Lexi heard the words leave his mouth, the pride that crossed his face as he mentioned the lifeboats. 'So, you still go out on the boats?' she asked inquisitively.

'Sure I do, only one or two shifts a week because of working here. We're stationed over at Seahouses these days seeing as we don't have a boat on the island any more.' He caught Becca casually by the waist. 'Anyhow...' He turned his attention to Becca. 'Come on, you. Place is a mess, but... I'm sure you'll organise me.' He pushed open the back door. 'And Lex, don't disappear on me. I won't be long. I need to speak to you.' He caught her eye, waited for the unspoken promise.

Glancing at the door as it closed behind them, Lexi wondered how easily she could leave, how guilty she'd feel. To see Harry entangled with another woman hadn't been the top of her list of things to do, and right now, she wished she'd never come back. She began to move towards the door, really wanted to see Maggie, the cottage, the blueberry muffins she'd been promised. The thought of food made her stomach turn with hunger, and she closed her eyes, tried to remember when she'd last eaten, remembered the untouched sandwich at The Barn and the way she'd been unable to sit still, the nerves and anxiety taking over until finally she'd pulled all their possessions out of the car, stacked them in rows on the gravel. And after staring at her possessions for what felt like an eternity, she'd tried to work out what she'd packed, but most of all what she'd forgotten, and chastised herself for not having had a plan, a grab bag, all of her and Isla's things just ready to go.

Yet that morning she'd sat skimming the news, only half believing how much danger she was now in. Danger that should have been more than obvious to see. Picking up her phone, she began to scroll the news, look for announcements, for breaking news, for any indication that the killer had been caught and that her flee for safety had been an unnecessary trip, one she could easily reverse and go back home. Knowing that it was a wish too far, she sighed, clicked in and out of different screens and finally, after much searching, she rolled her jaw in annoyance and threw the phone back into her bag.

'So, you missed the crossing?' Harry's voice brought her back to the present as he reappeared behind the bar, placed a white porcelain coffee cup down in front of her, poured the coffee, added a scattering of caramelised biscuits to the plate. 'Eat these, you look like you need them.'

'Thanks...' She looked at her watch. 'I didn't think to check the times. Tide was just rolling in as I pulled past The Barn. I could have just about made it across if I'd tried. And a few years ago, I'd have probably given it a go. But I had Isla to think of, and with the car being full of our things, it was a bit on the heavy side and when I did get to cross, the workmen were moving back in. Looks like the repairs will go on for a while.' She thought back to that moment, when she'd seen the water lapping at the edge of the causeway, the desperation she'd felt when she'd realised how much damage Storm Arwen had caused, and the way the island had looked standing in the distance, so close, yet so very unreachable. She sipped at the coffee, opened a biscuit, ate it hungrily. Staring everywhere but at Harry, she concentrated on the noise coming from the kitchens, wondered who was in there, whether she knew them. 'Where did Becca go?' She searched the bar, now lacking in tourists. She tried to give him a genuine smile, hoped he wouldn't see through her.

Pulling a pint of Guinness, Harry passed it to a man who sat at the bar, then turned back towards her. 'Yep. Apparently, it caused a lot of damage to the island. Plenty to do once the causeway is repaired; the church took a bit of a battering too. I don't think there will be a service this week and Becca, she's gone for a lie-down. Had a busy few days lecturing at the uni in Leeds, managed to escape early this morning,' he said thoughtfully.

She looked him up and down, appreciated the man he'd turned into. 'Harry. I'm gonna go. I've had a bad couple of days. I didn't know about you and Becca...' Again, she looked away. 'And right now, I need to see Maggie, and Isla.' She gave him a half-smile, momentarily closed her eyes.

'Lex, you and Nate. I need to know.' Harry's hand was suddenly on hers; a heat travelled up her arm and she snatched it away as though he'd burned her. 'What's happened, have you left him? Is he likely to show up?' His eyes searched hers.

Jumping down from the bar stool, she squeezed her eyes tightly together, the pressure behind them almost overwhelming. 'I don't know, Harry. All I do know is I love him. He's a good man.' She knew it was true, knew she'd done him an injustice, wanted to speak to him. Needed to put things right.

'So, why didn't you marry him? He asked you to get married, didn't he? Yet here you are, still single.'

Feeling uncomfortable, Lexi pulled at the neck of her jumper. 'Harry, you know it's not that simple.' She looked over her shoulder, made sure no one was listening. 'I've never told him about my past, about who I am, and the longer we were together, the harder it got and now...' She shook her head, stepped away from the bar. 'Now I don't know what to tell him and I can't marry someone who doesn't know my real name, can I?' She looked down at her feet, then directly at him.

Nodding, Harry moved from behind the bar, moved towards her. Pulled her back into his hold. 'I know it hurts, but you do owe him the truth. You have to tell him everything. Warts and all.'

Feeling him sigh, Lexi looked up, into his eyes.

'And Lex. I deserve the truth too.'

Grateful that the pub was almost empty, she felt it begin to spin around her. Her breathing altered; she grabbed at air as the urge to run took over her mind and she pushed herself out of his hold. 'Harry, I need to go...'

Leaving the bar, she slammed the door behind her, looked over her shoulder, and wished that life had turned out differently. She knew that coming here had been the right thing to do – it was the only place she'd ever felt safe, even if that meant she had no choice but to put a few ghosts to bed or face each of the demons she'd left behind. But first... first she had to phone Nate. Harry was right, she had to tell him the truth – even if that wasn't a truth he wanted to hear.

With Isla half asleep on her knee, all cosy in her fleecy pyjamas, Lexi inched backwards, snuggled into the soft grey sofa, and sank into the piled-up cushions of every shape and colour that Maggie had collected over the years. They covered the whole settee and made Lexi smile at the memory of being a very small child who could easily hide beneath them, her perfect 'go-to' place, when all she really wanted was to disappear from the world.

'Just throw them on the floor,' Maggie whispered. 'They're old. I only kept them for the kids, but since I stopped fostering, I should have probably got rid.' She gave a half-smile, a thoughtful gaze. 'I just wouldn't know what to do with them, it's not like we have a charity shop on the island, and it'd be a shame to throw them in the landfill.' She paused. 'Do you remember that pop-up tent we had, how the kids would take all those cushions in it to lie on? They'd spend hours out there, pretending to camp.' She stopped speaking, stared dreamily at the Christmas tree, at the way the fairy lights chased each other around in a pattern.

'I remember the cushions, and the blankets. All the hours we'd stay out there till it got cold or started to rain. Then we'd run for the warmth of the house and get all cuddled up in front of the fire.' She glanced down at Isla, wondered how long it would be before she'd be camping in the garden and, if she did, which garden it would be in.

'And Stanley. Do you remember, he always ended up bringing them all back in?'

Raising her eyebrows, Lexi stared into the fire, brought the memories to the forefront of her mind, smiled wistfully as she imagined Stanley's smile. 'You're right, he did. He'd grumble and moan, but he loved every minute.' She stared at his chair, the one seat in the house where no one ever sat. Not since Stanley died.

'He only did it so he could start the cushion fights,' Maggie dropped in. 'He'd instigate a battle with you lot, every single time. Get you all stirred up, then disappear down to his greenhouse. Leave me to sort you out and get you to sleep. Which was easier said than done and normally meant we'd all end up watching late-night films and drinking hot chocolate.' She held on to her stomach, began to laugh. 'Why did I do that? You know, pump you kids full of chocolate and sugar in the hope you'd sleep?' She pondered the thought. 'Saying that, you were so thin, I'd have given you anything to get you to eat.' Her hand reached out between the chair and settee, gripped Lexi's hand. Squeezed.

Closing her eyes, Lexi could easily see the blue and yellow tent. The garden. The constant supply of hot dogs, cake and soft drinks that had appeared from nowhere. The way Maggie would stand in the kitchen, her arms crossed firmly under her bosom, the way she leaned on the bottom half of the stable door, constantly watching each child as though her life depended on it. 'Everything was fun, back then, wasn't it?'

'Hey,' Maggie continued, 'if you were happy, then so was I.' She smiled as Agatha jumped down from the chair, sauntered across the floor, all the time with one eye glaring at the Christmas tree, until she reached Maggie's feet, jumped up beside her. 'It was always good to hear you all laugh, it melted my heart, so it did.'

Lexi felt her heart swell with love. This woman had given up a huge portion of her life to look after her, to look after the others. And she was right, she had always been at her happiest when the children were having fun. She'd taken in so many of them. All small, all vulnerable, all who needed love, a place to be. She'd protected them all, including her. And then, remarkably, at a moment's notice, all these years later, she'd done it again. She'd opened her door as wide as it would go, given both her and Isla the sanctuary they needed.

Looking down, Lexi stroked her daughter's cheek, watched her eyes as they drooped into a peaceful sleep, could literally feel the unbreakable, invisible thread of love that connected them both. A thread so strong it could have easily been made from steel. A thread she should have shared with her own mother but didn't and now she knew she never would. She felt a deep ache within her, the feeling of being let down, abandoned by someone who'd been supposed to love her. There had been a million different questions she'd wanted to ask. Wished she'd had the courage to post the letters before time had run out, before someone had taken her options away, and then, as though that hadn't been a big enough blow, they'd come to her home, caused her to pack her belongings, leave everything behind and run for her life.

Stirring, Isla wriggled and held her arms out to Maggie, who reached across to pull her onto her knee, cuddled her in, gently kissed her on the cheek and began rocking her back to sleep.

Wistfully, Lexi tipped her head to one side, watched the love they shared. It had always been her wish that Isla would have a better start in life than she'd had, to surround her with people who genuinely loved her and wanted to protect her. She knew that being here, on the island, had been the right thing for her and for Isla.

But in bringing her here, she'd had no choice but to leave Nate behind and once again she looked at her phone, thought of all the attempts she'd made to call him and the repeated sound of his voicemail, which she'd grown sick of hearing.

Sitting back and into the comfort of the cushions, she felt her eyes begin to flicker. Felt the flashbacks begin. Her dad, Isla, her mother, Nate, the scarf, Isla. Each image bursting out and before her eyes like fireworks exploding. They were slow at first, then came faster and faster, in rapid succession, causing a tsunami of nausea to surge through her, making her quickly sit forward, snap her eyes back open and, determinedly, she stared at Isla. Watched as she slept peacefully on Maggie's knee, and fearfully she wondered how she'd ever sleep again, how she'd ever feel at peace. And how her last memory of her mother's face and the way it had appeared on the front page of every single newspaper in England would haunt her forever.

On a normal day, she'd have devoured every one of the nationals. She'd have loved everything about them, was always looking for new ideas, for how other reporters had told a story. And took a special interest in it if it were a story similar to one she'd worked on. Yet that morning, while waiting for the tide to go out, she'd had no choice but to head into Seahouses, shop for all the things they'd forgotten, and had managed to avoid them until Isla had pulled her towards a newsagent's, where rows of papers had been stacked prominently for all to see on a rack outside. And although it had been a moment she'd expected, it was one she'd never thought to prepare herself for, and as she'd come to a stop outside the shop, she'd stared at the pictures as the blood drained from her face. Every part of her had begun to tremble with anxiety, her legs had become weak, she hadn't felt capable of walking, and held tightly to the shop doorway, while all the time staring at the front page, at the woman she'd once called Mummy.

You're safe now. She tried to convince herself, as she thought of the home she'd left behind. The home she'd created and shared with Nate and of how he'd be feeling. *You did what you had to do. You kept Isla safe. He'll understand.* She nodded, kept her eyes fixed firmly on Isla, used the words as a comfort blanket, tried to convince herself it was true. Closing her eyes, she could feel the island closing in around her, protecting her. *Nothing bad ever happens here. This island, this house, the people, no one ever hurt you.* She repeated the words internally, gave herself a half-smile, watched as Maggie ran a hand over her daughter's hair, saw Isla settle until her thumb was once again pushed firmly into her mouth. It was a habit she'd never really gotten out of and a constant reminder of how very young and vulnerable she really was.

Standing up, she walked to the window, looked at the island beyond, could imagine every tiny nook, every cranny, all the places where someone could live, or hide. There were so many small stone cottages, farm buildings or fishermen's huts that could be lived in without being noticed – a place where every day strangers walked the streets. A thought that sent shivers racing up her spine. A moment when she realised that the danger was real, even here on the island, a place where she'd previously always felt safe.

17

Just a couple of hours later, Lexi stood at the bottom of the stairs, listened to the gentle sound of Maggie singing Christmas carols while Isla splashed in the bath. She stood, ran her eyes along the hallway, along the numerous six-by-four frames. Each one held the picture of a child that had stayed here. All were either black-and-white, or sepia with age, all scattered randomly along the wall, with no real thought to order or synchronicity.

Recognising most of the faces, Lexi stared at each one individually. Read the words that had been slotted into the bottom corner of each frame, showing the child's name, age and year they'd stayed. One or two of the children, now adults, still came to the island, still paid Maggie a visit at Christmas, or met up in the pub for reunions.

Then there were the kids like Harry who had come back to the island and stayed. Staring at his photo, she thought of the day he'd turned up, a lanky teenager with ruffled hair, a cheeky smile and eyes that looked full of fury. Lexi had studied him for a while, quickly realised that his eyes told a very different story, a truth she'd immediately understood. Yet now, looking at the picture, she saw eyes that sparkled with laughter and Lexi tried to work out if the sparkle she saw was simply a reflection of Christmas tree lights that busily flashed in sequence behind her, to give the image a life of its own where it danced joyfully and magically before her eyes.

Pulling on her boots, Lexi hesitated, took a final glance over her shoulder, stared at the chair where Stanley used to sit, and in her mind's eye she could still see him sitting there, his pipe hanging out of his mouth, his book resting across his knee. Tried to work out what he'd say to her, what advice he'd give. And then, with a small wave to his ghost, she stepped through the door, took in the rain-soaked tarmac beyond, where a chill gripped the air, and the smell of woodsmoke drifted inland from the beach. 'Maggie, I won't be long,' she shouted, 'I need to phone Nate, he... it's only right that I let him know where I am, where his daughter is.' She paused, held the doorknob tightly in her hand. 'That's if he ever answers his damned phone...' She swallowed hard, felt the need to hear Nate's voice, to know he was OK. That no matter what she'd done, or who her father was, he still loved both her and Isla.

Taking a deep breath in, she turned the phone over in her hand, saw her screen saver light up and smiled as the image of Nate and Isla appeared, could immediately see the love they shared. It was more than obvious to anyone who saw them that Nate loved his daughter. That was without doubt. But her insecurities took over her thoughts and, fearing the worst, she tried to work out what he'd say, how he'd react once she told him the truth and knew that she had no choice but to tell him who she really was. She just prayed that once he knew, his opinion of her wouldn't change and, for the hundredth time that day, she wished she'd told him everything on the day they'd met. Before things got complicated, before they'd invested all they had on a house, had a child, bought a kitten.

Glancing nervously over her shoulder, Lexi stared at the cottage. She noticed the soft lighting in the upstairs window, where Isla would be put to bed, surrounded by teddy bears and a kitten who'd barely left her side since leaving Whitby. Feeling torn and guilty, she took in a deep breath, turned away from the window as the urge to speak to Nate became much too strong, and whether she liked it or not, it wasn't a conversation she could have in the cottage, not with Isla listening.

While keeping the cottage firmly in her view, she stepped slowly between the random puddles that had scattered themselves across the tarmac, walked slowly past the old stone houses and took pleasure in the familiarity of the street she'd walked a million times. Then, as she stood on the corner, she stared at The Ship Inn, listened to the sound of the evening's jovialities, the Christmas carols that seeped out of the window, noisily beckoning to all the people who dared to pass.

Leaning against the wall, she watched a group stop in their tracks. They were trying to decide whether or not they should go inside, out of the wind and the threatened rain, or continue on their way towards the castle, the lime kilns and the beach beyond.

Looking in the direction of the beach, Lexi could see the orange hue of bonfires that lit up the sky, a sight she'd seen every year since arriving on the island. A sight she'd always looked forward to, until now. Now she felt nervous. Could feel the danger. The way it lurked around every corner, behind every stone wall, hid itself in every sand dune. Stopping, she purposely kept herself within running distance of the cottage, knowing that if anything happened, if anyone approached her, she could get back to the house, let herself in, scream for help.

With her back to a wall, she listened to the island. Felt a flood of memories seep through her mind and remembered the first winter she'd been brought here. The first year she'd ever seen the bonfires and the way Maggie had led her along this very street, to the beach. They'd taken the same walk night after night just to give her a familiarity, an understanding of the island. 'See, it's just people having a party,' Maggie would say. 'They're having fun; it's nothing to be worried about.' She'd squeezed her hand in a kind, loving way. 'When you're older, you'll probably join in with the dancing, just like I did when I was a girl,' she'd said. 'Or you might simply lie on the beach with the one you love, stare up at the sky and count the stars.' She'd sat down on the damp sand and laid back as though ready to prove a point. 'Look up, Lexi, look at the stars. They're beautiful, aren't they? Each one has a story, each one a promise of things to come and there are so many, you can barely count them.' She'd paused, patted the sand beside her, waited for Lexi to sit down, look up at the constellations. 'All you have to do is wish,' she'd whispered, 'then all the good dreams, they'll all come true.'

Hovering, Lexi glanced between the pub, the walkway and the deserted coastguard station. Nervously, she looked at her phone, hesitated before pressing Nate's number, wondered if he'd answer.

'Hey, Lex, are you coming down the beach?' Harry's voice came from nowhere as he quickly jogged towards her, a small crate perched on his shoulder. Laughing, he swung the crate down and into one hand. 'We needed more beers; everyone's down there.' He stopped, dropped the crate to the floor, shuffled uncomfortably from foot to foot. 'Are you coming?' He beckoned, looked towards the castle, which was now lit up in gold fluorescent lighting.

Waving the phone around in the air apologetically, Lexi shook her head. 'I need to phone Nate. I need to tell him what happened, hope he understands.' She stared at the pavement, felt her stomach turn with nerves. 'I couldn't do it in the cottage, felt the need for a little privacy.' She gave him a twisted half-smile. Stared at his boots and sighed. Having Harry so close hadn't been a part of her plan. She hadn't known he'd be here, and now that he was, now that they were both back on the island, it was something else she had to deal with.

'Right.' He went to pick up the crate, changed his mind and ran a hand through his hair. 'I'll give you some space 'cause, well... I left Becca down on the beach along with her sister, and to say they don't like each other much is a bit of an understatement...' He rolled his eyes, looked just a little bit more than uncomfortable. 'Plus, I kind of owe you an apology.' He paused. 'I didn't know, you know, that she was coming back. Well, I guess I did. Her sister had told me. I just didn't know it'd be today.'

'So, what are you apologising for?' She shook her head dismissively and furrowed her brow as she looked back at the cottage, noticed the way the upstairs lights suddenly had dimmed, felt sure that Isla would be asleep and, knowing Maggie, she'd be lying protectively in her bed beside her. 'You moved on, Harry, and so did I. It happens and there's nothing wrong with that – people change.'

Pulling his thick quilted jacket tightly around himself, Harry zipped it up. 'Well, not quite everything.' He laughed. 'Ship's still the same.' He nodded thoughtfully. Looked wistfully in the direction of the pub. 'Same gin, same food, same floorboards, same atmosphere.'

'Well,' Lexi responded. 'If I'm here long enough, I might pop in, check it out.' She laughed. 'I have to say, I do like the gin.'

He spun on the spot, stepped towards her, placed his hands on her shoulders. 'What do you mean – if you're here long enough?'

'Harry. I'm really scared. What if I made a mistake, what if by coming here I've put Isla at even more risk?' Again, she paused, fought with the confusion in her mind. 'I have no idea who I can and can't trust.' She stared deep into his eyes. 'I don't even know if I've done the right thing by coming back here.'

'Hey. Don't ever say that.' He pulled her into an easy hold. A moment of familiarity between them as his arms tightened around her, rocked her gently, rhythmically against his body. 'Of course you should have come back. This is your home. Nothing's going to happen to you – you do know that, don't you?' he whispered sincerely, affectionately kissed the top of her head. 'Maggie told me what happened, with your mum. She asked me to look out for you.' He took a step back, held her at arm's length. 'Which quite honestly isn't a chore, Lex, because you know... you're one of my all-time favourite people and...' He gave her one of his smiles, cheekily tipped his head to one side. 'You need to come down to the beach, because I can't look out for you if you're up here and I'm down there, can I?'

Wiping the dampness of tears from her cheeks with the back of her hand, Lexi stared through the darkness. Caught the look in his eyes, saw the mischief within. 'And if I don't?' she teased.

'Well, I'd probably have to throw you over my shoulder and drag you.' He laughed, winked. 'Come down the beach...' he begged, leaned forward, pointed to the crate. 'Because if I have to carry you, I'll have no choice but to leave the beers behind and then, well... that'd be a shame, wouldn't it?'

'I can't. I... I have to get back.' She gasped, swallowed hard. She rolled the phone over in her hand, tried to focus on the call she had to make, thought about the way Maggie had insisted on taking Isla up to bed. 'I'll look after her, don't you worry,' she'd whispered as the soft tone of the Christmas carols had begun and, for a moment, Lexi had simply stood there at the bottom of the stairs, listening to that familiar sound of her voice, wished she were a child again and longed for those nights when Maggie had lain with her, protected her, promised her how beautiful life could be. 'It doesn't matter where you start in life, my girl,' she'd said, 'it's how you turn out that matters, and you're smart, and you're beautiful, and if you put your mind to it, you can be just about anything you want to be.' They were words she'd repeated over the years. They were words that had given her hope, made her feel as though she could achieve and for many years after, she'd often stared up at the stars, feeling as though she could quite easily grab one out of the sky, just because Maggie had insisted she could. 'And you... you have to get back to Becca. Didn't you say she was down there with her sister, waiting for the beers?' Lexi glanced up at the sky, where clouds circled moodily above. She wondered how long it would be before the rain came down.

'Yeah, they're down there, by the lime kilns. I left them in charge of the fire basket.' He began to move slowly away, leaned against the exterior stone wall of the gallery. Nodded. 'Lex, I'd love for you to get to know her.' He lifted a foot to press against the wall behind him. 'Don't let all the designer clothes put you off; she's got a heart of gold and I just know you'd love her, given the chance.'

'Do you love her, Harry?' The words simply fell from her mouth, and she wished she'd never asked, felt the colour rise to her cheeks. She wanted the floor to swallow her whole. 'Cause if you love her,' she said in an attempt to backtrack, 'then I will too.' She smiled, knew she was telling the truth, simply wanted Harry to be happy and even if that meant she'd have to make Becca her very best friend, then that's what she'd do. Harry would be happy, for once, even if it killed her.

'Look, I have to phone Nate.' Once again she waved the phone around in the air.

Striding on ahead, Harry waved. 'I'll be waiting on the beach for you, you know, once you're done.' He turned as he walked, gave her a smile. 'And don't be long, 'cause I'm gonna throw you a burger on the barbecue and you don't like them burnt, do you?'

She watched him walk into the darkness, watched as he began to disappear in and out of the sea fret that was creeping in from the sea. Finally, as he disappeared completely, she leaned on the wall, heard a rustling sound in one of the gardens behind her, felt her spine prickle with nerves, and had a feeling of being watched. Nervously, she pulled her jacket tightly around her as a gust of wind blew in from the sea, making her shudder with fear.

'Harry, wait up...' she shouted as the phone was pushed into her pocket, 'I'm coming with you.' She hurriedly ran through the sea fret, towards the castle. Hooking her arm through his, she looked over her shoulder, kept her eyes on the house she'd just left behind, thought she saw a movement, a shadow that moved slowly around the edge of the garden and then, as quickly as it had appeared, it disappeared into the darkness, and for a moment she simply held her breath, listened for any noise that might follow, any sound that might tell her who it had been, where they were going.

'You all right?' Hitching the crate further up his shoulder, Harry caught her eye, furrowed his brow. 'You've gone a bit pale.'

Shaking, Lexi held tightly on to him. 'I'm fine,' she lied, smiled anxiously. Every part of her wanted to run. To go back to the cottage, to lock the door, to never come out. But to do that would mean running past that garden alone, past the shadows that lurked in the bushes. 'I think I'm just going a bit paranoid. I...' Once again she glared at the house, the garden, waited.

'Do you want to go back?' Harry stopped in his tracks, stared into Lexi's eyes.

Pausing, Lexi weighed up the options. Looked from Harry to the beach, then back into town. 'No... no, I'll stay with you.' She gave a half-smile, a nervous laugh. Knew that being with Harry she was safer than being alone, and the chances of anyone attacking them both while they were together was more than remote. 'I'm just being silly, I thought I saw someone...' Staring at the garden, cloaked by the sea fret, Lexi waited. Wished for the movement to happen again, or for a cat to run out from the trees. For anything that would give her the answers, and sadly she realised she'd probably never get them and that she'd spend the rest of her life living with her own vivid imagination, her own paranoia, while watching the shadows, waiting for someone to alter the course of her life.

18

Leaning against the wall of the lime kilns, Lexi slid to the floor, happily sat on a long narrow blanket that had been spread out, and gratefully she wrapped herself in another that Becca had enthusiastically given her.

'Wow, you came well prepared, didn't you?' Lexi relaxed into the blanket, smiled as Becca fussed around her, and watched as she tossed burgers while jiggling to the music.

'Now, drinks. What do you want? We have lagers, hot chocolate...' Becca picked up a flask, waved it around. 'I mainly bring it for me because I don't drink very often, well... barely at all. Not unless it's a big celebration.' She laughed, grabbed a styrofoam beaker from her bag, filled it with the steaming hot liquid, passed it to Lexi. 'I make it according to Maggie's recipe, with just a tot of brandy to warm the cockles.'

'Oh, Lumumba, I'll have some.' A young woman walked to her side, pulled a fur-lined hood up to cover her dark auburn hair, gave Becca a sidewards look, then smiled awkwardly at Lexi. 'I'm Vicki.' She held out a gloved hand, then took the flask from Becca, who reluctantly held out a cup, watched as Vicki filled it. 'If there's one thing my sister can get right, it's making a spiked hot chocolate.' She laughed, sipped at the drink, then walked away with the cup in her hands and stood by the water's edge, looking out.

Bristling, Becca pressed her lips tightly together. Ignored the comments and continued to flip the burgers. 'Some of us should make our own,' she finally said as she eased herself into Harry's arms with a smile. Looking away, Lexi felt herself blush unnecessarily, looked up just in time to see Harry drop a kiss tenderly on Becca's lips, before holding her in his arms as though his life depended on it. To Lexi, they were like polar opposites. Yet the embarrassment of earlier had now gone and in its place was a look of love and contentment and it occurred to Lexi that for the first time in years, Harry looked truly happy. The fury he'd had as a teenager had gone and in its place was a dreamy, hopeful look that was emphasised by the glow of the fire baskets, which had been placed randomly along the grass incline. It was a position not normally used, but with the weather pulling in, they'd made the camp nearer the kilns; it was just a few meters from the beach but a little more sheltered from the wind that now whipped around the headland with the ferocity of a hurricane. Yet tonight, even with the wind, the area looked peaceful, almost serene, and Lexi stood up and looked up to take in the bright golden lights of the castle, which gave the area a soft amber glow.

'Harry, put me down, you're getting sand all over my jacket.' Becca squealed as she brushed the sand from the expensive-looking coat, then adjusted the scarf that had been expertly twisted into a loop around her head. 'You're being terribly rude to Lexi and we...' She hooked an arm through Lexi's. 'We have a lot of catching up to do, maybe even a shopping day to plan.' She spun around, turned her face into the glow of the bonfire, caught Lexi's eye and then squealed again, as once again Harry's arms went around her waist. 'Lexi, tell him to put... me... down.'

Not wishing to get in the middle of a domestic, Lexi waved her hands in the air. 'Oh, well. Of course, I normally would but, you know, I have a call to make.' She stood up, held her phone in the air, and with the blanket still wrapped around her shoulders she moved into the shadow of the kilns where she hovered in the entrance, tapped at the phone's screen, and felt her stomach turn with nerves as she heard Nate answer her call.

'Lex, where the hell are you?' Nate suddenly snapped. 'I got home and, Jesus, the house looks like we were burgled. Do you know how many of the neighbours took great delight in telling me how you'd packed the car, and threw everything in, the moment I'd gone to work this morning? Do you know how smug Mrs Baker next door looked and how that made me feel? Christ, Lexi, I could have crawled into a hole and died.' He caught his breath, didn't give her the opportunity to speak. 'I did nothing to deserve this, abso-lutely nothing.' He paused momentarily, took deep heavy breaths. 'I've worked my goddamn balls off to give you and Isla a good life, Lexi, and... and you, you take her away from me, right before Christmas.' She heard a loud thud, followed by a yell. 'She's my daughter too; you can't do this. You can't just take her away from me and not tell me where the hell she is.'

'Nate, don't... please don't punch walls.' Closing her eyes, Lexi walked deeper into the kilns, to where the darkness loomed, and the only light was that of the moon that shone down and through the old broken chimneys, where protective grilles had been attached to the structure, to create thick black shadows that crossed the floor.

'What the hell do you expect, Lexi? I'm furious.' There was another thud, another bang, another yell.

'Nate. I didn't mean to hurt you and I'm so sorry. But I had to leave, I had to protect Isla, I had to keep her safe.' She closed her eyes as she said the words, couldn't work out what to say next, how she'd tell him. Noticed that during his rant, he'd only been annoyed that she'd taken Isla and had never once mentioned her, or them and, painfully, she gripped a hand to her chest, felt herself sob deep within.

'Lexi, what the hell are you talking about? Isla doesn't need protecting; she was perfectly safe here, at home. With us.'

'Oh, Nate, there's so much you don't know. I'm so sorry. I've kept so many secrets from you... I just don't know where to begin.' The tears sprung to her eyes, the shame of what her father had done, of who he was. 'It's something I should have told you years ago, before Isla was born and, well... we need to talk, I need to explain, but not like this, not over the phone.' She spun on the spot, checked the darkness for shadows, spotted a courting couple pressed tightly against the wall and, embarrassed, she reversed in the opposite direction.

'Talk. I don't even know where the hell you are.' His voice grew in both volume and temper and Lexi held the phone away from her ear, knew she had to tell him where she was, who she was staying with but felt the anxiety rise within her, the knowledge that once she'd told him, she couldn't take it back. Hoped that by doing so, she wasn't making a mistake. Swallowing, she counted to ten, suddenly felt an overwhelming need to see him.

'Nate.' She hesitated, caught her breath. 'I'm on the island. Isla is safe. We're staying at Maggie's.'

19

Moodily, I watch clouds circle over the sea to form a dense, practically impenetrable coverage of the sky. One or two stars desperately try to poke out from behind, to show themselves, and even though most of them don't succeed, the odd one appears like a tiny diamond that shines as bright as it can, even though the night is filled with frost, making everything feel much colder than normal.

The small amount of light given off by the moon and the stars lights up the tips of the waves. They have an eerie, ethereal look, and I watch as they throw themselves haphazardly up and towards the beach where the stone stacks stand, patiently waiting to be knocked over until a new family turns up and rebuilds them into a tower that has no real meaning.

Even though I'm standing close to the fire baskets, my feet are cold, and I stamp them repeatedly, wish that the weather had been better; on a good day, it would have been just a little warmer and we'd have been able to set up on the beach. Instead, we're in the shadows of the cliff side, where the sheep tend to graze around the edge of the kilns and, instinctively, I watch where I stand and pull my coat tightly around me in a desperate attempt to stop the night air biting at my cheeks.

Obsessively, I watch you. You're hovering in the darkness of the tunnels, and I take delight in the obvious pain that keeps crossing your face, at the way you keep swiping at your eyes with a tissue. Seeing your pain makes me happy, especially after watching my family go through a similar torment for the past twenty years and, because of that, you deserve to feel pain too. Deep down, I wish that I could hurt him, your father, but I can't. I can't even tell him how I feel when I imagine what he did to my sister. How frightened she'd have been and whether she'd have known she were about to die. Every millimetre of my body aches with the knowledge that I'll never see her again, that my mother died wishing she could hold her in her arms just one more time, or watch her dance like she used to, while her face lit up with laughter. Instead, she had no idea what happened, died imagining the worst. And in my view, it's something he has to pay for, he has to feel that pain. He has to know exactly how it feels to lose someone at another's hand, at a time when he has no control.

Glancing around, I pull myself out of my thoughts, look at the last remaining people who stand between the kilns and the beach. They're huddled together like penguins in the snow, without having so much as an inch between them. And as the weather gets colder, I can see that they're giving up, leaving in search of warmth, and now only the diehard remain, along with a few courting couples who are slowly disappearing to the more remote areas of the nature reserve. And then there are the ones who still need to leave the island, who will make a mad dash for the causeway before the tide floods back in and leaves them stranded for another six hours.

Slowly, I cup my gloved hands in front of my face, blow into them in an attempt to warm my cheeks, but instead I feel the first drops of rain that fall. There's an icy coldness within each drop, and I move to the side of the kilns, use the cliff as a shelter, pull the hood up on my coat, and hope that the rain stops as you walk past me at speed. Following your shape through the darkness, I watch the way you saunter slowly along the water's edge, kicking out angrily at the tide, with a blanket still wrapped around your shoulders and, in a way, I hope you fall, I hope you trip and drown. But that would be far too easy, wouldn't it? And once again I try to comprehend what I'm about to do, how I'll do it and whether I'll take just your life, or that of the others around you. There are so many things I could do and with a surge of adrenaline I feel happy in the knowledge that your mother's death was just the first necessity. I had to hurt him, had to show him what it was like and it was a means to an end that got your attention. It frightened you into coming here, to the place where you think you'll be safe. And I watch as you meander along the beach, through the piles of stones, knowing you couldn't be more wrong and, while tipping my head to one side, I notice you stop abruptly and once again, you swipe defiantly at your face. It's an indication that you too are having the nightmare of your life. That your pain and misery are a feeling you have no control over, just as we had no control over ours, the moment my sister was taken from us.

The problem is, your nightmare is only just beginning and by the time I've finished with you, you'll wish your father had been just about anyone else in the world apart from the father you ended up with.

20

With her mind clouded by emotion, Lexi walked along the edge of the water, allowed the waves to lap against the tips of her boots, kicked angrily at the stone stacks and bit down on her lip in temper. The conversation with Nate hadn't gone as well as she'd hoped. And now, she chastised herself for having made the call, wished she'd made it earlier. Realising now that standing in the shelter of the kilns with the wind howling all around her really hadn't been the best environment. She'd been barely able to hear what Nate had been saying and she shook her head angrily, pressed her lips tightly together and tried to control the emotion inside.

Suddenly, she ached for home, for her own kitchen, her own fridge with barely anything in it and, most of all, the comfort of her own bed. A huge part of her wished she could turn back time, to go back to the days before she'd heard the news about her mum. To a life when she'd been completely naïve in the thought that she could get through her life without the shadow of her father's crimes lurking around every corner, waiting for her, haunting her thoughts. Just two days ago, her life had been simple; her mornings had begun with those few minutes after the alarm had gone off, when she'd lie in Nate's arms, with her head on his chest, listening to the gentle, rhythmic sound of his heartbeat. It had always been one of her favourite times of the day and right now she wanted it back. The question she couldn't stop racing around her mind was... did Nate want her back too? Because after how angry he'd appeared to be, she couldn't work out whether he was simply angry that she'd left, or just angry that she'd taken Isla with her.

Closing her eyes briefly against the breeze, she felt the sob erupt from her throat. 'No matter how much I want to go home, no matter how much I want it back, I can't have it, can I?' she whispered to the sea, and with a sudden realisation she snapped her head back in retort. 'You don't have a home. You left it behind and you can't go back.' It was true, she'd left everything behind and, with Nate's words spinning around her mind, she kicked out angrily at the water.

'So, you're at Maggie's, back on the island, are you?' he'd screamed. 'Jesus, Lex. What did you think? Did you think I'd run after you? Well, do you know what? I can't. I have a job. A contract. If I don't complete it, I don't get paid. Simple. I can't risk that happening, not at this time of year. We have a mortgage to pay.' He'd paused, slammed a door. 'Oh, and I take it you found Agatha? Did you take her with you?'

Feeling shocked and wounded that Nate was more worried about her taking the cat, she had tried to explain. Tried to find a way to get him back on side. While all the time walking further and further away from the shelter of the kilns.

'Nate. I didn't mean to hurt you... I had no choice. I had to protect Isla, I had to keep her safe.' The words she'd said went over and over in her mind, spinning around like a whirlwind that wouldn't stop. But equally and with just as much force, she thought about the anger he'd shown and in retort she'd tried to explain. 'You have to believe me,' she'd shouted over the sound of the wind, 'this wasn't about leaving you... it was... it was so much more than that.' She'd tightened the blanket around her shoulders, but still felt cold, hollow and empty inside. 'And whatever you might think right now, I do love...' Her words had broken off, the phone bleeped, then went silent. Shaking it, she'd looked expectantly at the screen, saw nothing. No lights. No name. No signal. The call lost. The phone dead.

Stepping out of the kilns and back onto the grass, she'd angrily headed towards the beach, furious with herself for not having recharged the phone, for not having checked it before she'd made the call.

'Hey, where are you going?' Harry had shouted as she walked past at speed, dodged his hand as it lurched outwards to catch her by the arm and missed. 'Lex, slow down. I'll come with you.'

'Leave me alone, Harry. I need a minute – alone.' She shrugged him off, marched past, didn't quite hear the response he'd thrown back as the sea rolled in, threw itself at the shoreline and swallowed his words whole.

Keeping Isla safe had been the right thing to do, but with tears filling her eyes, Lexi thought of Nate. She tried to imagine how he'd be feeling, how much of a shock all of this would have been, hoped wholeheartedly he'd heard the words she'd spoken and didn't think she'd just put the phone down, or cut the call short. And he'd been right, he hadn't deserved this, and for what felt like the hundredth time that day, she considered going back to her car and heading back to Whitby in the hope that she could repair the damage she'd caused. Once again wished she hadn't kept hidden all the secrets of her past. Deep down, she hoped Nate really did love her. Even though at times during the conversation it seemed his focus had been more on the fact that she'd taken both Isla and Agatha than it had been on her leaving herself.

Reeling with indecision, she had no choice but to go over and over what had happened. How after finding Agatha, she'd panicked, packed the car, took everything with her. With confusion spiralling around her and circumnavigating her mind at speed, she continued to walk, continued to follow the isolated shoreline, stumbled over the rocks that lined the beach with only the moonlight to light her way; she twisted her fingers tightly together and formed fists of frustration with both of her hands. Angrily, she wondered how much of a mistake she'd made, that by leaving she'd put both her and Isla in even more danger and, undoubtedly, she wondered if she should have taken the responder's advice, locked the doors and stayed where she was, because in the process of trying to protect what she had, she'd probably ruined it all, and by taking their daughter away from the only home she'd known, she'd lost Nate's trust too. A trust she wasn't sure she'd be able to retrieve, even if they both wanted it.

A sudden, violent shiver that brought her back to reality, Lexi felt the chill of the water seep into her boots. It was a feeling that made her quickly step backwards, look over her shoulder and stare at the castle that stood lit up in the distance, like a brightly tiered beacon. It was a sight that made her realise just how far she'd walked over rough terrain, and with dread in her mind, it occurred to her how easily she could have tripped, hurt herself in the darkness, and a sense of unease rippled through her as her breathing altered, and she began to panic.

Scrambling along the shoreline, she looked for sturdier ground, for something familiar. Then felt a sense of relief as an old fishing boat came into view, along with the upturned boat sheds, lobster baskets and fishing nets that had dominated the shoreline for as long as she could remember. It was a sight that gave her both pleasure and pain. Seeing the boats made her realise how close to home she was, but even though she could almost see Maggie's cottage in the distance, she still had a long walk to get her around the harbour, which meant either heading along the Heugh, through a field and past the priory, or back towards the road that led to the castle. Both directions involved a long isolated walk, with little or no light. Taking in her bearings, she gasped for air, tried to work out whether it would be easier to turn around, to go back the way she'd come or to continue through the darkness of the harbour. It was a moment's indecision as the first drops of rain hit her in the face, rolled down her cheeks and, with a quick scan of the terrain, she stumbled through the rain and around the harbour.

Watching every shadow, she slowed her pace, pulled her coat tightly around her, used the blanket Becca had given her as a temporary umbrella. Listened for noise, for footsteps, for any indication that she wasn't alone, and as she inched her way past the darkness of the boat sheds, she began to tiptoe, heard a noise, jumped backwards and held her breath as a black cat ran out from behind the shed, scarpered across her path, then watched as a lobster basket began to topple before dropping from its position and, while holding her breath, she watched as it hit the floor and broke into pieces.

21

Running past the boats that had been moored by the water's edge, and up the grass verge, Lexi felt her feet slip and slide beneath her. Steadying her pace, she dropped the rain-drenched blanket; it was no longer protecting her from the rain, which now fell in torrents and formed fast-flowing rivulets that poured down the roads and into the fields beyond.

Stumbling blindly through the darkness, she aimed for the lights of the village and felt a small amount of relief as she reached the ornamental fishing boat that stood on the junction. She leaned forward, held on to it, brushed her rain-soaked hair out of her eyes and caught her breath, then glanced up and down the now-deserted road and, while feeling fearful of every noise and every shadow that surrounded her, she tried to keep moving, felt the burn in her lungs, headed inland. Passing The Ship, she allowed herself to breathe, slowed her run to a walk and took the snicket that led between the cottages, suddenly desperate to get home, to see Isla.

As she rounded the corner, she hesitated outside the cottage, and with her hand hovering above the doorknob she homed in on the commotion within. It was a mixture of shouting, laughing and the shrill sound of Isla screaming and, with her heart pounding in her chest, every scenario of what was happening flew through her mind at speed. The thought that Isla was in trouble filled her with fear and without any thought for herself, she burst through the door, ready to face whatever was happening behind it.

Stopping in her tracks, Lexi took in the scene before her. Noted the mass of bodies that were all in a heap in the middle of the carpet with a triumphant Isla bouncing up and down on Harry's back. 'I win, I win,' she shouted with glee. 'Play again. Come on. Again.'

Spotting Lexi, Isla gave off another squeal. 'Mummy, come play.' She ran to her, grabbed her hand. 'We're playing Twister, and Howie, he's cheating.'

Catching Isla by the waist, Harry leaned forward, scooped her up. 'I did not cheat, madam, it was you.' He poked her in the ribs, tickled her until she laughed and wriggled. 'Somehow, you managed to put this tiny little foot of yours on all the colours. All at once.'

'Ahh, stop! Mummy, tell him no.' Throwing her arms around Harry's neck, Isla cuddled in and held tightly to him. It was a sight that melted Lexi's heart, brought back distant memories of the days when Harry had been a teenager, when younger children had been brought here to stay. Each one had been just a little bit lost or broken in one way or another, yet somehow Harry had always had a way of getting through to them, taking them under his wing, making them laugh. They'd naturally gravitated towards him, so much more than they had to her, and now it was Isla's turn to love him, just as they had.

Kneeling by the door, Lexi pushed it to a close, kicked off her shoes and simply watched the game from a distance.

'Ah, you're back. We were wondering where you'd got to.' Maggie paused, smiled at the way Harry now rolled on the floor, with Isla sitting on his back. 'I'm making hot chocolate.' She disappeared back into the kitchen, reappeared with a mug, the steam rising from it.

'Well, if you'd jumped in the sea and swam, you couldn't have got much wetter; let me get you a towel.' Maggie passed her the mug, shook her head with the pretence of annoyance. Smiled as Becca jumped up, ran into the kitchen.

'I'll get it.' She gave Lexi a genuine, easy smile, then disappeared into the kitchen, returning just a few seconds later with a towel tucked under her arm, more mugs, and a sippy cup for Isla. 'Here you go, baby girl. Maggie made you this and... apparently, this is your special cup. Isn't it?'

Standing up, Lexi gratefully took the towel. Rubbed her hair, then glanced up the stairs. 'I'd best, you know, get changed.' She ran up the stairs, dried herself off, quickly pulled off the wet clothes and replaced them with clean, dry joggers, and an oversized sweater. Suddenly overwhelmed, she closed her eyes, listened to the childish laughter that drifted up the stairs. It was a sound she'd heard many times before, a time when children had laughed, when Maggie had dished out gallons of hot chocolate, and days when the fire would roar in the grate, warm the house and steam the windows.

Returning to the living room and picking her mug up from the fireplace, Lexi settled into one of the settees, surrounded herself with cushions. 'Hey, Agatha.' She reached out, stroked the kitten who'd suddenly appeared from under the tree, and had sauntered across the room to stretch herself upwards before leaping up and onto the chair, where she pummelled the familiarity of Lexi's knee with both paws and claws. 'Ouch, that hurts,' Lexi cried as she ran a hand over the kitten's fur and felt grateful when she finally circled, curled into a ball and slept.

'And you...' Lexi poked Isla in the ribs as she ran past, picked up a new game. 'I thought you were in bed?'

Laughing, Isla shook her head. 'I got up again.' She passed the game to Harry. 'Here you go...' Dropping the game, she disappeared into the kitchen, only to reappear a moment later clasping a gingerbread man. 'Look, Mummy.'

Tipping her head to one side, Lexi smiled at her daughter, looked over her shoulder and into the kitchen where Maggie was leaning over the oven, the door wide open. 'What's Maggie cooking now?'

'She's putting jacket potatoes in the oven,' Becca dropped in. 'You know, she's doing what she does best: feeding us all till we burst.' She furrowed her brow, leaned in close to whisper. 'She did seem a bit upset when you didn't come back with us. God knows why, I told her you're a grown woman, but Maggie was ready to call the police, send out a search party.'

Once again feeling guilty for having walked off alone, Lexi made her way into the kitchen, caught Maggie wiping the corner of her eye on the edge of her apron. 'Maggie,' she whispered, 'I... I'm sorry. I had a row with Nate, and I know it was stupid, taking off, but I needed some space.' She paused, rested a hand on Maggie's shoulder. Felt the tremble within her. 'I really didn't mean to worry you.'

'Oh. Ignore me, I'm just being a silly old woman...' She paused, picked up the tea towel, once again dabbed at her eyes. 'But when you didn't come back with the others, well... I just thought. Oh, never mind what I thought, you're here now... that's all that matters.'

Pulling Maggie into her arms, Lexi rocked her back and forth. 'I spoke to Nate. He deserved to know where Isla was.' She rolled her eyes. 'Apparently, I'd worried him sick. Which isn't surprising. I left the house in a right state.' She paused, thought about her words, saw the worry in Maggie's eyes. A worry that wouldn't normally be there and a guilt spread through her, knowing she didn't need that kind of stress, not so soon after Stanley's death. 'Seems like I'm worrying everyone just lately.' Leaning against the door jamb, Lexi saw the way Maggie pressed her lips tightly together and avoided her gaze. It was her way of not giving an opinion, of keeping her thoughts to herself and, instead, she concentrated on the contents of a pan, which she stirred with a lot more enthusiasm than it deserved. 'He's coming at the weekend, to see Isla... we need to talk,' Lexi continued, then stared at the floor thoughtfully. 'I did do the right thing, Maggie. Coming here. It was the right thing to do, wasn't it?'

'Honey, you did what you had to do. You shouldn't question yourself for that.' She turned, picked up the black pepper mill, twisted it over the pan as the rich aroma of chilli filled the room. Lexi felt her stomach turn with hunger. 'Now then, will Nate be staying over?'

Sighing, Lexi thought about Nate spending the night. She hadn't really thought about what would happen, or where they'd sleep. 'I... I hadn't given it much thought.' She rolled her eyes to the stairs, thought of her childhood bedroom, couldn't imagine sharing it with a man, not even with Nate. 'Maybe... maybe I'll book a room, at the hotel, you know...' She took a breath. 'So we can talk.'

Giving a wry smile, Maggie turned to the cooker, picked up a wooden spoon and stirred the pan. 'I've made a chilli, to go on the potatoes.' It was a typical Maggie comment, a way of giving her blessing, without any other comment or judgement. 'I'll keep Isla here with me, shall I?' She paused. 'At the weekend.'

'Maggie, could you come in here and referee these two?' Becca giggled as she appeared in the doorway right behind where Lexi leaned. Resting her chin on Lexi's shoulder, Becca pushed out her bottom lip in childlike fashion. 'They're doing my head in, arguing about who won the game and right now I'm not sure which one of them is the two-year-old.' Turning back to the room, Becca slumped down to sit on the floor, grabbed at the cushions, pushed them against the settee, then smiled as Isla escaped Harry's clutches and jumped on her knee.

Gripping Becca's face, Isla planted a kiss on her cheek. 'I won, didn't I?' she whispered cheekily, then smiled and as though noticing Becca's shoulder-length hair for the very first time, she dreamily ran a hand through it. 'Amorrow. Will play again, amorrow. Promise.'

Laughing, Lexi stood up, held her arms out to Isla. 'Come on. Leave Becca alone; she might be busy tomorrow.' Pressing her face as close to Isla's body as she could get, Lexi closed her eyes, took pleasure in the scent of strawberry bubble bath and freshly washed pyjamas. 'Mmm. You smell so good. I could eat you.'

The words made Isla squirm in her arms. 'No, Mummy. I wanna play with Becca.' Her whole body heaved with a sob, her eyes filled with tears and her bottom lip wobbled dramatically.

Giving Becca an apologetic look, Lexi tried to work out what to say, knew that Becca would most probably have plans for the following day and didn't want her to feel obliged to take the whims of a two-year-old into consideration.

'Look, as I said, Becca might be busy tomorrow. And... let me think...' She rolled her eyes to the ceiling thoughtfully. 'I know what we should do.' She pulled a face, shook her head. 'No, maybe not. I bet you wouldn't want to play hide-and-seek with your mummy, would you?

Excitedly, Isla beamed back a smile, nodded with so much more enthusiasm than the comment had deserved, until, protectively, Lexi placed a hand on her head to slow the intensity of the movement. 'You do love to play hide-and-seek, don't you?' She looked towards where Becca happily sat in the crook of Harry's arm.

'Can I play?' Harry chipped in, with his gaze fixed on Isla. 'I'd like to play too. In fact, I bet I could win the game.' He began to laugh. 'I always win.'

Wriggling out of her arms, Isla ran to Harry. Straddled his knee and placed a hand at each side of his face while staring intently into his eyes. 'I win, me.' She looked up, over her shoulder. 'Don't I, Mummy?'

'Well, you could end up with quite a game, because Isla certainly does find the best places to hide, and believe it or not, she somehow manages to stay really quiet. Nate and I had to practically tear the house down, she was so well hidden, we literally couldn't find her.'

'And where did you hide?' Becca asked Isla inquisitively. She leaned towards her and took delight in the way Isla immediately reached across, moved from Harry's knee to hers.

'Hey, you... nice try at staying up late. Come on, bedtime.' Holding her arms out to Isla, Lexi picked her up, tucked an arm under her bottom and wrinkled her nose as Isla automatically leaned in, tucked her head under her chin.

'Come on, Lex. You have to tell us where she hid,' Harry pleaded. 'It's only fair – I can't have a two-year-old beat me, can I?'

22

After tossing and turning for most of the night, I creep as slowly as I can down the stairs and through the front door and, with a shudder, I realise how cold it's become, how the frost crunches below my feet on the pavement and how the air bites cruelly at the back of my throat. Even so, I have an overwhelming need to watch you, to see what you're doing, to know whether you too are awake, tossing, turning, thinking about your life. About what has already happened, and what is yet to come.

Climbing into my car, I use it as a shield against the elements and while waiting for the heater to warm the car, for the ice to clear itself from the windscreen, I pull my coat tightly around me. And, ironically, I wrap my warm woollen scarf around my neck, smile as I do so. Leaning back, I close my eyes, take pleasure in the warmth that now blows directly on my feet, but still feel the cold in my fingertips and flick open the glovebox to look for a pair of gloves that are no longer there. Slamming the box closed, I sit forward in my seat, shuffle back and forth, put my foot on the accelerator and literally move the car just a few feet until I'm parked behind a wall, with the cottage firmly in my sights.

Staring at the window of the cottage, I see you. You're sitting pathetically in the window seat, wistfully staring at the street, with just a dim light behind you to show that you're there. And for a while I watch the way you skittishly glance from spot to spot, checking every shadow, every noise. And even though you think you're alert, you're actually oblivious to the real world, to what's happening outside, or to the fact that I'm here, watching you, watching me.

With a need to get closer, I climb out of the car, step quickly from foot to foot, and duck from one gate to the next, using the overgrown bushes and trees to hide behind. Then curse loudly as I bump into the trunk of a tree, feel a shower of rainwater fall from its branches and, angrily, I glare at the sky. The weather seems to have cleared, the clouds have dispersed, and the early morning sun is just about to rise in the distance, making me hopeful of a good and productive day.

As a discarded can rattles past my foot in the breeze, I lean forward and, without thought, I pick it up and throw it in a wheelie bin that's standing by someone's gate. Then catch my breath as the lid slams down and, while ducking behind the wall, I look up to see you turn; you study the road, look in my direction, and I chastise myself for having made a noise, for alerting you to the fact that I'm out here. Annoyed, I wait until you turn away; I see your attention go to the stairs, and I use your distraction to my benefit as I quickly head back to my car, where I jump inside and slump childlike against the leather of my seat.

Determined to keep focused, I pick up my phone, begin to flick through the photographs until I come to the last few I took of my mother. It was at a time when she'd completely withdrawn, the mumblings had become worse, and her nightmares had changed from sobbing in her sleep to screaming and shouting. Tormented by the past, she was unable to leave it behind as her body gave up and diminished with a sickness that took over her mind. Even in sleep, tears dropped from her eyes. And in the hours she was awake, the torture remained within them. And I noticed that each time I pointed the camera at her, she stared into space, and never once looked directly at it.

I press my finger against the screen, trace the shape of her face. Feel *the tears in my eyes as I notice how pale and translucent her skin had become. It was a look that had made her seem old before her time and I now realise just how ready to leave us she'd been. The weight of my task lies heavily on my shoulders and even though she never said it, I know she'd have happily taken my place, taken the revenge herself. Made you wish it had been your father that had died that night, and not her daughter.*

23

Sipping at the mug of steaming hot tea, Lexi made her way to the window seat, plumped up the cushions that were scattered along it and, with one held tightly to her chest, she settled herself to watch the early-morning sunrise that was just about to poke its head above the horizon. It was a time of day that Lexi loved the most, a time when the house was still quiet, before the chaos of day began and even though she was exhausted from tossing and turning all night, she still wanted to enjoy that hour of solitude, of coming to terms with her own thoughts and trying to find answers to the questions that had spun around her mind during every minute of the night, giving her no time to rest or to sleep.

With her eyes fixed on the almost deserted street, she listened to the wind as it howled relentlessly down the chimney. Grabbed at a soft woollen blanket and pulled it tightly around her cold, pyjama-clad shoulders. Shuddering, she focused on the street, on the odd pieces of litter that rattled across the tarmac at speed and smiled wistfully as the street lights dimmed. Then, slowly – one by one – they turned themselves off. Watching the island spring back into life had always been a pleasure, and even though the night had been long and exhausting, she curled her shoulders upward to stretch, suddenly feeling as though she were coming out of hibernation and, at some point, soon, the sun would shine and all in the world would be good again.

Except it wasn't, and with her imagination running wild, Lexi breathed in slowly, almost protectively as she stared through the dusk while constantly searching every shadow, checking its size and shape in minute detail and, almost instinctively, she kept an eye on each and every corner, every parked car, along with the small cottages opposite, their overgrown gardens, and one house in particular where the outdoor security lights flicked on and off repeatedly, an indication that someone or something was around – she just didn't know what.

Looking out from Maggie's cottage, she couldn't believe how vulnerable and terrified she'd felt, just the day before. Whereas now she felt both safe and warm, and looking out from within was a sight that felt both comforting and eerie, all at once. It was a stark reminder that the world still existed outside of this cottage, even though at times she felt as though this island was cut off from the world, in a protective yet isolated bubble. And without a doubt, it could be the safest place on earth, but on the other hand she also realised that once the tide came in, almost anything could happen and, worryingly, she knew that help couldn't and wouldn't arrive, even if she wanted it to, not until the tide retreated and the island was released from its natural captivity.

Grabbing her handbag from where it hung on the newel post, Lexi yawned and dug to the bottom until she found the letters she'd written to her mother. They'd been one of the last things she'd grabbed before she'd left the house, simply hadn't been able to leave them behind, and slowly she began to read through each note, starting with the oldest first, which had been written on childish notelets that Maggie had bought for her. On the matching envelopes she'd written her mother's name, her address and, on the back, the words 'Sender: Alexandra'. The early letters had been much shorter, and much more tentative than the ones she'd written as an adult, and for a moment she wondered at which point she'd stopped wishing for her life to go back to the way it had been, to a time when she'd had a mummy and a daddy who she thought had both loved her. Or when she'd realised that life would never be the same again, that her daddy would never come home, and that the reality was that her mother had been selfish and cruel, in a way she could never forgive.

Considering the letters in her mind, she tried to understand the logic she'd had as a child, along with the way she'd practically begged her own mother to love her. Flicking through the letters, she found the one she'd written to her the day after Isla had been born, after becoming a mother herself. She still couldn't understand why she'd even considered adding a picture of Isla and, angrily, she tapped the palm of her hand against her forehead, wondered how stupid she must have been. Whether she'd have actually considered allowing her mother back into her life, to visit her grandchild, or, deep down, she wondered if her notes had been more of a wish list, in the knowledge that she'd never post any one of them. Not one had ever been received or read. And in the back of her mind, she tried to understand if it had simply been her way of putting one or two ghosts to bed, tucking them in and leaving them to rot. Exactly where they belonged. In her past.

Smiling as Agatha woke, stretched and sauntered over, Lexi patted her lap, then tipped her head to one side and, with one hand stroking the kitten, she dug back through her bag, pulled out her phone and began flicking through the missed calls and unanswered messages. Most had been from the office, from Simon, and it suddenly occurred to her that she needed to feign an illness, a reason for why she wasn't at work this morning, and to let him know that she most probably wouldn't be going back, not this side of Christmas. After all, her life had altered, and now, going back to Whitby might not be an option. Sighing, she tapped out an email, a brief explanation, and held her breath as she pressed the send button, all the time knowing that her picture could hit the newspapers at any given moment, that the connection could be made and that once again her life could be spread across every front page of every national in England.

A noise on the staircase made her jump and turn to see Maggie moving slowly down the stairs. She gave Lexi a look of concern that was quickly followed by a smile.

'Now then, my lovely, how long have you been sitting there?' She dropped a hand lovingly on Lexi's shoulder, stared deep into her eyes, nodded. 'You've been there half the night by the looks of you; you're cold,' she whispered, scooting past to kneel in front of the fire. 'Why don't I get this lit? Make the room all nice and warm for when our Isla wakes up.' She began to screw up newspaper, added sticks, a log, a few pieces of coal, then lit a match. 'It shouldn't take long to warm you up.' She moved across the room to where the Christmas tree stood and lay on her stomach to reach underneath. 'God knows why we always stand it here. This damn switch is so difficult to reach.' Grunting, she began to laugh as Agatha ran to the tree, protectively sat beneath it and then, with wide-open eyes, she jumped backwards as the tree began to randomly flash, filling the room with bright LED lights of every colour.

'Thanks, Maggie. You're so kind and Isla will love it.' Staring wistfully into the lights, she wished she'd put the tree up at home, made the house more like Christmas, just as Nate had insisted. And now he'd be sitting there alone, with both the tree and the Christmas presents still up in the loft, still in need of wrapping.

Standing up, Maggie stretched. 'I just looked in on her; she was fast asleep, absolutely flat out.' She laughed. 'Could be there for hours.' Making her way to the kitchen, Maggie flicked the kettle on to boil, pulled open a cupboard and studied the selection of mugs. After what looked like much thought, she finally grabbed at two, dropped a teabag in each. 'I'll make some tea, shall I? Give us chance to catch up.'

'Oh, Maggie. I wouldn't know where to start.' Lexi pondered the past two days. Nothing was as it had been, and she pressed the flats of her hands to each side of her face and briefly closed her eyes, tried to think. 'I just want my life back. I want to protect Isla, make sure nothing will ever hurt her, give her the best childhood ever, and constantly running away isn't doing that. I feel as though we're always going to be running, always watching our backs, waiting for the past to catch up.' She stopped, paused. 'It doesn't seem fair, dragging her away from her home, away from Nate.'

Sighing, Maggie passed her a mug. 'I hate what this is doing to you, hate that you feel so out of control. But don't ever think you're not doing your best. You are protecting her and no one knows you're here. It's the safest place you could have gone and until the killer is caught, this is exactly where you should be.' She smiled, threw herself at the settee, tossed the cushions to one side and patted the seat beside her. 'Come on, take a seat. Let's stare into the flames, shall we, watch them dance? You can make a wish if you like.'

With a half-smile, Lexi curled up beside Maggie, laid her head against her shoulder, closed her eyes, breathed in the familiar perfume and thought of that very first day she'd sat on this settee, read a book, cuddled up to this woman. 'Make a wish,' Maggie had said, while holding the book open. 'Go on, all you have to do is say it out loud and it'll be real.'

Lexi gasped as she remembered her response, the way even as a small child she'd spat the words with venom. 'I don't want to see her, not ever again. They won't make me, will they?' She'd looked up and into Maggie's eyes, felt the love and warmth within them. It had been a feeling she'd been so desperate for Isla to know. A feeling that had meant she'd taken her away from the only home she'd ever known and, in doing so, she'd cruelly left Nate behind. She knew she still owed him the truth. But had no idea how to tell him what had happened, that someone had been so close to her own front door that killing her and Isla would have been easy. It was a fear that sent shivers down her spine and caused her mind to spiral violently out of control and, with endless images of what could have happened, she felt herself sinking deeper and deeper into the darkness until suddenly she was travelling at speed. Hurtling through the Underground, with platform after platform flying past, each one tormenting her thoughts as she tried to guess when it would stop, where she'd get off and, when she did, who would be waiting.

24

'Well, look at you, you just look just like a princess, and your pretty tiara – are they real diamonds?' Becca's overexcited voice drifted in from the kitchen to infiltrate Lexi's sleep-filled mind and, with confusion, she rubbed at her eyes, rolled her shoulders backwards in an awkward stretch, snuggled deeper into the blanket that covered her and, while still in a half sleep, for just a few seconds she submitted to the exhaustion and allowed herself to simply lie and listen.

Perplexed, Lexi finally opened her eyes, focused on the dying embers of the fire, realised she'd slept for much longer than she'd thought and, with a feeling of annoyance, she pushed herself up much too quickly and immediately felt the whole room spin as though it were rotating on an axis. Holding on to the settee, she clung to the cushions, closed her eyes, took slow, deep breaths as she waited and hoped that the feeling would pass.

'Twinkles. My shoes... they twinkle,' Isla squealed excitedly. 'You... you put them on.'

Lexi could imagine Isla bouncing around, wearing her pale blue princess outfit, holding out her sparkly shoes up for someone to try on, along with her plastic sparkly tiara. Since watching *Frozen*, Elsa had been Isla's favourite person in the whole world and wearing her dressing-up outfit dropped her straight into a world of make-believe, where life never got much better and where a two-year-old seemed to get away with a whole lot more mischief than normal.

'Oh, thank you. Do you think your shoes would fit me?' The voice came from another woman; it wasn't Maggie, nor was it Becca and, puzzled, Lexi forced herself to sit up and listen intently as Isla gave off shrieks of delight while pretending to be Elsa and firing shards of ice from her fingers.

'Isla, come here, show it to me,' Becca interrupted. 'I think you'll find that Vicki is going home; she doesn't want to play.' The tone in her voice was unmistakably hostile and Lexi felt herself bristle nervously. She'd briefly met Vicki at the beach the night before, remembered the harsh way Becca had spoken to her then. At the time she hadn't thought much of it, she'd been too immersed in her own problems with Nate, but now she tipped her head to one side, listened, couldn't understand why one sister would be so constantly unkind to another. Inquisitively, and with her mind working over-time, she concentrated on what was being said, felt aggrieved that the door had almost been closed, with only a small gap left to peep through.

'Here you go, I'll even open the door for you,' Becca sang out as the back door was opened and a gust of icy winter air blew through the house, making Lexi shiver violently, lift her feet from the floor, move on to her knees and lean against the back of the settee to glare pensively at the kitchen door.

'Come on now, let's shut that door. I haven't warmed this house all morning for you two to let all the cold air in.' Maggie sang the words; it was her way of never offending anyone, and of always keeping the peace, but ultimately, it normally got her what she wanted. 'Now, who wants a lovely mug of tea?' she asked as the back door was firmly closed. 'And how about...' Maggie continued, 'how about I make you some eggy bread? Would you like that?'

'Yay, eggy bread!' Isla squealed as the sound of her feet ran at speed around the kitchen, leaving Lexi to imagine how she'd be circumnavigating the long, narrow dining table. Using it as her own personal roundabout, most probably, making everyone else in the room dizzy and wishing she'd stop.

'Oh wow. Do you like eggy bread?' Vicki questioned. 'Well, sometimes, and just for a treat, we have eggy bread at school,' Vicki said. 'You could come and take a look at the school if you like, maybe stay for lunch one day. That'd be nice, wouldn't it?' She paused as Isla mumbled a reaction. 'Of course,' Vicki continued. 'You can bring your mummy. I think she'd like school dinners.'

'Urgh. I don't think anyone ever liked school dinners,' Becca chipped in. 'Besides, I don't think Isla wants to go to school. Not yet. Do you, Isla?' Pausing, she then added abruptly. 'Plus, your mummy, she likes you to be at home with her. Doesn't she?'

Perplexed by the obvious animosity in Becca's voice, Lexi slowly stood up, threw the blanket from her legs and, still in her pyjamas, she uneasily padded across the room, peered through the crack in the door that led to the kitchen, took in the chaos that was Maggie's kitchen. It was a large room, the full width of the cottage, with racks on the wall, every spice you could name and shelves that were crammed full of odd china, ceramic teapots, vases full of plastic flowers.

'Maggie...' Isla yelled. 'You come to school.' Watching, Lexi saw Isla run across the room, jump into Maggie's arms, nod enthusiastically. 'They play at school.' She rearranged her tiara, gave Maggie the cutest smile. 'Big girls go. Don't they?'

'They sure do and you're gonna be a big girl real soon.' She caught Becca's eye, furrowed her brow in question. 'But do you know what I used to say to your mummy when she was little?'

Closing her eyes, Lexi could hear the words before Maggie said them; she'd heard them all a million times before, said to many a foster child that followed, all of whom had wanted to grow up much before their time.

'You should never rush growing up...' Maggie began. 'Your life, it isn't a race, and being young is something you should want to last forever.' She whispered the words wistfully, nodded. 'I wish I were young again.'

'Do you?'

'I do.' She paused thoughtfully. 'And if I were, I wouldn't rush a single thing. I'd make sure every minute lasted for as long as I could make it.'

Moving her position, Lexi closed one eye, looked at Vicki, who sat at the table, thoughtfully sipping from a mug. Taking more notice than she had the night before, she saw the similarity in looks to Becca. She was in her late twenties, wore barely any make-up and had straightened her long dark hair and tied it back with an elastic.

Giving Maggie an apologetic smile, Vicki lifted her mug in salute. 'Well, maybe you'd consider talking her mummy into coming over; we're having a nativity this year. First one since the pandemic,' she said. 'I'd love for Isla to take part. She'd make a fabulous angel.' She leaned forward and whispered, 'In truth, we don't have enough kids on the island. I could do with recruiting a few.'

Maggie shook her head, dropped Isla to the floor. 'Well. That isn't my decision. You'd have to ask her mummy. I don't think... I mean...' Turning to the toaster, Maggie dropped two slices of bread into the machine, clicked it down, then turned to a pan where a slice of bread that had been dipped in egg was lowered into the hot oil, causing smoke to rise up and fill the kitchen.

In an obvious move to gain Isla's attention, Becca grabbed her by the arm, lifted her up, pulled a face, gave her a mischievous smile, then pulled her in close, blew a loud, vibrating raspberry into the crook of her neck. 'Ahh, gotcha.'

Squealing, Isla wriggled in her arms. 'Becca, don't.'

'Oi, you two, let's not wake your mummy up,' Maggie whispered as the dishwasher was opened, plates and cutlery were taken out. 'She had a big day yesterday and she must have been really sleepy.' Playfully, Maggie poked Isla in the ribs, laughed as she squirmed.

'But why... why is she sleepy?' Isla quizzed as she slipped back to the floor, wandered across to the table, picked up her sippy mug, flopped to the floor in true spoiled-princess style and took a drink.

'Oh, I'm not sure,' Maggie faltered; she looked from Vicki to Becca. Smiled. It was more than obvious she was trying to dodge the question and Lexi found herself stepping from foot to foot, nervously trying to work out whether she should go into the room and say a quick hello or run upstairs and jump in the shower.

'Now then, Isla, eggy bread's ready. So, how about you sit at the table for me while I cut it up for you.'

Hearing the short rattle of a box, Lexi closed her eyes, knew Isla's routine and that she'd insist on feeding the kitten before eating breakfast herself. Cursing, Lexi wished she'd mentioned it the night before. 'Thank you. I'll take those,' Maggie chipped in. 'Now then, let's all go and sit at the table.'

'I wanna feed Agafa,' Isla yelled. 'Maggie, nooooo... they for Agafa.'

Pushing open the kitchen door as quickly as she could, Lexi stepped into the room. Held her arms out to Isla. 'OK, OK, calm down. Mummy forgot to tell Maggie. It's OK, Agatha won't starve.' Watching Isla push out her lip, Lexi snuggled her in, gave Maggie a look of apology. 'She's always fed her right before breakfast. It's kind of a ritual and she won't eat hers till Agatha's had at least a biscuit or two.' She paused, wiped the tears from Isla's face. 'I think it's Isla's way of making sure Agatha doesn't pinch all her food. Isn't it?'

'Hi. Do you remember me? I'm Vicki. We met at the beach.' Becca's sister gave her a soft but radiant smile. Picking up her mug, she nervously took a sip of the drink. Gave Isla a smile, but kept her eyes firmly fixed on Becca as she spoke. 'I didn't get the chance to tell you last night, but yesterday, I bumped into Maggie and Isla. Maggie told me that you might be staying for a while and, well... I work over at the children's centre. It's attached to the school, and I was wondering if Isla would like to come across, meet some of the other children on the island, maybe take part in this year's nativity. It'd also give me and you a chance to say hello properly.' She spoke at speed, without taking a breath. 'We have a playgroup, breakfast club and childminding facilities... it's lovely. You'd really like it.' She took a short, sharp breath, pressed her hands tightly together, steepled her fingers hopefully. 'We could really do with a few more children, children who might like to be angels or one of the three kings.' Laughing, she leaned forward as Isla danced towards her. 'We seem to have a lack of youngsters on the island these days and, well... as soon as I met Isla yesterday, it occurred to me she'd make the most perfect angel.' Looking up, she caught Lexi's eye. 'What do you say, can I borrow her? She'd be in safe hands, look.' She held her hands up in the air, wiggled them around, laughed at the joke.

With panic flooding her mind, Lexi caught the look in Becca's eye, fought the urge to run from the room, take Isla with her. 'Thank you. That's... well, that's a really kind offer.' She inched to the door, gave Vicki an apprehensive smile. 'I'm sorry but...' She used a hand to indicate her pyjamas. 'I need to shower, get changed.' She paused, looked to both Maggie and Becca for help. 'Isla, can you be a good girl for Maggie while Mummy gets dressed?'

'Well, I think you can call that a no... so, if that's all...' Becca chipped in with a smirk, leaving Lexi to run for the stairs. Making her way to the bedroom, she took deep inward breaths. The thought of Isla going off with anyone, even to the local school that she'd attended as a child, gave her palpitations. She held a hand to her heart, felt the way it raced. She could barely breathe and forced herself to sit on the bed, tried to calm herself down. But couldn't. Slowly, and for something to do with her hands, she began to pull clean clothes out of the wash basket. Began thinking about Vicki, Isla, how one day she'd have to go to school and how, very possibly, Vicki would be her teacher. It was something she'd have no choice but to come to terms with; the last thing she wanted was to be an overbearing helicopter-style parent and, whether she liked it or not, there would be a day when she'd have to let Isla go. She just knew that that day was not today. Her mother's murderer was still out there. They'd found her once and could find her again; it was only a matter of time. She just had to pray that the police would work out who it was, and when they did, they'd put him behind bars and, quite literally, they'd throw away the key.

Trying to compose herself, Lexi walked down the stairs, felt her emotions bounce off the walls and realised that it took all of her effort to conjure up her bravest smile and, with it fixed firmly to her face, she entered the kitchen, fully expecting Vicki to still be sitting there, still at the table with the mug in her hands, but she wasn't. 'Oh, where did she go?'

'Who, the teacher from hell?' Becca replied.

'Why do you call her that?'

Shrugging, Becca kneeled down, began to fuss Agatha, who was leaning in, purring loudly, taking the cat biscuits one by one from her fingers. 'She's annoying, never leaves me alone; not only did she follow me to the island, but she also decided to stay, get a job and now she hovers around me – all the time.'

'She's your sister.' Lexi furrowed her brow, shot a perplexed look at Maggie, who lifted her shoulders, took an obvious deep breath in before turning back to the cooker where she continued to stir the contents of a pan.

'She might want to be with you and it's really nice of her to offer about going to the school and all that, it's just...' She glanced at where Isla sat busily eating her eggy bread. 'I'm not ready to let her go. She's still a baby and... what if I bump into her around the island? What if she asks again?'

Drying her hands on a tea towel, Maggie pushed a mug of tea into Lexi's hand. 'Well, I think she got the message. It was more than obvious you didn't want her to go. I doubt she'll ask again.' She paused. 'And you won't bump into her today; she was heading to the mainland. Before the tide came in.' Turning to the cooker, Maggie lifted a poached egg out of a pan, placed it on a plate with a slice of toast. 'Here you go, get that down you.'

With her fingers gripping the plate, Lexi stared into Maggie's eyes, shook her head, was more than aware that Becca was listening, and although she was Harry's girlfriend, she was completely oblivious as to why Lexi had suddenly landed herself on Maggie's doorstep, what had happened to her mother and how terrified she felt at the thought of Isla going anywhere, with anyone. 'I... I don't want her to go to school, she's far too young. She... she still needs me.'

'Then don't let her go. It is your choice.' Filling the dishwasher, Maggie waved a spoon in the air. 'It'd be lovely to see her all dressed up, though, wouldn't it? She does love dressing up.'

'For what it's worth, I think she was being pushy, which is normal. She just loves to take control.' Becca sipped at her drink, placed the mug back on the table, picked up her phone, stepped away and pointed the camera towards where Isla sat. 'Isla, smile for me.'

'No,' Lexi yelled, held a hand out in front of the camera. 'Please, I'd...' She didn't know what to say, how to explain. Didn't want Isla's photograph taken, plastered all over social media for the world to see, for her mother's killer to find. 'I'd just rather you didn't. Sorry.' Feeling the colour rise dramatically to her cheeks, Lexi furrowed her brow and sighed. Inching her chair in front of Isla, she picked up a small piece of her toast, waved it around in the air, pushed it in her mouth. 'And if Isla wants to dress up, I'll buy her some more outfits and she can do it here. With me,' she said determinedly as her phone began to ring in her pocket. Jumping, Lexi ran from the room, pulled the phone from her pocket and felt her heart miss a beat as she saw the number that flashed up on the screen.

25

'Morning, I'm Detective Inspector Fiona Flowers; I'm trying to get hold of Alexandra Graves.' The woman's voice echoed down the phone as Lexi held it away from her ear and stared at the handset. It was the call she'd waited for. The call that could finally give her some answers. Overwhelmed, she closed her eyes, prayed that the killer had been caught, that her mother could be laid to rest with some satisfaction that her murderer would go to prison, serve his time.

With a mouth full of toast, Lexi repeatedly tried to swallow. Couldn't. It was as though the food had suddenly turned to dust, and was stuck in her mouth, churning around with nowhere to go and, with no other choice, she grabbed at an almost empty tissue box. Spat out the food and, frantically, she began to drag the air back into her lungs.

'Sorry. I... yes, speaking,' she eventually managed to say. 'What... what happened? Did you catch him? Did you catch her killer?'

'Sorry, Alexandra. No. We didn't.' The detective paused. 'But rest assured. We are doing everything we can, we're following every lead we have.' She coughed, hesitated. 'I'm calling because I need to see you. I could do with popping over to the island... to speak to you, about your father.'

The words cut through her. The palms of her hands went clammy, the back of her neck suddenly hot, and her mind spun with confusion as she reached for the stairs, sat down on the step. 'What about? What happened to him?' Every scenario sped through her thoughts and within seconds every image she'd ever stored up of her father flashed through her mind, along with every emotion, both good and bad. 'Is he dead?' She could barely breathe, shook her head repeatedly and began blinking away tears that wouldn't fall. After what seemed like an age, she heard the detective take a breath, knew she was carefully considering what she should say next, but the silence spoke volumes and Lexi dreaded what was coming.

'No... he's asked if you'll go to the prison. He wants to see you. Says he'll talk to us, tell us what we need to know, but only if you're there.'

They were the words she'd expected the least, and while reeling from the impact, she pulled the phone away from her ear, furrowed her brow in disbelief, stared helplessly at the screen.

'Alexandra...' She paused. 'I'm asking for your help. If he can give us just the tiniest piece of information that leads us to the killer, it not only helps us catch your mother's murderer, but it means you're safe too.' The words could only just be heard, and Lexi imagined them being shouted through the loud and violent storm that had taken a hold in her mind, where volcanos erupted, lightning struck and thunder roared. It was a constant noise that caused her to drop the phone in her lap, push her fingers in her ears, rock back and forth in an attempt to block out the present.

'Lexi...' The short, sharp sound of Maggie's voice made her open her eyes, stare at Maggie, who began walking towards her, wringing her hands tightly around themselves with a look of concern crossing every inch of her face. 'Are you OK? Can I do anything?' Her hand reached out, gently touched her on the arm.

Looking up and holding Maggie's gaze, Lexi stared into her deep, loving eyes, felt the tenderness within and, slowly, Lexi shook her head, grabbed the phone from her lap, then watched as Maggie gingerly reversed out of the room, went back into the kitchen and closed the door behind her.

'I can't. I... I don't want to...' Lexi felt the breath leave her body. It was as though she'd been punched in the gut. Couldn't comprehend why he'd suddenly ask to see her; after all, it had been over twenty years since she'd last looked at his face, touched his hand or kissed his cheek, and even though she knew many people did get visitors in prison, it had never been something she'd considered or wanted to do, and the thought of seeing him now, of looking into those steel-grey eyes, filled her with a dread she couldn't explain.

'Alexandra, Alexandra. Listen to me.' Fiona continued to plead her case. 'This could be the key we need to solve your mother's murder.' She paused; the sound of tapping could be heard at the other end of the phone and Lexi could imagine her tapping a pen angrily against her teeth. 'He's made it very clear that he'll only speak to you.' Again, she paused, tapped. 'I wouldn't ask if there were any other choice. But there isn't and if he has just the tiniest shred of information that helps put this lunatic away, I'd have thought you'd do it.' Pausing, she took a breath; it was obvious that she was clutching at straws, trying to pull on any emotion she could find within Lexi to manipulate her thoughts. 'Lexi. Listen. If we catch the killer, if we put him behind bars where he can't hurt you, or your daughter, you'd be able to go home. You'd like that, wouldn't you?'

Feeling the need to see Isla, to check that she was OK, Lexi used the banister to pull herself up, felt her legs weaken beneath her and, with shaking hands, she fell forwards and towards the window seat, where she allowed her whole body to flop forward to lie against the cushions with the phone still held tightly in one hand.

'And Lexi, do you know what? When all is said and done, he's still your dad. I mean, come on, how bad could it really be?'

The words were harsh, almost cruel, and Lexi found herself staring across the room at the dying embers of the fire, wishing she knew what to do, how to respond. She lifted a hand to her neck, imagined it being a scarf getting tighter and tighter. Tried to consider the fear her mother would have felt, the terror she'd have gone through, those last moments as the air had dissipated and the darkness descended.

'OK, I'll go. But...' She needed a caveat, didn't know what to say, what caveat to put in place, just knew she needed an out, should she decide to take one. 'But if it gets too much... if I want to leave, I can, can't I?'

'Brilliant, I'll organise everything.' The detective bounced into action, her voice now almost joyful as she continued to verbally list all the things she needed to do. '...and I'll need to get a visitor's order. Under the circumstances, the prison governor should expedite it and hopefully we should get access to the prison either tomorrow or the next day.'

With all the last-minute instructions that Fiona had given circling her mind, Lexi stared out of the window, felt Agatha's paws as they pummelled her knee before curling up and making herself comfortable and, for just a few minutes, Lexi made a fuss of Agatha and concentrated on the present. It was a short time of getting her thoughts together, of trying to work out what the visit would entail, how it would be, how she'd feel and, deep down, she realised that she was worried that she wouldn't feel anything at all, that she'd stare into his eyes and see him as the cold-blooded killer he really was. Rather than the father who as a child she'd adored with every piece of her heart.

Closing her eyes, Lexi purposely slowed her breathing, listened to the sounds that were coming from the kitchen, the opening and closing of cupboard doors, the constant chatter, giggles and the occasional shriek that came from Isla.

'Come on, Isla, get your coat on,' she heard Becca say. 'If we don't go soon, it'll start raining and then we'll miss our chance to go down the beach, stack some stones, give your mummy an hour's peace and quiet.' She paused; the coat cupboard was opened and closed. The sound of coats being wafted back and forth filled the room, making Lexi run to the kitchen.

'What's happening, where are you going?' She held onto the door jamb, then held her arms out to Isla. 'Isla, come to Mummy.' Furrowing her brow, she buried her face in Isla's hair, took in a deep breath, and closed her eyes, hoping that the panicked feeling deep within her would pass.

'I promised Isla I'd take her down the beach,' Becca said. 'I... well, that is OK, isn't it?' She looked from Lexi to Maggie, saw the glance that was passed between them.

Struggling with her thoughts, Lexi put Isla back on the floor, held out a hand and gripped Maggie's with hers. 'Maggie and I, we'd like to come to the beach with you. Wouldn't we?' She tried to sound enthusiastic, looked at Becca and gave her a genuine smile. 'If you give me a minute, I'll get our coats.'

26

With the ground squelching underfoot, Lexi led the way across the field, tried to keep to the path and laughed at the way Isla jumped over each of the puddles, fearful of any tiny bits of mud splashing her bright yellow wellingtons. Each time it did, it was as though the world was about to end and Isla would push out her bottom lip and give off a long and pitiful wail.

'Mummy, they dirty.' She stood, pivoting on one leg, while precariously holding the offending boot up and in the air, all the time at risk of landing on her bottom and causing an even bigger drama. 'Quick, Mummy. Wipe them.'

'Why don't you walk on the path?' Lexi suggested as she wiped the boot with an overused tissue, then held out a hand to take Isla's in hers. 'Here, let Mummy help you.' It was a simple gesture, a loving touch. One that was quickly shrugged off and Lexi sighed as Isla trotted off, tripping over her own feet and finally, after much wobbling, landing hands first in a puddle. 'Isla, come here. Walk with...'

'I can do it,' Isla insisted as she wiped her hands down her coat, immediately stumbled across the uneven ground, stopped in her tracks and squealed with delight as a small liver-and-white spaniel pup bounded energetically towards her. He was all ears and paws; his tongue lolled out to one side, drool slopping from his mouth. 'Good doggy, sit. Sit now,' she yelled, then giggled, then watched with much amusement as the puppy spotted a seagull and ran towards it, with its owner jogging behind, his face bright red with exertion.

'Sorry. So sorry. I swear, when I finally catch up with that pup, he's going back on his lead. Permanently,' he shouted over his shoulder, then disappeared over the ridge, his voice yelling and shouting in the distance.

Taking in a deep breath of sea air, Lexi felt the breeze bite her skin. Pulling her hoody up and around her ears, she spotted the boat sheds. It was a familiar sight and she smiled at the way the fishermen piled their lobster baskets up, one on top of the other. They were the same pots that had fallen over just the night before, but they now had piles of fishing nets strewn across the grass beside them, where an older man sat on an old milk crate, checking the nets for holes, his hands working fast in the cold, repairing as he went. And beside him, as normal, there were always one or two boats standing up high on stilts. They'd been taken out of the water and were waiting for repairs of their own. The whole scene was a stark reminder of island life and of the huge amount of work involved just to keep the men working, and the traditions of the island maintained.

'What's that?' Isla pointed excitedly to the lookout tower that stood high on the Heugh. 'Can I look?' She wriggled around in a dance, clapped her hands in delight. 'Can I, Mummy? Can I?' Suddenly, the mud splattering her boots didn't seem to be a problem as Isla set off at speed, leaving Lexi to glance over her shoulder to where both Becca and Maggie held on to one another, making it more than obvious that the walk was one of endurance rather than fun.

'Looks like we're going to the tower,' Lexi shouted, picking up her pace to follow Isla along the path that led up the embankment and to where the last crumbling remains of the old fort still stood, and central to it all was the old coastguard tower that had been refurbished to look resplendent against the most beautiful coastline.

With the wind getting stronger, Lexi had no choice but to hold her hair away from her face with a hand. She dug around in her bag for an elastic with the other as she cautiously looked from left to right, and felt her skin bristle before rolling her gaze up the tower and to where windows encircled the top of the building, which gave a panoramic view of the island. Finding the much-needed elastic, she tied her hair back and squinted. She thought she could see a face, someone close to the glass. It wasn't unusual for someone to be up there, not in normal times. But since the pandemic, the tower had been closed and uneasily she realised that just about anyone could be inside, looking out, watching them all, without ever being seen or really noticed by anyone.

'Isla, don't go in there, not without Mummy.' Shouting nervously, she watched Isla retreat, stare down at her wellingtons and, in anticipation of the wail that was about to follow, Lexi quickly pulled what was left of the tissue from her pocket, wiped them clean. Then, respectfully, she strolled across to the war memorial, placed the palm of her hand against it, closed her eyes and whispered a short, silent prayer. It was a habit she'd got into from being a very young child, a tradition that had remained with her from the times she and Maggie had sat on the grass beside it, staring out to sea, to St Cuthbert's Island or Bamburgh Castle, while Maggie had told her the stories of World War One, and Lexi remembered the way she'd always placed a hand to her heart as she spoke, and touched the stone with the palm of her hand before she left.

Keeping her gaze on the mainland, Lexi looked southward along the east coast, wished she could see Whitby, the harbour, the place where her home used to be and, with a sigh, she pressed her lips tightly together, wondered what Nate was doing, whether he'd slept or eaten. Anxiously, she felt her lip begin to quiver, reached for her phone and considered making a call as Becca slid up beside her, placed a hand next to hers on the monument, and without making conversation, she began to read the names carved on it.

'I wonder who they all were?' she whispered. 'I mean, I know the names, and that they're all soldiers and all that. But they must have had a life, a family, people who loved them. Yet they went to war and at such a young age...' She stared wistfully at the stone. 'And if they hadn't gone to war, I often wonder what they'd have done, how old they'd have been, don't you?' She lifted a hand to pull her hair back from her face, tucked it behind her ear, only to tut moments later when the wind caught hold of it again, whisking it up and around her face.

With one eye always on Isla, Lexi smiled at how she'd crouched down out of the wind and was looking through what appeared to be a perfectly placed peephole in the fort's remains. 'Isla, be careful,' she shouted over the sound of waves; they were crashing against the rocks below, a sign that the tide was in, that the island was once again cut off from the mainland and Lexi breathed out a sigh of relief, knew that if the protective cloak of the tide had surrounded them, she could relax, albeit just a while. No one could get to her, hurt her, attack her or her family. Unless, of course, that someone was already on the island. It was a thought that over the past two days had often crossed her mind, a way of keeping her on her toes and, for a moment, she thought of the logic. Knew how quickly she'd run to the island, but also knew that for the killer to have followed, or to have known where she was going, he'd be someone who knew her well. She pondered the thought. *If that were the case, he'd have already killed me by now.* The words went slowly around her mind as she ticked off all the people who knew her past, knew her history, knew where she'd run to and, with frustration, she shook her head, turned into the wind, stared at St Cuthbert's Island, now surrounded by the sea. *There's no one.* Closing her eyes, she allowed the wind to blow in her face, and prayed for the safety this island had always offered and hoped that bringing Isla here had been the right thing to do.

'Will you two slow down?' Maggie staggered towards them both, gasped for breath and, with a hand on each knee, she stared out to sea. 'For a minute, I thought you were going up the tower.' Lifting a hand, she pointed to the old coastguard station with a wry but mischievous smile. 'Look, Isla, it's Elsa's house.' Biting down on her bottom lip, she caught Lexi's eye. 'What do you think, Mummy? Do you think Elsa might live there?'

They both looked at Isla, fully expected an explanation as to why her favourite Disney character couldn't live in the tower, but instead they saw her turn and disappear down the embankment.

'Isla… no…' Lexi scrambled across the grass, lost her footing as she went, heard the sound of a woman's voice coming from the other side of the Heugh.

'It's OK, I've got her.' Emerging from behind the tower, Vicki walked towards them, a wriggling Isla held tightly in her arms. 'She was making a run for the edge. I only just caught up with her before she toppled right down the embankment.' She tapped at the wellingtons. 'And these, these are much too big for you, aren't they?'

'Oh, for God's sake, that's all we need, the bloody teacher from hell turning up every two damn minutes, giving us a lecture on the size of kids' welly boots,' Becca whispered out loud, then saw Maggie respond by flashing her a stern look of disappointment.

Picking up on Maggie's annoyance, Lexi turned her back to where Vicki stood, looked Becca in the eye. 'She's your sister,' she whispered. 'Why don't you like her?' She heard the words fall from her mouth, couldn't help the reporter within her. Turning, she looked from one to the other, wanted to ask so many questions but bit her tongue as Isla ran past and to where Maggie held out her arms, lovingly pulled Isla into a hug and began to walk along the Heugh. 'You might as well have it tattooed across your forehead,' Lexi continued.

Embarrassed, Becca pulled her hoody up to cover her cheeks. 'She's just always there, hanging around, and I don't want her round me all the time – is that OK? Besides, she said she was going to the mainland, yet here she is, annoying us.'

Giving Vicki a genuine smile, Lexi studied her face, felt sure she'd met her prior to the brief interlude they'd had in the kitchen and, once again, without knowing why, she felt her skin bristle uneasily, and instinctively she held her arms out to Isla, took her from Maggie, who seemed to be struggling to walk. 'Are you OK?' she whispered, turned into the wind. 'You've gone painfully white.'

'Oh, don't you worry about me.' Maggie lifted her arms up over her head as though trying to prove a point. 'I'm absolutely fine. All I need is a nice cup of tea and a piece of that ginger cake that I made this morning, and I'll be as fit as a fiddle.'

For the first time since arriving on the island, Lexi observed Maggie. She watched how she walked, how her hand constantly wiped her brow, or went to her chest as though she were struggling to breathe. They were all classic signs of illness, of someone not being as well as they pretended to be and although she didn't want to interrogate her, Lexi knew that something was wrong and made a mental note to speak to her later, to do all she could do to help her, possibly convince her to see a doctor, or at least a pharmacist, which would mean a trip to the mainland, to Seahouses, a place

Lexi didn't really want to go. But even so, after all the years Maggie had helped her, looked after her when she had no one else to do it, it was the least she could do.

Overwhelmingly, she wanted to do nothing more than keep both Maggie and Isla safe, and protectively she wrapped her arms tightly around her daughter, kissed her repeatedly, felt a need to hold on to her forever, but felt Isla resist and wriggle until once again she was standing on the ground, kicking out at the ruins with her foot.

'Hey, don't do that,' Lexi snapped, as Becca began to frantically jump up and down on the spot, making Lexi turn quickly to try and see what she'd spotted.

'Look, Isla. Can you see the lifeboat?' Becca began to run excitedly along the embankment, towards the beach. 'It's over there, do you see it?' She stood on her tiptoes, swung Isla up and into her arms, looked into the distance. 'Do you... do you see the boat?'

Nervously, Lexi ran to her side, stood on a bench, kept her eyes on the water. 'I wonder what's happened?' Within seconds, she spotted the man who'd walked past earlier. He paced anxiously across the rocks, his phone in his hand, a look of desperation on his face, and inquisitively Lexi listened in to what he was saying.

'That's right, he's liver-and-white, he's just a pup, I told your colleague a few minutes ago. He was chasing a damn seagull, it looked wounded, was resting on the water and for some reason he went after it, and just kept on bloody swimming.' He paused, gasped. 'I kept shouting for him to come back. But... it was windy, he didn't hear me, and... now he's too far away. The tide must have taken him.' A hand went to his face to wipe his eyes. 'I can't see him. I just can't see him.'

'The boat keeps circling.' Maggie watched thoughtfully as the engine slowed, moved carefully over the waves, kept close to the island. 'I'm sure Harry said he was working today. Do you think he could be on board?' She pointed to the three-man crew with their white helmets and bright yellow drysuits. Each seemed to be kneeling on the side of the boat, keeping as high as they could to see as much of the water as possible. Then, as one of the crew held their arm outward, fingers flat and pointed, the boat swerved to the right and set off at speed.

'That's the sign. They've seen something. I just know they'll find him. They just have to,' Becca whispered as she stepped forward, rested a thoughtful hand on the man's shoulder. 'Are you OK? Do you want me to phone anyone for you?'

With a shake of his head, the man once again wiped at his eyes. 'He's just a baby, around six months old. I doubt he can swim that well and the water, and... it's cold right now – no one, nothing would survive out there for long, would it?'

'Hey, I'm sure they'll find him. Our friend, he works in the boat, and he always gets there in time. Doesn't he, Maggie?' Pressing her lips tightly together, Lexi felt Isla snuggle in to hide her face deep within her jumper. She was getting tired, grumpy, and it was something she always did when she wasn't sure what was going on around her, and with a comforting squeeze, Lexi kissed her cheek. 'You OK, sweetie?' Watching Isla's response with one eye, Lexi kept a worried eye on Maggie with the other. She was still pale, still held a hand to her chest, looked out of breath. 'You all right there, Maggie?' she shouted over the sound of the oncoming wind, caught Becca's eye, and moved slowly towards where Maggie stood.

'Oh, I'm fine. You know me. Tough as an old horse, I am.' She gave a genuine smile, leaned against the tower. 'Now, you go and make sure that poor man is OK. He looks terribly upset, doesn't he?' she said as Vicki moved slowly towards them.

Tipping her head to one side, Vicki held out her arms to Isla. 'She looks heavy; would you like me to take her for a while? I don't mind, you know, if you want a rest from carrying her.'

With a jolt, Lexi spun to face her. 'No. I... I'm fine. What the hell makes you think I need a rest from my own daughter? I thought you were going to the mainland?' The words fell sharply and embarrassingly from her mouth, making the colour immediately rise to her cheeks. 'I... I'm sorry. That came out wrong.' Lexi apologised but carefully watched every move Vicki made. She appeared to be friendly but the obvious tension between her and her sister made Lexi uneasy, and she made a mental note to speak to Becca properly, to try and find out what had caused the animosity, and, with them sharing such an obvious deep-seated dislike of one another, what Vicki's reasons were for persistently hanging around.

Laughing, Vicki persisted with holding out her arms. 'It's OK. I'm used to kids, and their parents,' she said with her tongue firmly in her cheek. 'And yes, you're right. I was off to the mainland... but at the very last minute, I saw the tide coming in, and after Storm Arwen, the men were still working on the causeway and people are queuing to get past. I weighed up the options and, in the end, I didn't dare risk it.' Sighing, she eventually dropped her hands, pushed them into her pockets. 'I was just heading back to the car when I heard the commotion. News sweeps around the island fast when the boat goes out, so I thought I'd head this way, take a look and then I saw you lot.' She gave a wide, disarming smile. 'Thought I'd join in with the fun.'

Again, Lexi looked across at Maggie, could see the beads of sweat forming on her brow, and began to quiver fearfully. The thought that Maggie could ever be poorly made her stomach turn. It was a feeling she'd never previously experienced and, quite selfishly, one she didn't want to think about because the thought of ever losing Maggie was something she simply couldn't bear. After all, Maggie had always been there for her, the one who'd always been strong for everyone else and, even after the loss of Stanley, she'd carried on being the matriarch of the family. The thought that

that might end, that one day Maggie might not be there, made Lexi stop in her tracks and, while taking in deep measured breaths, she felt tears immediately spring to her eyes, and quickly she turned into the wind, did her best to stop the tears from falling.

'I'm sorry Vicki, but' – Lexi caught her breath – 'you might have to excuse us. Maggie doesn't look too well, and Isla and I, well, we're going to take her home and insist she sits on the settee with a duvet and watches *Frozen* with us. It's Isla's favourite film and, well, you know what kids are like – we haven't watched it for at least two days.' She kept her gaze on Maggie, hoped for a fast retreat. 'Maggie, did you hear that? We're heading back; Isla wants a duvet day. She likes us all to get snuggled up while watching a movie.' Noting the relief on Maggie's face, Lexi furrowed her brow with concern, watched the way Maggie strode on purposely ahead, but also noticed the way her shoulders drooped. For once in her life, she knew that Maggie was the one who needed to be looked after, the one who needed to be surrounded with all the love she'd constantly given.

'Oh, I know that feeling,' Vicki persisted. 'In nursery, we watch the same films over and over. But I haven't seen *Frozen* for a while.' She smiled hopefully, pulled the hood up on her coat, cupped her hands in front of her face, puffed up her cheeks and blew warm air onto them.

Feeling uneasy, Lexi sped after Maggie and with raised eyebrows she gave her a look. 'Maggie, let's go this way. We'll walk along the Heugh, see if we can spot what's happening with the dog.' Walking away, leaving Vicki behind, she made her way along the ridge, and with the watchtower now well behind her she kept her focus on the water that surrounded St Cuthbert's Island, praying that the dog survived the tide, found a sandbank to stand on.

Placing Isla back on the ground, Lexi felt Maggie sidle up close, squeezed her hand. 'Look.' She pointed to the lifeboat, to the way it circled. Slowed. 'The man's dropped his arm. He's leaning over the side, pulling something out. I think they've got him.' As the dog bounced up and down in the lifeboat, Lexi felt the relief flood through her and ran back along the Heugh, where she shouted to the man who still paced along the shoreline. 'They've just pulled him out of the water... he's alive, he was a long way offshore, but not long now and you can get him all dry, warm yourself up with some coffee.' Elated, she felt the tears spring to her eyes. Couldn't imagine what the man had gone through, didn't want to even contemplate how it would feel if Isla had disappeared even for a minute and watched as, emotionally, the man dropped to his knees, and with drooped shoulders, he simply kneeled there, staring at the water as it lapped up on the shoreline before him.

Relieved, Becca clapped her hands together. 'Did you mention coffee? What a good idea.' She leaned forward, swung Isla up and into her arms. 'How about we go and see if they do hot chocolate at Pilgrims?' She rubbed her nose lovingly against Isla's. 'They are open again after the storm, aren't they?' She looked from Maggie to Lexi, who both shrugged their shoulders. 'I hope so, because the chocolate there is legendary... and then, once we've warmed up a bit, and only if you fancy it, we might go and stack those stones on the beach.' Nodding, she smiled, caught Isla's attention. 'What do you say, would you like to do that?'

Laughing at the comical way Isla did a jig in Becca's arms, Lexi rolled her eyes in submission as she noticed Vicki speed up to walk beside them. 'How about we go another day? Maggie doesn't look too sparkling, and we were kind of hoping to get tucked up in front of the telly. We're going to watch a movie, aren't we, Maggie?'

'Great,' Becca said loudly so Vicki could hear. 'Is the teacher from hell coming to watch the movie too?'

27

Looking beyond the dark and moody sky, I lean against the priory ruins, keep my gaze to the east, and at a time when most of the island sleeps, I watch the sky, take delight in the sunrise as it slowly changes colour and I marvel in the way the dark, sullen grey horizon becomes tinged with deep reds and burnt oranges. Each colour moving fluidly together, like the colour palette of an artist when the smallest drop of water allows him to swirl his brush around, from one colour to the next until just for a second the colours merge perfectly, before mixing more than they should and turning a thick and dingy shade of brown.

Smiling, I notice that each colour reflects against the castle walls, against the water beyond, giving the whole scene both height and depth and making it twice as dramatic as it would be if I were standing in the valleys, with the fields and hills stretching out before me.

Reflectively, and even though the rain has begun to fall, I slowly turn and make my way through the churchyard. I snake between the gravestones and casually allow my hand to run across them; the roughness of each one shows its age, the way the weather has eroded them over the years, and I feel delight as I notice the different shapes and sizes that stand before me. Some of the stones stand proud and tall. Others lean precariously with age. Yet interestingly, and even though most have stood in the same position for hundreds of years, the names and dates are still just about distinguishable on them all. They were words once written in a loving memorial to mark the resting place of someone's mother, father, brother or sister. It is something I've been denied, a simple act of marking a place for my sister, so everyone knows who lies there, who she was.

As I wander aimlessly, it's not the old stones that I'm drawn to. It's the newer ones at the other side of the church that attract me, and as I reach them, I run a finger over the top of smooth black marble, admire the bold gold lettering as it glistens with the morning rain and I nod, knowing that this is the type of stone my sister would have had. It's the type my mother would have paid for, on which she'd have lovingly chosen the words. That was providing my father would have allowed it and, for a moment, I close my eyes, see the way he used to sneer, the way he turned bright red and curled his fists in a vicious, deep-seated anger that would brew within him. 'You need to get over it,' he'd scream. 'She's gone, you need to get out of that damn chair and stop wallowing. It isn't good for you, and I won't have it, do you hear me?' The more he shouted, the deeper into herself my mother became with her constant rocking and sobbing and the way she'd stare into the sky for hours on end, all the time refusing to eat, to acknowledge anything else around her. His cruelty was a part of life for many years; he is just one of the people from my past that I truly don't miss and just the thought of seeing him again makes my skin crawl with anxiety. As with everything else, my history is a part of my story. My siblings were the people I should have been able to rely on the most. But that one night, that one day changed every part of my life, undoubtedly altered the path I was supposed to walk and turned my mother into the kind of woman I barely recognised. She was no longer the woman she'd been before that night. The love, the affection, everything I'd previously loved about her had gone. And then, on that final night, the night she rocked and sobbed just once too often, I listened to her words. 'I just want to die,' she whispered. 'I did so much wrong, so much of this is my fault and...' The still grey of her eyes flicked to the door, to where she knew my father would be. 'He'd kill me if he knew. He'd take my last breath without a thought.' Her words spun around my mind, like the continuous loop of an old record that has become stuck to repeat the words, over and over. It was then that I moved slowly towards her. 'Here, let me make you more comfortable.' I whispered the words in a soft, loving tone, while all the time looking over my shoulder. Listening to the sounds of the house. To my father's snores, a clear sign that he'd fallen to sleep and that right now the sound of the television would mask what I knew I was about to do. 'Let's have those pillows?' Closing my eyes, I can still see the look she gave me as I plumped up the pillow. It was as though she were giving me permission to end her pain. With eyes that begged for a forgiveness I didn't and couldn't understand.

Kneeling beside the gravestones, I look from one to the other, realise that most of the new stones are well cared for, most are tended on a regular basis, with new flowers and tiny ornaments. One in particular catches my eye and I read the words upon it.

Stanley Jakes

Loving husband and father to Henry.

A golden heart stopped beating.

Hard-working hands at rest.

It broke our hearts to see you go.

God only takes the best.

January 1946 to February 2021

Also:

Henry Jakes

Died in childbirth.

Much-wanted son of Margaret and Stanley Jakes.

August 1987

The words answer so many questions, make a lot of sense and give all the reasons why this couple gave their lives to loving other people's children, and for a moment I feel their pain, know what it's like to lose someone, and I smile at the way the grave is lovingly tended. It's a grave well cared for and deep down I hope that someone somewhere is caring for the spot where my sister is buried, the place where twenty years later she still waits to be found. Deep down, I long for that moment, wish that I could sit by her stone, place flowers on it daily, and slowly, I whisper a meaningful prayer. But now, after what I've done, I know that my past will catch up with me, and my freedom will soon be lost, and I dread the thought that my life will soon become one of constant monotony. A time when the days and weeks will blend into one, and I try to convince myself that the small, restricted rooms will become bearable, that my claustrophobic nature will disappear and that my time inside will be short, that a judge will realise that I've suffered enough and that my actions were brought on by trauma, rather than being acts of random violence.

With my focus turning to the bell turret of the church, I stare at the structure, the damage left behind after the storm, and wish for the bell to toll, for it to wake me up from this constant feeling of need, of longing for something I can't have, for a closure my mother so desperately needed, a closure I finally had no choice but to give her. Even the rise of the sun doesn't help me, not today, and wistfully I stare at the ruins, at the way the priory is perfectly aligned end to end with the church, and the way each part blends with the other.

Every part of this island seems to take on its own battle that arcs between the weather and the wildlife. Both give it natural beauty, a rugged yet perfect appearance. And, amusingly, I feel my mood change as I watch a small robin who hops along the wall before me. He looks directly at me, studies me and for a moment I envy his lifestyle, I wish for his freedom, for the way he can go wherever he wishes, and laugh as he hops, tips his head to one side, and gives off the most beautiful, shrill morning call. It's as though he's singing just for me and, euphorically, I *walk to the ridge, stand with the full force of the easterly wind in my face and I close my eyes, hold my arms out straight and pretend I can fly.*

'You all right there, love?' an older man's voice shouts harshly over the breeze, brings me back to reality and I lift a hand, wave in his direction. He's walking past the old fort, a part of the island that screams of its history, of the way that battles would have been fought, won and lost here. And as I watch him, happily throwing a stick for his dog to chase, I feel a surge of guilt, an overwhelming rush of adrenaline as I realise that if my wish goes to plan, if I gain my revenge, once again this sacred island will have blood spilled on its shores, and I wander along the priory wall, all the time looking over its edge and at the rugged shoreline that stretches out below.

Slowly, and regretfully, I walk away from the graveyard, through the streets, past the cottage where I know you sleep and, with my hand resting against Maggie's front door, I take a deep breath in and sense your presence. It's a house I've been in so many times before and right now I feel the need to open the door, to walk right in and to infiltrate your day, and I begin to laugh in the knowledge that I can so easily do that and of how I've already become a part of your life. You just haven't realised it yet.

28

Stretching out, Lexi immediately ran a hand between cold cotton sheets, stopped when she reached the edge of the single bed. Felt sure that Isla had previously been there, curled up in a tiny ball, attached to her in the same way that a limpet would grab hold of a rock. Her not being there caused an immediate panic, making her sit up in bed, hold a hand to her chest as her heart began to pound wildly and, even in the darkness, she knew that the room was empty.

'Isla, Isla. Where are you?' Throwing back the duvet, Lexi leaped out of bed, and turned as quickly as she could to scan the room, taking in the shape of the wardrobe, the chest of drawers and the chair that was full of teddy bears. Swiping at the light switch, she had a strong feeling of déjà vu as she threw the wardrobe door open and scoured its insides. It was only a couple of days since she'd searched her home for a kitten, just a couple of days since her life had turned upside down and now, here she was, once again searching, but this time it was for her daughter. 'Isla...'

'She's down here, with me,' Maggie shouted up the stairs. 'I found her snuggled up next to me in my bed, so we got up and made some dippy eggs.'

Sitting down on the edge of the bed, Lexi tried to draw air into her body; every time Isla went out of her sight, she felt as though she'd lost the ability to breathe and, quickly, she closed her eyes, couldn't imagine ever having another day in her life when she wouldn't panic over her whereabouts, felt relieved that she was in the house, with Maggie. For the life of her, she couldn't imagine ever taking her to school, leaving her with Vicki, or any other teacher who'd be in full charge of her well-being, and Lexi's thoughts kept going back to Vicki, to how she'd kept going on about the school, the nativity. 'I... I think she's far too young,' Lexi remembered saying, giving Vicki her best smile. 'Maybe next year. You know, if we're still here. Maybe by then she'll be big enough.'

'Do you want a cup of tea?' The sound of Maggie's voice bellowed from the bottom of the stairs to break her thoughts, just as the shrill sound of the telephone echoed noisily through the house.

Inquisitively, Lexi pulled on her dressing gown and a pair of slippers that Maggie had loaned her before stumbling to the top of the stairs, where she wondered who was on the phone at such an early hour and stood, guiltily listening to the exchange.

'I'm sorry. I can't. Not today and yes, yes, I know I promised.' Leaning against the wall, Lexi saw Maggie's shoulders slump, the palm of her hand momentarily covering her eyes. She wiped at her cheeks. 'It's Lexi, she's had a hell of a week, you saw what she was like yesterday. She needs me right now and what's more, she probably needs to spend time on the island. A crowd might just be a bit too much.' Maggie paused, moved across the hallway, perched on the bottom step, listened. 'Oh no, I doubt it. Not even with me. Santa or not, she'll want to keep Isla here, on the island where she can keep an eye on her.'

Turning, Maggie looked over her shoulder, up the stairs, saw where Lexi stood hovering on the top step, gave her a loving smile. 'It's Becca,' she whispered. 'She wants to go to that Victorian market over in Berwick; apparently there's a Santa, and a grotto with elves and everything.' Again, she turned to the phone. 'It's Lexi, she just got up; I was telling her about Berwick.'

Crouching down to sit on the top step, Lexi listened to the way Maggie busily made excuses. It was more than obvious she'd just reluctantly changed her plans to stay at home, rather than spend the day with Becca, doing the type of things she'd always done, the markets and craft fairs she'd always gone to, and Lexi's mind went back to Nate, to the way she'd constantly made excuses to him and all the reasons why she hated Christmas so very much. Never once had she told him of the nights she'd spent, cold, frightened and alone, following her father's arrest. Or about the hours she'd stared out of the window, watching everyone else have fun. Instead, she'd pretended that she didn't have the time to put up the tree, to dress the house or to make the big day exciting. Inside, she hadn't allowed herself to become immersed in the magic of Christmas, knowing then that no one could take it away from her. Not like they had. Not ever again.

But now, as she sat alone, listening to Maggie's disappointed voice, she could hear Nate's words echoing in the back of her mind. The way he'd constantly asked her to make more effort, to make everything magical and to give Isla the Christmas she deserved. Swallowing hard, she felt the wave of guilt building up within her, until like a punch to the stomach, she caught her breath, held on to the banister for support and wished wholeheartedly that she could make herself love Christmas. Placing a hand to her heart, she promised herself that for Isla's sake, she'd do all she could, and that Isla would get the Christmas she deserved. Even if it killed her.

'Maggie, you really don't need to stay home to babysit me. Honestly. Why don't you go with Becca?' She forced herself to smile. 'Me and Isla, we'll be fine. Providing the weather is dry, we'll go for a walk. We didn't get back to the beach yesterday, or the castle, and I'd like to stack a few rocks and take in a bit more air. Show Isla all the places I used to go.'

'No, my lovely, it's fine. I still feel a bit tired. And I just think Becca was a bit excited, thought Isla might like to go and see Santa?' As Maggie said the words, Lexi saw the hopeful look on her face, the way her mind calculated all the possibilities. 'Or, if you fancied it, we all go? It'd be fun if we were all together. Safety in numbers and all that?'

Catching her breath, Lexi immediately shook her head. 'We couldn't, I couldn't...' She thought about her wish for Isla to get the Christmas she deserved. At just two years old, she deserved to have all the magic. One with gifts, twinkling lights and a belief that Santa would come. It was a Christmas that Nate had desperately wanted, and now, she thought of how he'd be getting up for work in an empty house, with no tree, no decorations and all the gifts they'd bought together, still unwrapped, still in the loft.

Determinedly, Lexi marched down the stairs, took a moment to stroke Agatha, who ran straight to her, thrust her tail in the air and arched her back in welcome. 'Hey there, Agatha, are you settling in?' she whispered, then followed Maggie into the kitchen where she leaned on the door jamb, took pride in the way Isla looked up from her eggs, gave her the biggest, most hopeful smile. 'Look. You're right. We should all go,' she suddenly blurted out, knowing that Maggie was right. She would be safer if they all stuck together and the chances of someone attacking her would be more likely to happen while she was here, alone, rather than in a crowded market, where thousands of people were gathered. 'We should all go and take Isla to meet Santa.' Taking delight in Isla's excitement, Lexi nodded, crouched down, accepted the toasted soldier that her daughter offered. 'Mmm, that's good, isn't it? Now, you eat it all up, dip all of these soldiers in your egg.' She raised an eyebrow, peered into the half-eaten egg. 'And Mummy and Maggie will take you to see Santa. How about that?'

Nervously, she thought about what she'd just promised, the fact that by going to Berwick, she'd be leaving the sanctuary of the cottage, the safety of the island. She'd be immersing both her and Isla back into a world where people got murdered and kittens became suspiciously tied up in red silk scarves and were left in dustbins to die.

She tried to think logically. It was a trip that could potentially put them both in danger: if the killer saw them, he could follow them back to the island; her sanctuary could be short-lived; her life could be in danger. With her breathing accelerating out of control, she quickly grabbed at her phone and for what felt like the millionth time that week, she began scrolling the news, looking for clues, for anything that might say that her mother's killer had been caught and knowing that if he hadn't, the chances were that he could still be out there, still following her, to leave her feeling like a wild and defenceless animal.

As she felt the panic course through her, she quickly left the room, headed up the stairs and to the safety of her bedroom, where she opened the window, lay on the bed, twisted the bed sheets around her fingers, buried her face in the pillow and listened to the sound of Isla excitedly running around downstairs.

'Maggie, Maggie...' Isla yelled, 'my mummy, she said we're gonna see Santa!'

The words pierced her heart. She had to give Isla the Christmas she deserved, but already knew that taking her away from the island was a mistake and with every wish left in her, she wished she hadn't said it, wished there were a way out, a way that meant she didn't have to go.

29

With every thought, every scenario flashing through her mind, Lexi pushed herself up on the bed, anxiously began to flick through her phone, and with her reporter's mind in gear, she analysed as many news reports as she could. She studied pictures of her mother's face, each one a mixture of shame and a steely determination she'd often had. Then, she looked at her father. That same moody, unsmiling mugshot with his ruffled, unbrushed hair and the bruise that covered one side of his face. It was an injury he'd picked up during his arrest but this had been the one picture all the nationals had used to depict him to the outside world. Then there had been the pictures of her six-year-old self and, uneasily, she enlarged one after the other. Felt grateful that because of her age, the press had been restricted, that her face had been blurred and the only images they'd managed to take of her had been from a distance and, with that in mind, she tried to work out if anyone could possibly recognise her now. Whether the tabloids had people in place, trying to work out who she was, where she was, whether or not they could get the next big story. After all, it was what they did and Lexi knew that someone, from at least one of the newspapers if not all of them, would be looking for her.

'Mummy, come on... come now,' Isla shouted in a soft Irish lilt, ran into the room, tugged at her hand. 'We'll go without you.'

Giving her a nervous half-smile, Lexi pulled her blue quilted jacket onto her shoulders, took in a final deep breath of fresh air, and then closed the window she'd previously opened. 'Give me a minute.' She reached forward, lovingly moved a curl of hair away from Isla's face. Felt a rush of love as she immediately fell into her arms, and scattered kisses all over her face.

'Mummy. I love you.'

Wrapping her arms around her daughter as tightly as she could, Lexi wished for it to always be like this. For Isla to always need her. To love her. 'I love you more than all the stars in the sky,' she whispered back, stared into Isla's eyes, and smiled at the instant retort.

'And the fishes. All the fish... in the sea.' Her words stuttered as her hand pretended to be a fish.

'OK, I know you have your pull-up pants on, but how about we try and go to the toilet, you know, before we set off?' Lexi jumped back into mummy mode, knew that once they were in the car, there wouldn't be too many places they could pull off, didn't want Isla sitting in wet pull-ups for hours on end. 'Go on, ask Maggie to help you,' she shouted as she heard a loud, thunderous knocking on the front door. It was a sound she'd heard before, an unmistakable knock that took her back to being that six-year-old child, the one who'd shrunk into a corner, feeling terrified and completely alone as the stampede of police tore through the house like a herd of elephants, not stopping for anything.

Barely able to breathe, Lexi felt her throat close with anxiety as she made her way to the bottom of the stairs, heard the officer's voice.

'Sorry to bother you, is it Alexandra? I'm Detective Inspector

Fiona Flowers, Northumberland Police. I rang you yesterday. I said I might come.' She waved a piece of paper in the air. 'I have the visitor's order. It has to be today.'

Closing her eyes, Lexi felt her whole body shrink. She took a step backwards, puffed up her cheeks and carefully blew out, slowly. 'I... I didn't realise it would be so soon.' She held tightly to the banister, sat down on the step, as Becca rushed in.

'What... what the hell's happening?' Becca looked the woman up and down, took note of the expensive suit, the polished shoes and the briefcase that was held tightly in her hand. 'Is everything OK?'

Holding the detective's gaze, Lexi gave a short sharp shake of her head. She didn't want Becca to know why Fiona was here, certainly didn't want her to know that her arrival meant that for the first time in twenty years, she'd be going to see her father or that, imminently, a killer could turn up and all their lives might be ended. It was a thought she tried to supress. Something she didn't want to believe, and felt the implication spin around her mind in never-ending circles, until it became a fast-spinning hurricane, one that could and would come to an abrupt stop the moment she laid eyes on her father.

'It's nothing.' Maggie waved a hand dismissively in the air. 'Our Lexi, she saw an accident on the way up here yesterday; this nice detective just needed to take down some notes on what happened. Now, how about we get our coats on and go wait by the car.'

Catching her eye, Lexi gave her a thankful smile. Realised how many times throughout the years this wonderful woman had jumped in, diverted questions about her past, saved her from multiple explanations. Stepping forward, Lexi pulled her into her arms, held a hand to her cheek, and stared into her eyes as though her life depended on it. 'I love you so much,' she whispered in her ear, 'but please, this could take a while, you... you go without me.

Take Isla with you.' Letting go, she ran up the stairs, dug around in Isla's bag. Found the wrist link she'd been looking for and passed it to Maggie. 'This is a godsend. I use it all the time.' She gave her a knowing look, smiled. Then kneeled down to speak to Isla. 'Now then,' she whispered, 'why don't you go with Maggie? She's going to take you to see Santa.' She swallowed hard, felt the invisible thread of love stretching between them; it was a thread that connected them all. But today, it felt different. Today it felt like a long piece of elastic that was ready to snap and, quickly, she offered an alternative. 'Or... or maybe you'd like to stay here, with me. We could go to the beach, play with the rocks, maybe even pop into Mr Palmer's next door, see if we could borrow his doggy?' She held her breath, knew she'd quickly backtracked, hoped that Isla would take the second option, then felt her heart shatter into a million shards as Isla grabbed Maggie's hand and headed to the door.

'Mummy... come and see Santa... he's waiting.'

It was a single sentence that made Lexi realise just how much Isla needed Christmas. She needed the magic. The belief. The love. Along with all the sparkle that surrounded it. It was a thought that tore her heart from her chest, and left her feeling inadequate and cruel as a parent who would have quite easily denied her daughter the Christmas she wanted. And now, she vowed that the moment she saw Nate, they'd begin to make plans. She'd tell him the truth and they'd find a way of having a real family Christmas, just like he'd wanted. Although now, going back to that house would be impossible and their family Christmas would have to be somewhere new and not in the house they'd once called home.

'Maggie, come on...' Isla yelled. She tried to run ahead to where Becca still hovered in the doorway but was yanked back by the wrist link that Maggie had already attached, making Isla turn and give out a pitiful yowl.

With eyes that searched Lexi's, Maggie gave her a look of silent apology. 'Look, it's fine. We don't have to go, not if you don't want us to. We... we could all go down the beach, later this morning, we could build a sandcastle, or play hide-and-seek down by the lime kilns. I hear that Isla likes hide-and-seek, don't you?' She paused. 'And we could all go for a walk, while you sort this out.' It was typical of Maggie, the way she tried to please everyone, but Lexi knew that the detective wouldn't have come unless she'd got the visiting order and, reluctantly, she knew that going to see her father was the only way to catch the killer. The only way she'd ever get her life back. And the only chance she had of going home, of going back to Nate.

With her shoulders physically drooping with disappointment, Becca sighed. 'Look, shall I just go on my own? I've promised Harry I'll pick some of those Battenberg-type cakes. He loves them and if I don't get to the market early, they'll be all sold out.' She continued to cautiously look the detective up and down. 'Or... or... how about, we get off' – she used her finger, wand-like, to point between herself, Maggie and Isla – 'we go and get Harry's cakes and then we could get in the queue for Santa and, Lexi, you could follow on and meet us there?' She nodded, bounced up and down, clapped her hands together in a childlike fashion. 'See, we have a plan.'

Feeling the pressure build up inside, Lexi stared into her daughter's hopeful eyes; she knew she had to decide whether to let Isla go and see Santa or not and felt completely torn at the prospect of letting her go. Keeping her safe was her priority and keeping her close for the foreseeable future was imperative, but also impossible as Isla grew older.

'Promise me you'll keep her safe, won't you?' she whispered to Maggie. 'I mean, I know you will.' Tipping her head to one side, Lexi placed a hand on Maggie's shoulder and for a split second that seemed to last forever, they stared into each other's eyes, made promises without saying a word. She knew wholeheartedly that

Maggie had never allowed a single child to ever get hurt, that she wouldn't let Isla get hurt either. 'Seriously, I want you to go. I want you to have fun.' She looked down at where Isla continually pulled at the wrist strap. 'And... look at her, she needs it. She needs all that Christmas has to offer and more.'

Gripping her hand, Maggie gave her a knowing look. 'Keeping children safe is what I do, it's what I've always done.' A tear dropped down her face. 'I kept you safe, didn't I?'

Nodding, Lexi threw Becca the car keys. 'Here, take my car. It's insured for any driver and Isla, her car seat's already in there. Just be aware, she won't unclip herself from the car seat. You have to do it for her.' Kissing the tip of Isla's nose, Lexi resisted the urge to grab her, to hold her tight, and felt the emotion bubble up inside, where it constantly threatened to erupt. 'Now, go. You don't want Harry to miss out on those cakes, do you? And this one, well... I'd say she really wants to meet Santa...' The words began to choke her and, quickly, she held a hand over her mouth, felt the bile rise in her throat.

Looking down at the keys, Becca turned them over in her hand, then looked up at Lexi and furrowed her brow. 'But how will that work? If I take your car. How will you come and meet us? You... you won't get to see Santa.' A look of realisation and horror crossed her face. 'I mean, I could take a photo with my phone, and send it to you... but it wouldn't be the same, would it?'

Grabbing hold of Agatha before she escaped through the front door, Lexi puffed up her cheeks, blew out in a feeble attempt to control her breathing, then turned back to Becca with a forced smile. 'I'm not coming. This...' She caught the eye of the detective. 'This could take a while and, well... maybe I could have a dig around in the fridge or the freezer. Make something good for tea. Something hot and wholesome for when you get home?' She looked at Maggie for help. 'Do we have any minced beef? I could make a cottage pie. Everyone loves cottage pie, don't they?'

With a plan in mind, Lexi kept the fixed smile for as long as she could hold it, stood on tiptoes and felt her whole body ache with longing. Smiling at the way Isla continually looked up at Maggie, with a look of love and trust that was obviously shared between them, Lexi imagined an invisible thread of love stretch between them like a long extended zip wire. It was a thread she'd felt since the moment Isla had been born, yet the second they disappeared through the gate of the pub car park, she felt that imaginary thread physically sever, leaving her once again feeling anxious, lost and alone.

30

Fiona Flowers pulled her car up to the prison gate, showed her pass to the guard, nodded and drove forward. 'I'm sorry, Alexandra. But seeing him is the only way and I swear to God, we've tried everything else. But he won't talk. Not to anyone, apart from you. And if I'm honest, his health isn't as good as it used to be, so we need to do this now.' She paused, squeezed the steering wheel as tightly as she could. 'We're worried about him, worried about his mental health. He's made several attempts on his own life, he could quite easily take his secrets with him and if he does, his last victim, Melissa Jameson, might never be found.'

Lexi swallowed hard, felt her heart pound in her chest. The thought that her father might die too had never previously crossed her mind. She'd never before wondered about his health, or his well-being. Instead, she'd only ever focused on what he'd done, how his actions had affected her, her life and the lives of those he'd killed. It was twenty years since she'd seen him, and deep down she was prepared for him to look older, frailer, but had never contemplated the idea that his life could ever end. 'Is he that frail... do you think he could really die?' Holding her hands to each side of her face, she noted the way Fiona pursed her lips, kept her eyes averted. Her silence spoke volumes and Lexi held her fingers to her ears in an attempt to stop the banging that attacked the inside of her mind and vibrated like a bass drum on parade. In her opinion, it was a sure sign that the day was going to get so much worse before it got better.

Looking to her left, she took note of the bold white letters imprinted on the jet-black background.

HM Prison Frankland

She paused, looked up at the prison walls. 'I can hardly believe I'm here, right outside Monster Mansion. That is what they call it, isn't it?' Eyeing the gates, she tried to imagine what it was like to live within them. What her father's life had been like since he'd been driven through those gates, knowing the chances he'd ever get out were slim, and his annual escapade his only chance of seeing the world outside.

Lexi felt the acid burn her throat and took slow breaths to try and dispel the nausea she felt. Nothing had prepared her for actually visiting her father, for looking into his eyes. The same eyes she'd looked into as a child, with such love and hope for the future. She just hoped he'd give her the information she needed, anything that could lead them to the person who'd killed her mother, his wife, and surely he wouldn't want that person to kill her too. Would he?

'I don't know what to say to him, I... I haven't seen him since I was a child – since he was arrested. I wasn't allowed to see him after that and... well, I don't think I can do it.' She trembled with fear, squeezed the car seat until her knuckles turned white, and stared into the perfectly tidy footwell before briefly closing her eyes, taking comfort from the darkness, all the time trying to imagine his face, the way he'd look, the words he might say.

'Look, we'll be in a private room with a barrier between us and him. A glass screen.' Fiona turned, smiled. 'And before you ask, it isn't like the movies; you don't have to pick up a telephone to speak to him. There's a grille in the glass screen – you'll be able to speak normally, so he'll be near, but he won't be able to physically touch you.'

'I'm scared,' she said, but didn't know why. This man, her father, he'd never hurt her before, he'd never even sent her to her room or slapped her for being naughty. All the torment, the anxiety, the shame of who she was had come after he'd been arrested, not before, so why did she fear him now?

Pulling on the handbrake, Fiona turned in her seat. 'Lexi, he's your father. He's wanted to see you for a very long time and from what I can gather, you're the last person he'd ever want to hurt.' She sat forward, held tightly to the steering wheel with two hands, and stared up at the prison. 'There's something he isn't telling us; there's a key that will unlock the past. It will answer so many of our questions.'

'I know, but I'm still scared.' She thought of the last time she'd seen him, the way he held her gaze, stared into her soul; the words 'be a good girl for your mummy' had been etched on her mind.

Shaking her head, Fiona gave Lexi a half-smile. 'Alexandra, you don't have to be scared. You're here to help catch the killer that came to your house; they made an obvious threat against you, and your daughter. They wrapped a red silk scarf around your kitten's neck and left her in a dustbin to die. What's more, it was the same brand of scarf that killed your mother. You have far more to be scared of out there' – she pointed to the car park – 'than any fear you might have of him.' She pressed her lips together in a tight, formidable line. 'I know that visiting your father is something you've never done before. But this visit might just unlock the truth. He might just know who was in your garden and why they were there, why they killed your mother, because it's far too much of a coincidence that she died in the same way he killed.' She paused, took a breath. 'As I said on the phone yesterday, a team of officers went to see him. They questioned him for hours, but he wouldn't speak.' Again, she stopped, considered her words. 'He just repeatedly said that he'd only speak to you.'

'He said that?'

'He did.'

Lexi felt as though she were going into battle and screwed her fingers up, until they formed fists. She tried to understand the way she'd actually feel when she looked into his eyes and what she'd see when she did. A cold-blooded murderer, or simply the daddy she'd previously known and loved.

'If he'd asked to see me before, if he'd asked to speak to me, then why wasn't I told?' She held her hands out palms up, shrugged. 'I... I could have done that. I could have saved all of this from happening.' Her mind went to her mother, to the letters she'd written, the questions that would never be answered. 'I know my mother didn't deserve my love, not after what she did. But I wouldn't have wanted her dead and I could have stopped her from being killed.' Suspiciously, Lexi eyed the detective. 'I feared for my life. I really thought I'd be next, that my daughter would become a target.' She thrust her hands up and into the air. 'And we still don't know if that will happen. What his reasons are, or his motives. Does anyone have any idea why? Or was it simply because of who she was, who she'd been married to?'

'We don't know yet,' Fiona chipped in. 'And he's always wanted to see you. But that wasn't for us to instigate. Only you could decide if you wanted to come here, to visit him. And we didn't ask you before because that's not how things are normally done.' She pursed her lips, unclipped the glovebox, dug inside, pulled out a black leather wallet. 'I took a chance by asking you, but fully understand that if at any time you want to leave the room, do. Just stand up, let me know you want the visit to end. We knock on the door, and they escort us out.' She nodded in affirmation. 'Now then, did you remember your passport or driving licence?' She waved the leather pouch in the air. 'No one gets in without an ID, not even me.'

31

Standing in line and as close to Fiona as she could get, Lexi held a hand over her mouth as large groups of people swarmed past, all eager to get to the front of the queue. With them came the distinct odour of cigarette smoke and cheap perfume. Most were dressed up, with their hair perfectly styled, fingernails long and painted and stilettos so high they could have easily passed for stilts. Each one carried a mobile phone, busily swiped at screens and continually tapped out messages while moving forward. Occasionally, they'd look up, glared in her direction, allowed their stare to bore its way through her. It was as though they were judging her, just like she was judging them. They were keeping tabs on her every move, which made her more nervous and, anxiously, she too pulled out her mobile and, just for something to do, she mimicked them, began to flick from screen to screen.

'You a newbie, then?' the woman asked as she sidled past, chomping at her gum but giving a genuine look of concern. 'Just stay in the queue, do what they ask. Doesn't normally take too long.' She paused, looked Lexi up and down. 'Your fella just been banged up, then?'

Swallowing, Lexi looked everywhere but at the woman. 'No... I'm... I'm here to see my dad.'

'Oh bless, been a naughty boy, has he?' Pulling a lipstick from her bag, the woman used her phone as a mirror, applied the bright red colour. 'And this is your first visit, is it?'

Nodding, Lexi nervously looked over her shoulder, hoped Fiona would step in but she too had her phone to her ear, a last-minute call before going inside. 'Yes, sir. No problem, well, we're here now and hopefully I'll have something to give you within the hour.' She paused, rolled her eyes at the never-ending queue. 'Anything else I should know before I go in?' she asked as the queue surged forward. A guard pointed to the mobile, shook his head. 'Yes, sir, we're going in now. I have to go.'

Keeping to the left, Lexi could feel her heart speed up. The rhythm was now palpable, her movements slow, measured, and she knew that by the way she was acting, it was more than obvious to everyone else in the room that she hadn't been to the prison before, that she didn't know the rules. Sheepishly, she nodded persistently when asked a question, agreed to everything the guards asked for, stood patiently in line. Which was more than could be said for the other visitors, who crowded around, threw comments back and forth and jeered at the guards.

'Is it always like this?' she whispered to Fiona, who rolled her jaw in annoyance as she kept her eyes on all the people around them.

'Yeah, some days it isn't so bad, but today they look as though they're out for trouble. Just stay behind me; we'll be through it all soon.' She inched forward to where a set of lockers stood, opened one of the doors. 'Put your bag and your phone etcetera in here. You can't take anything in with you.'

Lexi thought of the letters she'd written to her mother, the ones still tucked into the depths of her bag, and for a few seconds she wondered why she'd never written to her father, why it had never occurred to her to write to him, to ask him why. And as the locker door slammed to a close and the key was turned, she suddenly felt the need to get the letters back, to show him what she'd written, how hurt she'd been. But instead, she twisted her fingers tightly together, until they formed fists that were ready to fight, fists she could defend herself with. Even though right now, she wasn't sure whom she wanted to defend herself against: the other visitors, the other inmates, or her dad?

Shocked by her thoughts, she wondered why she feared her father. He'd always been good to her, gentle and kind, and deep down, she knew he wouldn't hurt her now. Which was why it was so difficult to believe that he'd actually killed any of those women, that by his own hand and without a care in the world, he'd murdered them all in cold blood and then, to degrade them even further, he'd left them in the open, whatever the weather and, of all things, he'd placed a chess piece in the folds of the scarf, his way of categorising the kill in order of importance.

As the crowd began to disperse, Lexi carefully watched a guard. He stood with a clipboard, an earpiece and periodically he'd shout a name from the list, point to a door.

'Alexandra Graves.' As her name was bellowed across the room, other visitors went silent. All turned to look at her and, with an internal trembling that wouldn't stop, she held on to Fiona's arm, felt herself being led across the room until she stood before a large electric door. 'As the door opens, you move forward. OK?' the guard growled and once again Lexi felt herself nod as a loud bleep blasted out and the security door opened.

Feeling her body stiffen, she stepped forward, heard the door immediately close behind them. Biting down on her lower lip, she could taste blood. It seeped into her mouth and quickly she dug into her pocket for a tissue that wasn't there. With no choice but to patiently wait, Lexi wiped her mouth on the cuff of her jumper, saw the deep red stain and, while moving forward, deeper and deeper into the prison, she hurriedly curled the cuff over, hoped she'd hidden the mark, and glanced up to find herself standing in a room, probably four or five foot square, with a sealed vinyl floor, white uninviting walls and two well-worn royal-blue polypropylene chairs.

Feeling slightly claustrophobic, Lexi stared at the door on the other side of the screen and, with one hand, she tentatively pressed her fingers against the glass division, pushed once, twice, checked how sturdy it felt to her touch, then carefully she checked the grille, tried to work out how easily it could be spoken through, without being breached. Then, with her gaze fixed on the chair at the other side of the screen, it suddenly occurred to her that that chair was where her father would sit. That as soon as the door opened on the other side, he'd be in that room, looking back at her.

'I can't do it.' She jumped backwards. 'I don't want to. I can't.' She glared at Fiona, then lifted a hand to knock on the door as she grabbed at breath, felt her breathing accelerate faster than she'd ever known before. Closing her eyes, she thought about Isla. Thought about the threat to both their lives, knew she couldn't let her daughter down.

'Alexandra...' She heard the unmistakable albeit shaky tone of her father's voice. 'Is... is it really you? Did you really come?' Turning as slowly as she possibly could, she held her breath, could feel the involuntary shaking inside her body and, through squinted eyes, she looked him up and down, barely recognised the gaunt, brittle-looking man he'd become. 'Please...' He pointed to the chair with a long, spindly finger. 'Why don't you take a seat, we...' He looked as though he were struggling to breathe and Lexi noticed how tightly his fingers held on to the chair, how unsteady he looked on his feet, and she wasn't sure he'd be able to stand at all, if he were to suddenly let go. 'Please…' He gave her a crooked, uncertain smile. 'We have some catching up to do.'

By the time Fiona drove her back to the island it was just before six at night. There were only around thirty minutes left before the causeway closed; the contractors had already left, their machinery moved and the repairs to the causeway halted until the tide went back out and once again work could be safely completed. The safety tower's steps had been broken, removed and Lexi tried to imagine what would happen if someone ignored the tide, got stuck halfway across.

With the causeway snaking ahead, Lexi sat silently watching the road, hoped that Isla would be home and, with disbelief, she thought of all her father had said. How excited Fiona had been, and she knew by Fiona's actions that the information he'd given had been exactly what the force had needed, albeit not what she'd expected to hear, and now she was filled with a new and different kind of confusion, information she had to get her head around, understand and, while trying to comprehend it, she shook her head as she saw Maggie's cottage loom up in the distance.

Anxiously, she sat forward in her seat, searched the road for her car, realised it was missing, and with the briefest of goodbyes, she bounced out of the car and dashed into the cottage in search of Isla.

Twenty minutes later, Lexi ran out of Maggie's cottage with her phone in hand. The call with Becca hadn't been the news she'd wanted to hear and anxiously she headed through the darkness of the street and straight into the Manor House Hotel. It was almost empty with just a soft buzz of conversation between the one or two that remained, a sure sign that the tide was on its way in, and that once again the island was cut off from the mainland.

Standing on her tiptoes, she eagerly tried to spot Harry, but couldn't and, quickly, she ran to the bar and leaned over to look at the young barmaid who crouched down behind it. A crate of mixers stood by her leg, which she carefully lifted out bottle by bottle, wiped with a cloth and placed on the shelf behind the pumps.

'Sorry to bother you, it's Chloe, isn't it?' Lexi whispered impatiently. 'Do you know where Harry is? I... I really need to speak to him. It's kind of urgent and...' She once again glanced over her shoulder. Exhaled noisily. '...he just has to be here.'

Noticing the young girl blush at the mention of Harry's name, Lexi turned as she pointed to the hotel reception. 'He's in there. He's checking out some guests; they stayed here last night, but have a cottage on the island for the rest of the week. Couldn't get in until the deep clean had happened,' she rambled, then seemed to spot the concern on Lexi's face. 'Is all OK? You've gone terribly white.'

'I'm fine,' she lied. 'It's Maggie. She isn't well.' Rushing towards reception, Lexi stopped abruptly in the doorway and patiently hovered while Harry chatted to the guests, talked them through their bill, took their payment and finally gave them a cheeky smile as they dragged their bags behind them and headed for the door.

Sensing Lexi's unease, Harry rushed forward, immediately took her by the hands. 'What's wrong?' His eyes searched hers. 'You said something about Maggie?'

Taking in a single deep breath, Lexi began to explain. 'She isn't well. All the signs were there; she wasn't well yesterday. Becca said she had had a real funny turn and that when they'd got to the market, her heart had started racing for no apparent reason, she went all dizzy, almost collapsed, and Becca took her straight to the hospital where they've kept her in, put her on bed rest.' She took a breath. 'And, well, to cut a long story short, by the time Becca left the tide had started coming in, the causeway was already partially underwater, and she didn't dare risk the crossing.' Her hand went to her mouth as a sob left her throat. 'Harry, it's been a horrible day and now, now it's getting dark, and now Isla is at the other side of the causeway; they can't get back.'

Looking up at the clock, Harry furrowed his brow. 'OK, let's take a look.' He blew out a breath, moved to a chart that was hanging beside reception, ran a finger slowly down it. 'The causeway. It reopens at... crap, really?' He scratched his head. 'Midnight, which really isn't what you want to hear, is it?' He shook his head; life on the island had taught them both that if the crossing was missed, the only thing you could do was sit it out, wait for the tide to retreat.

'I don't know what to do. She can't sit in a car for five hours. It's freezing out there.' Lexi held on to the balustrade, stared at her feet, thought of all the times she'd been to nightclubs, with no alternative but to drive herself home. Because of where she'd lived, she'd always taken her car, stayed sober and, much to Maggie's annoyance, she'd always left it to the last minute before setting off for home, then the slightest of traffic jams and she'd miss the crossing, often having no choice but to pull her car into the car park at The Barn in Beal, where she'd spent hours staring at the island in the distance – unable to get home. After the second time she'd spent the night in her car, Maggie had insisted she packed a sleeping bag and pillow in the boot. A spare jumper, emergency chocolate and water to drink. And now, all these years later, she felt unbelievably sorry for the anguish she must have caused, the worry both Maggie and Stanley would have gone through, and could literally imagine them both sitting in the cottage, discussing ways of encouraging her to leave the nightclub just a little earlier in the future, in the hope she'd make the crossing.

Feeling her stomach turn with nerves, Lexi thought of the forced distance that now separated herself and Isla. With a fear that was now amplified after seeing her father, she could feel the pain tearing her in two. She wanted her daughter here, with her, where she could try and ensure her safety, because after what her father had said, she couldn't trust anyone. Not until the killer was caught. Closing her eyes, she concentrated on the beating of her heart, could feel it hammering at speed, going faster and faster until she could barely breathe. Overwhelmed, she sat on the staircase, swallowed hard, felt the colour drain from her face. Went over and over her father's words. Knew that the police would move quickly, that the body of his final victim would be unearthed and, when it was, the truth would come out. What Lexi didn't know was how the killer would take that truth, how they'd react. 'They're all alone,' she whispered, felt Harry squeeze himself to sit on the step, where, lovingly, he dropped an arm across her shoulders and pulled her towards him.

'Let's not panic. She's with Becca. They're both together.' He stood up, reached for his phone. 'If you want me to, I could give her a call. Make sure everything's OK.'

Staring, Lexi shook her head. 'I literally only just spoke to her. She seemed OK, completely in control. She told me not to worry, that Isla was absolutely fine. She even said that they were having fun, and that it was a bit like camping. But I can't get it out of my mind that there's a killer out there, they're all alone, it's cold and I didn't think to pack the car with the essentials. With all the things Maggie used to insist I took with me.' A sob left her throat. 'I'm a rubbish mum, Harry. The worst, and after today, I'm probably the worst daughter too.' She looked up, into Harry's eyes, wished things had worked out differently. More than anything she wished she could have loved him in the way he'd wanted her to... felt bereft that she could have hurt him so very badly, and that for all of these years, she knew that he'd been imagining that Isla could be his.

Shaking his head, Harry dropped a kiss on the end of her nose. 'You're not rubbish, far from it.' He stared into her eyes, then looked away. 'You couldn't have foreseen this happening, but... you've been away from the island all day. I came looking for you, wanted to chat to you but the cottage was empty. So, what happened for Isla to go and see Santa without you?'

'Oh, Harry. Everything happened.' She stopped. Closed her eyes. Tried to remember everything in order. 'We were all going to go to the Victorian market, to see Santa. Maggie, Becca, Isla and me. It was an outing that Maggie and Becca had arranged ages ago, but with my arrival on the island, Maggie was going to cancel, so I agreed to go too. But then, a detective turned up to see me. I was half expecting her. But hadn't realised she'd come so soon. So, we decided that Maggie and Becca should take Isla with them.' She paused for breath, gripped his hand as tightly as she could. 'Then, the detective, Fiona, she wanted me to go to Frankland, to see my dad.' She felt the heat travelling up her body until the burning sensation reached her neck, and her cheeks. 'It's the first time I've seen him, you know... since...' She paused, pulled a tissue from her bag, wiped the back of her neck, prayed that the front door would open, that the cold December air would infiltrate the room. 'They wanted me to ask him questions, to find out what he knew. Things he's never told anyone...'

'And he told you these things.'

Nodding, she could barely speak. 'He told us what happened, where the body is. They'll be looking for her, right now and he...'

Her voice broke, tears rolled down her face, sobs tore through her body.

'Shh... it's OK. You can tell me later; you don't have to say it all, not right now.' Protectively, his arm tightened around her and he pulled her close, rocked her against him.

'Harry, it still doesn't seem real. And... he looked frail and... he had a scar, right down one side of his face, looked like someone had taken a blade to him...' She shuddered, moved away slightly, used a finger to draw a jagged line down her own face. 'And it felt odd, asking him all those questions, but... but it was the only way.' She paused, saw Harry bristle, his face a mixture of emotions. He ran a hand angrily through his hair, unconsciously ruffling it to look like he'd just fallen out of bed. It was a look Lexi liked, brought back memories of him being a teenager and his opposition to ever using a hairbrush.

'Are they expecting you to go back, to speak to him again?'

Shaking her head, she thought about the way her dad had shaken with nerves. The way his eyes had pleaded with hers for forgiveness. 'It was all too much. He said so many things, things I didn't expect, things I'd never prepared myself for.' She thought of the way he'd leaned close to the grille, so close she'd been able to smell the sour odour of his breath as it drifted towards her. Between his breath and the scar that lacerated his face, it was a stark reminder of the life he now lived, the limited access to dental or medical care he had. He was no longer the parent she remembered. His mischievous smile had gone, the sparkle in his eyes had dimmed to a dark, sullen grey and the scar that dominated his face was something the newspapers hadn't previously spoken of, even though it looked to be quite fresh, and roughly sutured, with no care to how it might eventually look, once fully healed. But it hadn't been anything about his looks that had bothered her the most; it had been the words he'd used and her inability to believe anything he said. She knew that once the woman's body was found, the truth would be found with her. What Lexi didn't know was how the killer would react and whether or not the truth would put both her and Isla in more danger, or less.

Realising she'd been deep in her own thoughts, she looked up, placed a hand lovingly against Harry's cheek, saw the need within his eyes, realised how easily they could fall into old ways; she caught her breath, ran a hand over her face to wipe away the tears but couldn't tear her gaze away from his and could feel herself falling towards those deep, dark eyes.

33

'I've lost an earring. A diamond one.' A shrill voice came through the front door, shattering the moment. It was a shock that brought Lexi's thoughts back to the present, to the reality of what was happening in the here and now and, like a thunderbolt, her mind immediately went back to Isla, to how cold she'd be, and tried to remember if she'd left anything in the car that could easily be used to keep her warm.

Looking up, and without trying to attract any attention, she studied the woman who'd just rushed back in. It was the same guest who'd checked out moments before, but now she was bright red, panting and looking as though any moment now, she'd collapse in a heap and hit the floor from heart failure.

Leaning her rotund body heavily against the door jamb, the woman raised her eyebrows, shot Harry a look that demanded his attention, then glared at Lexi, who still sat on the stairs, leaning against the balustrade.

'You wouldn't be a love, would you?' She directed the question to Lexi. 'Just pop yourself up the stairs, see if you could spot it – it's about this big.' She held her fingers together to indicate a small but significant size of diamond, then sighed. 'It was a gift from my husband for our wedding anniversary, and I'd just hate to lose it.' She rubbed at her back and groaned. 'I'd go up there myself, but we were in room ten, right at the top of the house and those stairs... oh, they're a killer at my age and you're so much younger than I am.'

Slowly, Lexi gave Harry a half-smile, reached for the banister. 'Sure, I'll go up. I have nothing else to do,' she answered ironically, while keeping her eye on where Harry stood.

The woman shuffled on the spot. 'Come on, come on...' She wafted her hands towards the stairs as though trying to physically push Lexi up them. 'Before someone cleans the room. The thought that it could go up the vacuum cleaner – well, if I'm honest, it's giving me so many palpitations,' she added, and expectantly placed a hand on her heart for effect. 'I might need to sit down.'

With a look of annoyance that only Lexi would have spotted, Harry moved towards reception, pulled a key from a hook, jangled it around in his hand, then pressed his lips tightly together. 'I'll go. The girls aren't due to clean it tonight; it isn't booked out. So, there's no worry, it won't get cleaned until the morning.' He gave Lexi a look of concern. 'Why don't you go and, you know, get some coffee or ask Chloe to organise you some food. After the day you've had, you could probably use something good to eat,' he whispered, placed a hand against her arm. 'Whether you like it or not, Lex, I doubt you're gonna get any sleep, not even if you wanted to. So, personally, I'd take the time to relax a little. Kill an hour or so with some good food, read a book.' He went to walk past her, held her gaze for just a few seconds too long. It was a moment Lexi had hoped for, a way of her remembering the past, the time they'd shared, along with all the reasons she'd left the island behind and hadn't looked back.

Shaking her head, she grabbed the key. 'It's fine, I'll go, I need to keep busy, I'm still trying to process everything that happened today, and you know what I'm like when I'm thinking... I'm much better having something to do.' She began taking the stairs two at a time, headed upwards, and ran a hand lovingly over the oak banister as she went. She thought of all the times she'd been in this hotel, the memories it held. All the hours, days and weeks she'd worked here during the school holidays. Then, as she reached the final flight, she began paying attention, looking at every speck of dust on the heavily patterned carpet, climbed the steps slowly, one at a time, and even checked the area along the top of the landing, where a single chair stood by the linen cupboard, its door open and a pile of fresh sheets stacked in readiness on the chair, right next to the door.

Using the key, Lexi pushed the bedroom door open, switched on the light, continued to scour the carpet, felt her eyes drift to the dual-aspect windows, which in daylight would have given the most beautiful view of both the castle and the priory. It was a view she couldn't resist and as she walked past to look, she ran a hand lovingly across the antique telescope that stood just inside the door. It was just standing there, dominating the room, waiting for visitors to use it, to look admiringly at the view.

'Beautiful,' she whispered to the room as she tiptoed in. She felt almost too scared to walk across the floor just in case she stood on the earring and, gingerly, she inched to the French antique bed, allowed her fingers to caress the mahogany corner post, where, dutifully, she dropped to her knees and ran a hand across the carpet. Lying on her belly, she looked under the bed, the wardrobe and then kneeled beside the bed to check the duvet and the area around the table and chairs, which stood in a space just in front of the dormer window that overlooked the castle. Sighing, she rolled her eyes to the bathroom, wondered if it could have been lost in there, but instead of rushing forward, she stayed kneeling by the bed, in front of the window, looked through it at the ruins of the priory, which were now shrouded in darkness.

'Lex...' Harry's voice came up the staircase. 'It's fine. She's found it.' He fell through the door, began to laugh. 'She popped into the cloakroom by the bar and found that it'd dropped out of her ear and into her underwear.' He poked a finger down his shirt, pointed to his chest. 'It's a bra like an apple catcher, I think she called it.'

'Oh, right. So, all's good.' Relieved that the hunt was over, Lexi pulled herself up to sit on the bed and stared wistfully out of the window, where rain now hammered against it, only to be seen a few moments later dribbling down the pane in rivulets that caught the light. The castle, like the night before, was lit up in the distance with dazzling bright gold fluorescent lighting. 'It's so beautiful up here, isn't it? Almost dreamy.' She pointed to the castle, felt a deep ache within her. She felt the need to hold her daughter, to pull her close and curl her body protectively around her. 'Did you hear from Becca? Did she text you?' A sob left her throat. 'Oh my God, Harry, I'm so frightened, so out of control. I need to know she's safe, that Isla's safe.'

Slipping onto the bed beside her, he pressed his lips together in a cheeky half-smile. 'She's absolutely fine; I just spoke to Becca. She's taking Isla to Lindisfarne Inn for the night and should be checking in' – he looked at his watch – 'any time now.'

Surprised, Lexi threw her arms around his neck and felt the relief flood through her veins. 'Oh, that's... that's nice.' Closing her eyes for a beat, she imagined Isla having something warm to eat before climbing into a safe, warm bed, rather than sleeping in her cold, untidy car, with side pockets full of stale crisps and bottles of water that had most probably been there for over a week. 'Oh, Harry, you have no idea how happy that makes me and I... I'll pay her back.' She took in a deep breath, caught Harry's eye, and stared into the deep, sparkling onyx of amusement within. 'What...'

'Lex. I booked the room for them.' He raised an eyebrow, nervously pushed a hand through his hair and held her gaze. 'So, there's no paying back necessary. God only knows you bailed me out a few times in the past.' His hand went to her face, gently touched her cheek. 'I want them safe too.'

Using a single finger to trace the shape of her lips, Harry inched forward. It was a touch that lasted for just a few seconds but a touch that shot a surge of electricity through Lexi's body that was so strong she jumped backwards and collided with the corner post of the bed, and with a hand carefully rubbing the small of her back, she considered his words.

'Harry, thank you but... why... why would you do that?'

He shook his head in disbelief. 'Jesus, Lex. If you can't see it, I can... she's my double and... I know you say she isn't, but I'm sure...' He paused, furrowed his brow. 'I'm sure she's mine.' His hands went back to her shoulders. 'I'd love for her to be mine, Lex. For her to be ours, and you've got to admit, the dates, that last time we were together. It all adds up.'

'You... you're wrong. She's Nate's. He loves her... and... and...' Lexi began grasping at straws. 'She was born a couple of weeks early... that's why the dates add up and... and for no other reason.' Grabbing at breath, she stared into his eyes, could imagine Isla's looking back at her, felt his hands on her shoulders, pulling her towards him. 'Harry. Please... I need to think, I need to explain...'

'Oh, an explanation. Yeah, I think that'd be a great idea,' Nate's voice bellowed from the doorway. 'The totty behind the bar said the two of you were up here. Apparently, you're searching for an earring.' He nodded. 'And there I was, hoping it was true. But instead, I find you both curled up on the bed together, discussing my daughter's parentage.' He punched at the door, grunted with pain.

Jumping up, Lexi felt her heart accelerate. She didn't know what to do, how to react, even though every part of her wanted to run into his arms, hold him close, but the anger that seeped from him was palpable, making her take a step back and flash Harry a look. 'Nate, it isn't how it looks... I swear... it... oh my God, I'm so pleased you're here.' Biting down on her lip, she searched his eyes with hers.

'Are you really?' He curled his lip. 'Well, personally, I don't know why I bothered...' He screwed his hands up into fists until his knuckles went white. 'So, come on. That explanation... now you've had a moment or two to think about it, do you want to tell me what's going on? 'Cause from where I'm standing, it sure as hell needs to be a good one.' He looked from Lexi to Harry. 'I'm waiting.'

34

'Nate, please come back... where the hell are you going?'

Running behind him, Lexi stumbled down the stairs, through the bar, which was thankfully empty, and outside to where tall willowy trees arched in the north-easterly wind. The rain that had been previously bouncing against the window had now soaked the ground of the car park, where shadows from the priory loomed above and surrounded her like a cold and unwelcome blanket.

'You wanna know where I'm going, do you?' he yelled. 'Well, I think I'm gonna go sit in my car until that goddamned causeway opens, then I'll drive back to our house. You know the one, the one we used to call home and, when I get there, I'll do my best to salvage what's left of my bloody life.' He threw a look of disdain over his shoulder. 'I walked off the job, Lexi. I left the other guys to carry me, to do my work. I risked not being paid. Right before Christmas and why... why?' he yelled. 'Because I thought that by coming here, by coming to this godforsaken island, by running after you, just like you expected, I'd have a chance of saving our relationship and, crazily...' He threw his head back and laughed ironically. 'Crazily, I thought I'd be able to talk to you. Convince you and Isla to come home with me, so we could spend Christmas – as a family – together.'

'Nate. You can talk to me, and I didn't expect you to run after me. Not at all. Honestly. It was just that everything happened so quickly, I got scared and I had to make a quick decision. I didn't have time to explain and I had to make Isla a priority. I had to keep her safe.' She held her hands together as though in prayer. 'And that... up there. I know what you heard, but it's not what it seems. Harry and I were a long time before I met you.'

He turned, ran his hands angrily through his hair. 'Really?'

'Really. You know how far back me and Harry go. We grew up together and yes... we got close a few times but Nate... you have to believe me...'

'Do you know what, Lexi? Stop right there before you dig a hole so deep you can't get out. 'Cause right now, I have no idea what to believe.' He cut her off, stood his ground, stared directly at her. 'I know what I saw, Lexi, and I'm not deaf either. I heard what he said. So, I'll ask you this once. Is Isla my daughter?'

Lexi rushed towards him, grabbed his shoulders. 'Nate, look at me.' She manoeuvred her body until she held his gaze, saw the heartbreak within them. 'She's yours. You saw her born, Nate. And... I... I promise you, you're her daddy.' She looked away, then back at him. 'She loves you so much, Nate.' Closing her eyes, she whispered a silent prayer, hoped she wasn't making promises that couldn't be true. Knew there was a chance, albeit a small one, that Isla could be Harry's, that the life they'd been living had been a lie and, wholeheartedly, she wished she could remember the exact timeline, between her leaving the island, leaving Harry behind and meeting Nate. How long had it been? Days? Weeks?

'Where is she?' Nate pushed his hands into the pockets of his jeans, puffed out his chest. 'I want to see her – right now.'

35

Pouring two large glasses of whisky, Lexi searched through each of the crowded cupboards in turn, looking for a mixer. Considered going across to the hotel and buying some – but then thought better of it. Instead, she took a deep breath, went back to the living room, passed the glass of neat spirit to Nate, who sat on the settee surrounded by cushions, with Agatha curled up on his lap.

'Here, I found this in the cupboard. It might help.' She sniffed at the glass, pulled a face, took a sip. 'It's all I could find and I'm not sure about you, but I really need a drink.' She gave him an apprehensive half-smile, sat on the settee beside him, amidst the cushions that tonight felt warm and welcoming. They'd been something to hide behind and comfort her while reliving her story. She'd told him exactly who she was, who her father was, all the fears she'd felt after her mother had been killed and how she'd found Agatha in the dustbin tied up with the red silk scarf and, while telling him her life story, she'd simply prayed she didn't push him any further away than he currently was.

'So, the woman who was killed. She… she was your mother, your real mother?' Nate ran a hand across Agatha's back, then lifted the glass to stare into the amber fluid. He swirled it aggressively around the glass, lifted it to his lips and knocked the whole amount back, in one. 'Jesus, Lexi. Why the hell didn't you tell me?'

'Because... oh, I don't know, because I never had. When we met, I was embarrassed, cautious of everyone. I barely told anyone about my past and the closer we became, the harder it got and then, well... Isla was born, and it got more and more difficult.' She rested a hand against his knee. 'I swear to God, I didn't want to lie to you, Nate. I just didn't know how to tell you the truth. I was so unbelievably ashamed of who I was, and of what my father had done, it was simply easier to pretend I was someone else.'

Picking Agatha up from his knee, he gave her a kiss, placed her on the floor. 'Do you know what hurts the most? You... the one person who says she loves me, didn't trust me enough to talk to me, to tell me about her past.' He shook his head decisively and turned to the window. 'I think I should go.'

'Nate. Please... you can't go, and you certainly can't drive, not after necking a double whisky like that.' She took hold of his hand, pulled him back to the settee. 'Besides, the causeway. It's still closed and... well, I'm not the only one with secrets, am I?' She swallowed hard, thought about her words. 'You have secrets too.'

'What are you talking about?'

She shook her head in disbelief, pressed her lips tightly together. 'Nate. I know,' she yelled. 'I know there's something going on; why else would you step away from me rather than make love to me? You did it more than once and... you've been constantly on your phone, something you never do. All those messages. The texting. For God's sake, you even changed your passcode. God only knows who showed you how to do that, 'cause you, Mr I Hate Technology, wouldn't have a clue.' Tutting, she stood up, grabbed both glasses, poured more whisky. 'So, the day after my mum was killed, I found Agatha; she was wrapped in the scarf. It was obvious that whoever had killed Mum had been right outside our front door and it all got too much, I was scared and, to be honest, Nate, after the way you'd been acting, I didn't think I had much to stay for.' She caught her breath, sipped at the drink. 'My priority was keeping our daughter safe. I couldn't think about us any more; I didn't have time. I had to put Isla first.'

Watching him struggle to find the words, she saw the colour rise to his cheeks and, once again, he picked up the glass, knocked back the drink. 'Fine, OK. You're right.' He slammed the glass down on the table, held his hands up, palms out in submission. 'Do you want to know what all the secrets were? Do you?' He looked at her and raised his eyebrows in question. 'I was planning a surprise. A surprise for you. All our friends, all your work colleagues, all the guys from the site. They were all coming over Christmas Eve.' He nodded slowly. 'Stupidly, I'd organised it all, the party, the cake, the ring, how both I and Isla were going to go down on one knee.' He paused, took hold of her hands. 'I'd planned what I'd say to you, was going to get Isla to say something too. I was trying to do it as a family.' The colour continued to deepen on his cheeks. 'Which was why I was trying to encourage you to put the tree up, to decorate the house, for it all to look perfect. So it looked lovely for the party.' He furrowed his brow, stared wistfully into the dying embers. 'The only reason I changed my passcode was so you couldn't see all the organising I'd done, or the responses people were sending to the invites. There were so many, and they wouldn't only message once. They'd continually ask what was happening, whether or not you'd guessed, what I'd do if you said no. I think a few of them were holding a sweepstake as to whether you'd accept or not.'

Lexi rolled her jaw, felt her heart leap into her chest and for a moment she thought about his words, whether she would have accepted or not. Marrying Nate was the one thing she'd always wanted, but without him knowing the truth, without him knowing who she really was, it had been one wish too many. And now she knew how much she'd have hurt him, all because she'd kept so many secrets, told so many lies. Yet now, now he knew the truth, he knew who she was and now there would be no reason why she couldn't say yes – was there? She rolled all the questions around her mind, tried to answer each one in turn and knew that if they were going to move forward, she had to ask them all, and leave nothing unanswered. Considering her words, she sat forward on the settee, took hold of his hands. 'Nate, that night... the day my mother had been killed. I needed you. I needed to feel loved by you, for you to hold me. But you just pushed me away... I need to know why. I need to know why you did that.'

'I didn't know what you were going through.' His hand left hers, reached out to carefully touch her cheek. Looking into her eyes, he lovingly held her gaze. 'I swear, I didn't know...'

Suddenly, his mouth took possession of hers. Tentatively at first, but then with a passion so strong it took Lexi by surprise. Breathing in, she caught the strong scent of his aftershave. An earthy, musky smell. It was the new scent she remembered from her last night at home and she wondered if that had been part of his surprise, whether he'd gone as far as to buy new clothes, a ring. Feeling his lips momentarily leave hers, she gasped as they began to sear a path down her neck. His hands travelled quickly across her skin, touching every part of her with ease and with a skill that only an experienced lover could do. It was a feeling she'd missed, a feeling she'd longed for and, without inhibitions, she heard herself moan out loud with desire as once again his lips recaptured hers. This time, he was more demanding; his tongue began to tease hers and shivers raced down her spine as his fingers tentatively traced the curvature of her back, her bottom and her breasts. Closing her eyes, she felt a sudden overwhelming sensation. It was a mixture of love and lust that left her legs weak, her mind light-headed and her heart frantically beating with desire as, slowly, his lips left hers, leaving him to gaze tenderly into her eyes.

'I never meant to make you feel that way, Lexi. Honestly, I didn't. I... I was so afraid, I was having nightmares, convinced myself I'd blurt it out, you know... during the moment.' His words were little more than a breathless whisper, a kind of apology that hadn't needed saying. 'I'd gone over the words I wanted to use. I'd practised exactly what I'd say, so many times. I could imagine saying them out loud in my sleep.'

Standing up, she pulled at his hand, led him towards the stairs as she pivoted on the bottom step and kissed him seductively. Taking a man to her childhood bedroom had never been a part of her plan and, for a beat, she wished she'd tidied it more. Put her things away rather than leaving all the bags all over the floor. Wondered how he'd feel, what he'd think when he saw the things she'd taken with her, from the home they'd shared. But knew that taking him to her room was exactly what they both needed and, for just a few hours, until the causeway opened, she wanted to feel safe, to take pleasure in his arms and, more than anything, she wanted to take away his pain and give that pleasure back.

'I think I should mention, it's a single bed...' She felt a small laugh rise to her throat. 'But somehow, I think we'll manage.'

36

It was just before seven in the morning when Lexi jumped into Maggie's car, and after a passionate farewell, she followed Nate through the darkness to cross the causeway. He had no choice but to go back to work, to finish his contract, and she was insistent that she wanted to reach the inn with enough time to see Isla for herself, to collect her and to get back across the causeway before the tide came back in. It was a plan she and Nate had come up with, knowing that with Maggie still being in hospital, Becca might need to go back and, hopefully, would get to bring Maggie home.

Pulling into the car park beside Nate, she felt herself blush as he jumped out of his car and pulled her into a hold. 'I'll be back at the weekend, OK? First thing Saturday.' He repeatedly pressed his lips against hers, smiled, then eagerly looked over her shoulder and towards the hotel. 'Did you say that this Becca took your car?'

'Yes, she...' Lexi scanned the car park. 'I thought it'd be easier, because of Isla's seat.'

'Right...' Looking concerned, Nate began to stride up and down the cars, checked each one, shook his head. 'But it isn't here.'

'What do you mean it isn't here?' Lexi began to panic, paced up and down the car park behind him. 'She... she has to be here. Harry booked the room. He told me they were staying here last night. I... I trusted they would be.' She looked at her watch. 'And it's only just seven o'clock, there's no way Isla would be up yet, not unless...' She paused. Every scenario flooded her mind. She felt a surge of acid rise and fall in her throat as she considered what was happening. Isla wasn't where she'd thought, she was with a woman she barely knew, and immediately she grabbed at her phone, rang Becca's number, waited for the response that didn't come and screamed out loud as she heard the voicemail kick in. 'Why... why isn't she answering?' Feeling the panic drive through her, she tried to think logically. Tried to come up with any excuse rather than the one that dominated her thoughts. That the killer could have found them, killed them both, left their bodies out there in the weather, waiting to be found. It was a thought she couldn't bear. She felt the strength leave her legs and with a determined effort she went back to Maggie's car, leaned against it, tried to come up with another answer, another reason why Isla wasn't here. There had to be a simple explanation. Another reason why they'd left the room early; maybe they'd had a call from the hospital, gone back to see Maggie. Feeling a sense of relief, she nodded. Thought lovingly of Maggie, one of the only other women she trusted with her daughter. 'That's what it will be. They'll have gone back to the hospital. I bet Maggie was demanding to come home. That's why Becca isn't answering the phone.'

Raking his hand through his hair, Nate anxiously pulled his phone from his pocket, checked the time and bit down on his lip. 'Are you sure? 'Cause if not, I'll give the lads a quick call. Tell them I can't get back to the site.' He sighed, stared at the phone. 'As you say, Isla comes first.'

Shaking her head, she took his hands in hers. 'I'll find her.'

He moved uneasily around the car park, constantly looking,

checking, pursing his lips thoughtfully. 'She can't be far away, can she?'

Lexi took in a deep breath, gave him her most confident smile. 'Seriously, go to work. Finish the contract, come back Saturday and we'll spend the weekend, all of us together.' She reached up, kissed him firmly on the lips. Tried to hide the fear, the worry, the deep-seated sickness she felt as she said the words. 'Nate, there has to be a perfectly good explanation. No one disappears with a noisy two-year-old, do they?' She did her best to sound positive, fell into his arms. Held him close. 'So, why don't you get off. And as soon as I see her and we're back on the island, I'll phone you and get her to FaceTime you. How about that?' She paused, gave him a half-smile. 'You do know how to FaceTime, don't you?'

Letting him go was something Lexi soon regretted as she cast her eye around the bar of the Lindisfarne Inn, stared at the numerous residents who all sat, eagerly tucking into their breakfast, and as she'd feared, none of them were Becca or Isla.

'As I said, Miss, er... Jakes. She didn't check in.' The receptionist sat back in her chair, and annoyingly tapped a pen against her teeth. 'I've got her down as a no-show.'

Quizzically, Lexi took a step back, felt her legs weaken as once again she searched the dining tables in the hope that Becca would appear or that Isla would jump up energetically, run into her arms and plant her distinctive fairy kisses all over her face.

'Is there anything else I can help you with?' The woman swivelled in her chair, turned to her computer screen, began drumming her fingers on the desk, as though tapping them would solve the problem sooner. Scrolling through a spreadsheet, she lifted her eyebrows, then sat back in her chair, waiting.

'Actually. Yes... yes, there is something you can check.' Lexi held a finger in the air, laughed as a thought came to mind. 'The room. It was booked under a different name. My friend, Harry Miller. He

booked the room, and he paid for it.' She stepped forward enthusiastically, leaned over reception so far her feet lost contact with the
floor in the hope that she'd be able to read the screen for herself. 'Is
it there? Can you see it?'

'Yes, I see it. I have the booking, as you say it was booked by a
Mr Miller. It was room number eleven; he asked for a ground-floor
room because of the child.' She paused, looked up. 'And as I've said
before, the room is empty. The keys were never collected. Your
friends, they didn't turn up.'

Feeling her stomach turn, Lexi took a step back, felt the floor
move beneath her feet. Falling out of the reception, she stumbled
awkwardly. Pushed the door open, and almost slipped down the
rain-soaked step. Holding tightly to the wooden banister, she
glanced across to the other side of the car park, scanned the rooms.
'Room eleven. She said room eleven... she has to be there.' Running
across the tarmac, she banged on the door. 'Isla, Isla, it's Mummy.
Isla...' She held her breath, listened for any sound that might indicate that her daughter was inside, waited for a split second, then
banged again. 'Isla, where are you? Becca, open the damned door.'
Spinning around, she once again began to search the car park,
looked at each car in turn, hoped her car, the car that Becca had
taken, would miraculously appear and, without warning, her mind
spun violently around her; she felt her breakfast lurch in her
stomach and with no other option, she ran to the bushes and
expelled the food.

Leaning against Maggie's four-by-four, Lexi rummaged around
in her bag. It was full of all the usual things a mother would carry,
including a packet of baby wipes, which she tugged from the pack
and wiped her mouth with. Then, with shaking hands, she pulled
open the car door, sat down and searched in her bag for her mobile.

'You heard what I said, Harry. Your goddamned girlfriend, she
isn't here.' With the phone held to her ear and her mind racing,

Lexi paced up and down the car park, kept checking cars, checking number plates, felt sure she'd somehow missed the car. 'And if she isn't here, I want to know where the hell she is. I've tried phoning her, repeatedly. Damn call keeps going to her voicemail.' Again, she spun on the spot. Closed her eyes to see images of Isla's face, her cheeky smile, the red silk scarf. 'Oh my God, Harry, what if...' She couldn't say the words, couldn't even consider the thought. Tried to understand why she'd phoned Harry rather than Nate. 'And don't tell me to calm down; my daughter is missing. She's with Becca. She's supposed to be at the hotel, and she isn't and right now, I... I want to know where the hell she is.' She growled the words, kicked out at the kerb as she turned in the seat of Maggie's car and started the engine.

Turning left out of the car park, and towards the A1, she missed a junction she'd crossed a million times before and cursed as a wagon shot across her path, and the near miss made her hit the brakes, take a breath and study the road ahead.

'No, Harry, I'm sure she didn't drive past me. It was dark, but there was barely anyone on the causeway and I think I'd have known my own damned car, wouldn't I?' She paused, kept her eyes on the road. Felt the pressure build up inside her; it was like a pressure cooker about to explode, a volcanic reaction that wouldn't go away, not until she had her daughter back in her arms. 'The only thing I can think of is that she could have gone back to the hospital. But that could mean Maggie took a turn for the worse?' Again, the bile rose and fell. 'What if...' A sudden thought crossed her mind, and she knew that the only reason doctors would have called her back was if Maggie was in danger, if she were about to lose her life. 'Oh, Harry...' A deathly image flashed before her eyes.

'Lexi, please. Don't even think it. Now, think carefully. We need to phone the hospital. Which hospital did they take her to?'

In panic, Lexi searched her memory. 'I don't know. I didn't ask...

I was so worried about Isla and her being stuck at the wrong side of the tide. I didn't ask where they'd gone.' She paused, screwed her eyes up tightly together. Revving the car, Lexi lifted a hand, tapped her palm repeatedly against her forehead. 'I'm so stupid.'

'Don't torture yourself, Lex. You're not stupid...' Harry whispered thoughtfully. 'You're a good person, a good mum.'

Good or not, she felt like a failure. Maggie had been the one person who'd been there for most of her life. She'd been a parent, a mentor, a friend. She'd been the one to hold her, care for her when there was no one else to do it and, what was more, she'd even taken her in as an adult, along with her daughter, her kitten and her newly acquired fiancé. And now, now she was sick, and Lexi hadn't even asked which hospital they'd gone to.

'Berwick... or... or Cramlington maybe, I'd say either would have been a possibility?' Harry questioned. 'Try and remember, did Becca mention either?'

Trying to think, Lexi stared up at the sky, at the clouds that had begun to form in shades of grey and roll towards the island, with the promise of a storm coming with them. 'I don't know.' She considered her options, looked left, then right, tried to think back to the conversation they'd had. 'Come on, Harry, you need to help me out here, I'm at the junction of the A1 and I don't know which way to go.' Waiting for the answer that didn't immediately come, Lexi could taste the silence. It was deafening, lasted for what felt like hours and in the end Lexi screamed into the phone. 'Harry, for God's sake, say something, anything...'

'I'll try and phone her. See if she answers,' he said sulkily. 'She normally does. Seems a bit odd that she didn't, so as you say she's probably inside the hospital. Maybe she had to turn her phone off.' Again, he went quiet. 'Why don't I come across to the mainland. Before the causeway closes. You could go to one hospital. I could go to the other.'

'Harry... yes, anything... I just need you to do something.'

Again, the phone went silent. The only thing she could hear was his breathing, the slow, rhythmic sound that filled the phone, played with her senses. 'I wanted to do something last night, Lex. I wanted to kiss you, to love you. To show you how I've always felt about you.' There was the sound of a door slamming. An engine revved. 'Lex, I know you ran from the island a few years ago because you didn't think I'd commit. But it's different now, I'm older, wiser, I know how I feel about you. Yet, last night, I had to stand there and watch you run after him, all the time knowing you'd go back to Maggie's, to spend the night with him, to make love to him...' He paused. 'Do you know how that made me feel, Lex? Do you have any idea?'

'Harry, please. It's really not the time for big announcements, is it?'

His voice went distant; the car's Bluetooth took over as he put his call to hands-free. 'It's hardly an announcement; you must know how I feel about you and if you don't, ask yourself this. Why did you phone me, Lex, and not Nate?'

Hearing the blast of a horn behind her, Lexi jumped forward. Pulled Maggie's car onto the A1, headed towards Berwick. Tried to comprehend Harry's words, the way she'd run out the night before, left him behind without a second thought. 'Harry, you know I'd have never purposely hurt you.' She took in a breath, tried to calm the erratic booming that erupted from her chest. 'But you have to let this go, Harry. Nate, he's good to me, and last night...' She paused, didn't know whether or not to continue, but knew she'd have to tell him at some point. 'He asked me to marry him, Harry, and I said yes.' Again, she paused, fixed her jaw. 'But do you know what? None of that matters. Not you, not me, not Nate. Right now, I need to find my daughter. Because, right now, she's the only thing I care about.' She took a breath, knew she was being cruel, but couldn't think of anything but Isla. 'And I phoned you first because I thought you cared. I thought you'd help me because I need to know she's safe. And if you cared about either of us, you'd want to know she were safe too.'

'Is that so?' Harry yelled, making her hit the brakes and swerve the car as rapid images flashed through her mind. All she could see were red scarves, chess pieces and her father's dark, sunken eyes.

'Harry. Please. I'm sorry you're hurt but I'm so scared. Someone killed my mother. They crept up behind her and strangled her with a scarf. They came to my house, made sure I knew they were out there, that they were close. They knew where I lived. And now... now Becca has disappeared, and she's taken Isla with her and so help me God, Harry. If I don't find her... or if something happened to Isla, it'll kill me too.'

37

With her finger on speed dial, Lexi hit the number for Fiona Flowers, and quickly went over what had happened.

'I don't know what to do. I mean, it might be nothing, but she didn't check in to the hotel. She isn't where she said she'd be, and no one seems to know where she's gone. I'm terrified, 'cause wherever she is, she has Isla with her.' The fear shook through her words as she spoke. Her mind felt as though it had become filled with a self-protecting numbness, where nothing felt real, and the world was seen through a thick, impenetrable fog. 'I can't bear it. What if...' Slowing the car, she indicated and pulled to the side of the road, rubbed her eyes and tried to get the images of red silk scarves out of her mind. 'She's just a baby, just two years old.'

'Alexandra, let's not go there right now. Let me do some checks, and in the meantime, I need you to go back to the island, go back to the cottage. Wait for me there. As soon as I know something, I'll be in touch.'

'Lexi,' she snapped, 'my name is Lexi.' She paused. Took a breath. 'You keep calling me Alexandra and only he gets to call me Alexandra.' Her thoughts flashed back to her father, to the haunted look in his eyes, the crudely stitched scar on his face and the way he'd placed a hand against the grille, whispered her name repeatedly and all in the hope she'd meet his touch, hold her hand to his for just a second. And for what felt like an eternity, she'd stared at his thin, spindly fingers, remembered how as a child he'd held her hand so tenderly, in a protective and affectionate way. And while trying to convince herself that meeting his touch was the right thing to do, she could barely breathe and, instead, she'd twisted her fingers painfully around themselves until she'd had no choice but to sit on her hands. The whole hour had gone in the blink of an eye, and unsurprisingly she'd gone into a defensive mode. She'd refused to meet his eye as she'd asked each of the questions, the ones she'd rehearsed. One by one she'd got the answers the police needed and then, once Fiona had ticked all the points on her notepad, she'd stood up, abruptly called time on the visit, opened the door, and had ushered Lexi out of the room, leaving her father looking lost and bewildered, without an opportunity to say anything more. Closing her eyes as she'd walked along the corridor and to the first of the automatic doors, where she could still hear him yelling her name, then as the door slammed shut, his cries had disappeared behind it.

'Sorry. I didn't think,' Fiona replied apologetically. Paused. 'And of course, I'll use Lexi in the future. Now, please, go back to the island. Before the causeway closes. It's the best place you can be. It could be that Isla is already home, and if she is, you'll be there for her.'

'Fiona... what happens if she doesn't come back?'

38

With her hands gripped tightly to the wheel, Lexi turned the car, took in a deep breath and headed back towards the island while constantly checking each car that passed, hoping hers would come into view, that she'd see both Becca and Maggie in the front and that Isla would be safely fastened into her car seat in the back.

'Never again... no one takes her, not ever again,' she whispered through gritted teeth, indicated left, and scowled as she went past the inn. The place where Isla should have slept. Where she should have been warm and safe. But wasn't. Cursing, she knew she should have phoned Nate, didn't have a clue what to say, how to tell him their daughter was still missing, that she hadn't turned up as she'd expected.

Thoughts of the tide suddenly came to mind, and, quickly, she grabbed her mobile from the seat beside her, began to flick at the screen, knew she'd only had an hour to get to the inn and back again. Couldn't work out how long she'd been and looked at the time, felt her concentration dip, and jumped as the loud blast of a horn came from behind. 'Sorry, sorry...' Swerving, she felt her heart rate accelerate, threw the phone back down at the seat and as soon as she could, she pulled into The Barn's car park, then resumed her search. 'Twenty minutes...' She breathed a sigh of relief, and although she knew she had time to make the crossing, it was winter, the tide was volatile, and she felt her anxiety rise as she saw the water already lapping against the edges of the road, a queue of traffic meandering across bumper to bumper, all avoiding the construction workers who were hurriedly packing the trucks that still lined the causeway.

Determinedly, she set off across the road and felt the frustration rise as the cars in front slowed to take in the view, to watch the workers, to point and laugh at how the tide flooded in. Adamant that she had no choice but to get to the other side, Lexi sped through the shallow water, cringed as the spray splashed up from the tyres and sent dramatic outward arcs of water back into the sea. Holding her breath, she felt a slight sense of relief as she passed the tower, reached the home straight and headed for the causeway that snaked its way around the edge of the island. This was the most dangerous part; once she'd left the area between the island to the mainland there was no turning back and, without warning, it was an area where the tide could easily flood, especially when the moon was full and the tide was high.

Reaching the other side, she puffed out her cheeks, blew out a long, slow breath and anxiously pulled Maggie's car into the main car park. Then she set off on foot, over the dunes and towards The Snook. With the wind whipping her hair around her face, she used one hand to hold it back as she walked to the highest part, tried to calm her breathing and, longingly, she watched the road, prayed that her car would appear. That Becca, Maggie and Isla would make it through the causeway before the tide came back in and that the island wouldn't be isolated, not again. Not without them on it.

'Come on...' she whispered into the wind, kept her eyes on the tide, saw the way that with each wave the water got closer, deeper, more and more inaccessible. 'You have to come back. You just have to.' Wrapping her arms around her body in a hug, she imagined holding Isla, wished for her to be there, in her hold where she could take in the smell of her strawberry shampoo, and the sweet-smelling talcum powder she insisted on using each time she got out of the bath. But instead, Lexi shook her head; she felt as though it were a wish too many and sank down, to sit on the cold, damp sand, where she felt the harsh winter breeze cut through her jacket and, despondently, she stared out to sea, felt the anger build inside her like a volcano ready to erupt.

Screaming with frustration, she pulled her phone from her pocket and hit redial, and cursed as she heard Becca's voicemail kick back in with her normal, bright and breezy message.

'Hi, this is Becca. I'm a bit busy... so leave me a message and I'll call you back...' The words were sung down the phone; Lexi had heard them once too many and was in no mood to be polite.

'I'll leave you a message, all right – I want to know where the hell you are, where the hell my daughter is. How dare you disappear without a thought for others. How dare you take her with you.' She grabbed a breath, pushed the hair from her face, felt hot, angry tears scald her cheeks. 'I'll say this once, and only once. You bring her home and you bring her home right now. Or so help me God...'

With her phone bleeping, Lexi pulled it away from her ear, glanced at the screen, saw the call coming in, flicked to accept it. 'Becca, where the hell are you?'

'Whoa, Lexi, calm down. We're at Maggie's. We've been looking for you.' Becca's words hit her with force, relief spread over her like a tidal wave and, quickly, she stood up and set off running across the dunes and towards the car.

'You're at home. You're at Maggie's and... and Isla, she's with you.' The words came out in a rush; tears of relief filled her eyes. 'Why the hell didn't you phone me? I've been going out of my damned mind...' Stopping for a moment, she caught her breath. Swallowed hard and stared at the tiny town that stood in the distance. Her daughter was there, she was safe, she was at Maggie's and the relief that quickly spread through her was just a little more than overwhelming and even though she wanted to get home and quickly, she took a moment to lean against the wall of the car park, recapture her thoughts, and waited until her heartbeat slowed.

'Well, do you know what, I've been kind of busy. I've not only had an overactive two-year-old to look after – all by myself – but also Maggie, who's been terribly sick and as stubborn as a mule who won't do as she's told. I spent the night at the hospital in a really uncomfortable chair, being a temporary mattress for your daughter. But that's OK... We're all OK... Thanks for asking.' Her response was sarcastic, full of animosity, and Lexi pulled the phone away from her ear, tried to calm herself down.

'Becca, I appreciate that you looked after them, really I do, but seriously... you don't ever disappear, not with someone's child, not without checking in. It's just wrong...'

'Lexi, just back off. It's not like you didn't know what had happened,' she yelled back. 'I was stuck on the mainland. It's not my fault the bloody tide came in, is it?'

With the wind now circling the island like a hurricane, Lexi pulled her coat tightly around her, zipped it up and closed her eyes. It was more than obvious that a storm was brewing, that if she didn't get home soon, she'd be caught in the deluge. Counting to ten, she tried to imagine it from Becca's point of view. 'OK, OK... I'm sorry, can I speak to Isla?' As though to prove a point, Isla squealed in the background.

'There, you heard her. She's still alive and... Maggie is shouting for me too, so I'm gonna go.' She paused. 'But if you'd come home as soon as you could, it'd be greatly appreciated... I could do with some help.'

'Becca, please understand. I... I didn't know where you were and... oh my God, I phoned the police. They...' She suddenly realised that the whole of Northumberland Police would have gone on alert looking for a missing child, who was at home, safe and well.

'You did what? Why?'

'Becca, I'll explain later. I didn't feel that I had a choice.' Her eyes immediately went to the causeway, fully expected to see the blue flashing lights. The police cars thundering their way across with the incoming water dramatically spraying outward from the causeway. 'Becca, I... I need to call the police. I need to stop them storming the island...'

39

Listening to the monotonous on-hold bleeps that were interspersed with short messages, Lexi held the phone away from her ear, drummed her fingers on the dashboard and tapped the accelerator with her foot. On more than one occasion she debated putting the phone down and setting off for Maggie's cottage, which was literally just up the road, but knew that Fiona wouldn't have asked her to hold, not unless she'd had a good reason for doing so. Now she sat with every thought going through her mind, every unspeakable scenario, and her mind went back to her father, to the haunted look he'd had in his eyes, the evil that was obviously within and the knowledge that he alone had destroyed so many families, so many lives including her own.

'Sorry about that.' Fiona came back to the call, paused. 'I really need to speak to you but had to make sure the alert had been taken down first. No point having half the north-east force looking for a child, not if they don't need to be, now, is there?'

'I'm so sorry.' Lexi added, 'I panicked. I didn't know where she was, where Becca had taken her. They just seemed to disappear, and stupidly, I didn't know which hospital my foster mother had been taken to, so I couldn't even phone ahead and check.'

'No need to apologise, you did the right thing.' Fiona took in an obvious deep breath. 'As I said, I do need to speak to you. It's about your father and as you haven't already mentioned it, I'm taking it that you didn't hear the news?' Again, she hesitated, and Lexi could hear the tapping of her fingers on a keyboard.

'What news, what happened?' The way Fiona had spoken was slow, calculated and unnerving, and Lexi immediately thought the worst; she could still hear the way her father had yelled her name as she'd been ushered from the room and she'd spent the whole night wishing she'd turned, gone back, held her hand to that glass and given him the moment he'd obviously needed. 'Is he dead?'

'Oh no. Sorry. No. He... he isn't dead. But after he told us where to find her, where to find his final victim, I thought you should know: we've started the search.'

Taking in a deep breath, Lexi stared at the tide, the way the waves rolled in towards the island, tried to come to terms with what Fiona had said. What her father had told her. What it actually meant to her. To Isla. And whether the news would make the killer react, and with a sigh she looked back at the tide, felt relieved that it had come back in, and unless the killer was already on the island, they'd have at least five hours of tranquillity and safety, until the causeway reopened.

'... there's a team up there now, digging up the woods close to where you used to live. The ones that were right behind your house. Unfortunately, the news has got out and the papers, the radio, everyone's there... social media's gone crazy. I'm amazed you hadn't heard already and, well, I thought you should know.' Lexi realised she'd probably missed half of what had been said and for a beat she closed her eyes, tried to imagine how difficult it would have been for him to tell the truth.

Giving the details of where his last victim was buried, knowing that by doing so his annual excursions would end and that the chances of him ever leaving those prison walls again would be virtually impossible.

Putting the phone down, Lexi shuffled in her seat, stared directly at the radio and, with shaking fingers, she reluctantly switched it on, flicked through the stations until she found the news, then chewed at her bottom lip as she listened.

'Following a visit from his daughter, Alexandra Graves, serial killer Peter Graves has finally disclosed the burial place of what was thought to be his final victim, Melissa Jameson. The nineteen-year-old disappeared in 2001; her body was never found. Officers have descended on woodland close to the murderer's home in an effort to find her body; it's expected that the search will take several days and that every inch of the woodland will be searched before any further details are given.'

Striking out repeatedly at the radio until she managed to hit the off button, Lexi took a moment to take in the silence, felt the nausea fill her mind and, as though she'd been struck by lightning, she felt the same cloud that had hung over her for the past twenty years dramatically erupt. Every inch of her body began to shake with emotion; scalding-hot tears filled her eyes, cascaded relentlessly in torrents down her face until finally they dripped from her chin and were wiped away by the back of her hand.

'How the hell did they find out?' she screamed, thumped at the steering wheel. She'd worked in a newsroom for far too long, knew how the grapevine worked, how a small nugget of information would work its way in and somehow it would turn into a giant story that would end up on the front page the following day. But what she also knew was that for that headline to hit today's newspapers, the newsroom would have to have had that press release the day before and within hours if not minutes of her prison visit.

'No one knew. No one knew I was going. Goddamn it. Even I didn't know. Not until yesterday.' Anger tore through her mind as she went through the people who could have known, could have informed the papers. A series of images flashed before her eyes like photographs being dropped on a table. Fiona. The prison. The guard with the clipboard. The guard who'd shouted her name. Then there had been all the other visitors. Twenty or thirty of them, who'd turned, gasped and stared once they'd realised who she was. Any one of them could have blabbed to the papers. The story could have been on a news desk before she'd left the prison. And once one reporter knew, the story would have been sold on to others. Which would have given every reporter in England ample time to start digging for information, to look for a story, a new angle to use.

Drying her eyes, Lexi grabbed at her handbag, dug around for a tissue, and spotted the letters she'd written to her mother. She knew every word within them and couldn't help but wonder if there'd ever be a day when she didn't wish she'd posted them, got the answers to those questions. Or when her father's sordid past wouldn't infiltrate her life and make her feel as though he were dragging her down and into a deep, dark hole alongside him.

Thrusting the letters back into her bag, Lexi dried her eyes, and with the window down and the wind in her face, she drove the few minutes through town until she reached Maggie's. All she could think of was Isla, of holding her, loving her, keeping her safe, and felt a mixture of relief and excitement when she saw the car parked outside. There was smoke billowing out from the chimney and one or two walkers rushing along the road, looking for sanctuary as the weather came in. Taking deep breaths, Lexi stared out of the window, realised that even though her mind was spinning with its own personal turmoil, normal life seemed to be carrying on around the island and, eventually, she jumped out of the car and ran towards the cottage.

'Isla, there you are,' Lexi squealed as she saw Isla standing on the window seat, waving frantically, with her nose pressed tightly against the glass. It was exactly the sight Lexi had needed, making her throw open the front door, where she fell to her knees in the entrance and let out a long, happy sigh as Isla jumped down from the window seat and dived into her arms.

'Mummy, where... where did you go?'

'Where did I go?' Lexi asked. 'I was going to ask you the very same thing.'

'Me and Becca, we slept on a chair, didn't we?' The excitement of having a story to tell made her voice go high, her soft Irish accent a little more pronounced.

'Isla tucked Maggie into bed, let her borrow Teddy and... and we put the Christmas music on for her to listen to,' Becca added.

'She's poorly.' Isla pushed out her bottom lip in protest, but then gave Becca a playful, cheeky smile. 'We had cake... for breakfast.'

'Well, I think it was really lovely of Becca looking after you like that, wasn't it?' Holding her daughter at arm's length, Lexi stared into her eyes, saw how they sparkled with reflections from the Christmas tree. 'I'd say we all owe Becca a big thank you for looking after you all. Don't you think?' She smiled. 'Did you say thank you?' She prompted Isla with a tap on the bottom, and watched as she ran straight to Becca, threw her arms around her neck and promptly kissed her on the cheek.

'Aww, Isla, that was nice of you, wasn't it?'

For the first time since arriving home, Lexi realised that someone else was in the room, that Vicki was kneeling on the floor behind the settee and beside the fire. Standing up, Lexi smiled, noticed that although Vicki had taken off her shoes at the door to reveal her bright rainbow-coloured tights, she still wore her coat, draped with a matching rainbow scarf that was so bunched up it almost covered her face.

'I hope you don't mind me being here... Harry told me what had happened. I saw the car turn up and popped over to see if I could help.' Vicki pursed her lips. 'Thought I'd maybe see if you wanted me to take Isla down the beach for you or over to the school playground. You know, let her burn off some steam, while you settle Maggie back in.' With narrowed eyes that were directed at Becca, she shuffled uncomfortably on the spot and then pushed herself up from the floor, began pacing back and forth in front of the fire.

'And I told her, we're just fine,' Becca growled as she picked Agatha up and turned her onto her back as though cradling a baby. 'Maggie is in bed. This one's just been fed, and we have some beans and sausages warming up in a pan for Isla's lunch. So, I think I have it all under control. Don't you?'

Looking from one woman to the other, Lexi saw the bitterness that radiated from them both. Couldn't help but wonder what had happened to cause such dislike, such animosity between two sisters. Wished she'd had the chance to get Becca alone, to ask her what had caused the hostility.

'Look, Lexi. I'm sorry about last night, I should have phoned you,' Becca said sheepishly with a pensive smile. 'Everything happened so fast, and then, before I knew it, it was the middle of the night, Isla fell asleep on me and if I'm honest, it was such a relief that she'd finally stopped talking, I was terrified of waking her up again...'

'Forget it. It's done now. I just worry, any mother would, but you're safe, Isla's safe and that's all that matters. Now, how is Maggie?' Lexi glanced at the stairs, considered going up, seeing how she was for herself. 'I mean, the hospital, what did they say?'

'They said it's AF, atrial fibrillation. I think they said her heart is going too fast, much too often. They've put her on blood thinners, referred her to a specialist, said something about maybe having to do a cardio vascy... something. Sounded horrid, they stop and start your heart in theatre with one of those machines, and apparently it calms it all down.' She paused. 'Maggie will tell you all about it later; she seemed to understand what they were saying. In fact, it wouldn't surprise me if she hadn't already known how poorly she was.' With one eye peering anxiously into the kitchen, Becca tipped her head to one side. 'I'd best take the beans off the cooker.'

Making her way across the room, Lexi made the pretence of laughing at Agatha, who was now lying beneath the Christmas tree, one paw outstretched, tapping at the dozens of baubles that hung from its branches. Sighing, she thought of how this house was always cluttered, even in the summer. But at Christmas, it was more so, and while kneeling by the tree, she realised that the tension between the two women was palpable and, consciously, she placed herself between Isla and Vicki at all times, kept one eye on how the food was going down, how Isla was stabbing each sausage in turn, flying it around in the air like an aeroplane before pushing it mercilessly into her mouth, then giving out a cute but tomato-sauce-covered smile.

'As soon as Isla is finished, we'll pop up and see Maggie,' Lexi whispered, watched Becca lovingly pour juice into a beaker, then stop abruptly.

'Oh, no. No. I... I don't think you should. She's finally resting. And... you know what she's like, she's always worrying about the rest of us, and...' She looked at her watch. 'Even though the doctor said she should, I doubt she'll stay up there all day.' She paused, nervously picked up her phone, began flicking through the screens. 'Before you know it, she'll be doing her normal thing, making sure we've all had lunch, putting the kettle on and off for the rest of the day.' She gave a nervous laugh. 'She isn't happy unless she's feeding us.'

Tapping Isla on the bottom as she ran past, Lexi frowned as Isla grabbed the box of cat biscuits, shook them loudly, then squealed in delight as Agatha ran towards her, rubbed herself eagerly around her legs, all time purring, looking for treats. 'I thought you said you'd already fed Agatha today?' Standing up, Lexi grabbed the box. And with one eye on the way Becca and Vicki continually scowled, she uneasily headed towards the stairs, tried to work out what was causing the tension, perched on the bottom step and gripped it for support.

'Isla, come cuddle Mummy.' Without being able to explain why, she desperately wanted to keep Isla away from Vicki. Something wasn't right, she just didn't know what, and with a fear building up within her she glanced up the stairs, caught sight of the rows upon rows of black-and-white pictures, and with unshed tears, she saw them all blend into one. Each picture was a child, or teenager, who just like her had been brought to this house, to a place of safety. It was a house that had always felt like a sanctuary – that was, until today – and, disturbingly, she felt an internal trembling that vibrated through her and wouldn't stop.

Holding tightly to her daughter, Lexi tried to come up with a plan. A course of action that would distance them both, but with the storm thrashing down outside she couldn't even take the opportunity of going for a walk. 'Hey, Isla,' she suddenly said, 'how about me and you play hide-and-seek?' She purposely didn't invite either Becca or Vicki into the game, knew the game would take them upstairs. A place where she could take Isla with her.

'Yay… OK. I play.' Isla's eyes lit up with excitement; she struggled to free herself from Lexi's arms and bounced up and down on the bottom step.

'OK. How about you go and hide? And Mummy, well… Mummy will count to ten, then she'll come up and look for you.' She bit down on her bottom lip, saw the way Vicki paced back and forth in front of the fire, noticed the way her hands were twisting themselves tightly together. The way Becca watched her.

'Don't wake Maggie up,' Becca suddenly blurted. 'She's been awake most of the night. She'll be really tired.'

Lexi gave a forced smile. 'Becca's right. You can hide anywhere apart from Maggie's room. Don't go in there, will you?'

'Me?' Isla giggled.

'Yes, you. You be a good girl for your mummy and play nice, won't you?' As she said the words, they stuck in her throat; she could hear the way her father had said them to her, the way he'd looked at her, held her gaze, as though he'd known to hold that image in his mind. That it would be the last time he saw her, and now, staring at Isla, she shared his pain, felt the way her heart slowed, and pounded audibly. Wished that once again she could take Isla away, run somewhere, anywhere that was safe. Somewhere she could rid herself of this overwhelming feeling of helplessness and of a fog that had begun to descend, trapping them both in a world from which she wanted to escape.

'...seven... eight... nine... ten...' With relief that she could escape the tension of the room, Lexi crept up the stairs to follow Isla. With a storm crossing the island, the upstairs of the cottage had become dark and gloomy. Shadows fell through the doors of each of the four bedrooms that lined the corridor, apart from her room, which was the first on the landing. Hers was the only room with the door closed and, with a spring in her step, she flung it open and looked inside, fully expecting to see Isla hiding within. Suddenly, she remembered the night of passion she'd shared with Nate, the happiness she'd felt. It had only been the night before and, for a beat, she closed her eyes to see Nate's face, remembered her promise to phone him, for Isla to FaceTime and, with a hand on her heart, she made herself a pledge that they'd do just that. Just as soon as both Becca and Vicki went home.

Walking past each door, she peered in, looking for Isla. There were two other bedrooms still made up and ready to take children. They were children who had long since stopped coming and Lexi knew that Maggie kept the rooms fresh, on the off-chance that one or two of them, who were now adults, would drop by for a visit. It was something that happened quite often, and it had always been Maggie's way to make sure they were welcomed, that they always had somewhere to be. A place to stay.

Listening to the creaking of floorboards, Lexi took one short step after the other but couldn't help stopping and listening to the muffled voices that came from downstairs. The verbosity and ferocity of the argument grew, and Lexi hovered on the spot as she heard the slamming of doors, making it more than obvious they'd gone into the kitchen, the furthest-away point from where she was now. With her breath held tight, she slowly moved one step at a time towards where Isla's high-pitched giggles now gave her away.

'What did I say? Not in Maggie's room.' She tried to sound annoyed but loved the way Isla chuckled with delight, her soft Irish tones chatting away under her breath as Lexi slowly pushed the door open, and immediately felt the atmosphere change within the room. It felt uncharacteristically cold and dark, with just a sliver of light filtering in through the split in the curtains, and rain could be heard hammering against the window in sharp, sporadic strikes. Thunder roared angrily in the distance. It felt as though it were in direct competition with the arguments below and Lexi pushed the door to a close behind her, in the hope that Isla wouldn't hear the argument.

'Hide me, Maggie?' Isla's giggles continued, her delight of snuggling up to Maggie more than apparent, and Lexi found herself tiptoeing across the room, shaking her head and squinting in the half darkness. Maggie's room had always been full of the same mahogany furniture, the same antique carved bed, which had been a wedding present from her parents. The only changes Lexi had ever known was the colour of the duvet cover, which never matched the curtains. 'No one cares what colour the bedding is, do they?' Maggie had said one day while they were changing the beds. 'So long as it's clean, nothing else matters.'

'Isla... come out, right now.' Lexi sniffed the air, and without thought she went back to the window, pulled the curtain to one side, pushed it open. 'Isla...' Taking a step closer to the bed, Lexi felt her heart pound in her chest, her pulse quicken and her mind buzz with trepidation. After having a night in the hospital, Lexi was fearful of waking Maggie up, or even worse, giving her a start and making her heart condition worse. And now, as she padded carefully across the room, she regretted the game, the way she'd asked Isla to go and hide, and knew that by using the words 'and not in Maggie's room', she'd almost certainly put the idea in the forefront of the child's mind.

'Hey, Maggie. It's Lexi, how are you doing?' In the half-lit room, Lexi carefully moved the duvet to one side, held a corner up for Isla to escape. 'Come on, get out of there.' As carefully as she could, she reached under the covers, where Isla wriggled. 'Isla, come on, you'll wake Maggie.'

'But...' Isla's voice wobbled; her words came out as a sob as her hand appeared from beneath the duvet, the unmistakable shape of the white queen chess piece, lying between her fingers.

'Where... Isla, where did you get that?' she screamed, blinked rapidly, frantically scoured the carpet to look for other pieces. 'Isla?'

'Maggie had it.'

As the realisation hit, Lexi physically felt the floor move beneath her. The air rapidly expelled itself from her lungs like a fast-deflating balloon. She could barely breathe, her mind spun like a tornado, and she immediately tried to pull deep breaths into her body while all the time turning in circles. 'Isla...' Throwing back the covers, she grabbed Isla's hand, felt her legs buckle dramatically beneath her as her worst nightmare became a reality and she saw the red silk scarf that was wound tightly around Maggie's neck, her pale grey lifeless face staring back at her.

41

With sobs pulsating violently through her body, Lexi held a hand tightly over her mouth; she spun around, terrified that whoever had killed Maggie was still in the house, in one of the bedrooms. Moving to the open window, she leaned out, hoped for someone, anyone to be walking down the street, but with the rain still pouring in stair rods, the streets were deserted.

Keeping tight hold of Isla's hand, she pulled her close, held a finger to her lips, hoped Isla would see it as a game and, with adrenaline rushing through her body, she carefully and quietly opened the door, began to move slowly down the hallway until she reached her bedroom. It had always been a room where she'd felt safe, a place she could come to be alone. Yet now as she hovered in the doorway, it felt anything but; the walls were closing in around her until the two beds, the dressing table and the built-in wardrobe had all blended together.

As gently as she could, she stepped into the room, felt grateful for the lock that Stanley had fitted. 'Young ladies need their privacy,' he'd said as he kneeled in the doorway, chisel in hand. 'And you, you're all grown up now and sometimes you just need to lock a door and take a minute.' Little had he known that one day she'd use that same lock for protection, and that his wonderful, loving wife would be down the hallway, murdered in her bed, and that it would be all Lexi's fault.

Standing with her back to the door, Lexi blew out a long, painful sigh and while desperately not knowing what else to do, she looked for a weapon.

'Are we still playing?' Isla innocently danced around the bed, pulled her teddy from under the quilt, rocked it like a baby. 'Can Teddy play?'

'He sure can. I think Teddy should play hide-and-seek with you.' Moving towards the bed, Lexi pulled out the bedside drawer, dragged the contents out, threw the old quilts at the laundry basket. 'Do you remember, at our old house, you found that really good hiding place?'

Nodding, Isla began bouncing up and down, and pointed to the drawer.

'Well, Mummy wants you to hide again, like you did before, with Teddy. But this time, don't come out. Not till Mummy says you can.' Again, she held a finger to her lips. 'And you have to be really quiet. It's the only way to win the game, and you...' She poked her with a finger. 'You like to win, don't you?' She said the words Isla needed to hear, but her thoughts spiralled out of control and the words 'and stay alive' went over and over in her mind.

With Isla safely hiding in the drawer, Lexi looked out of the window, past the old oak tree and towards the priory. She'd spent so many years looking at this view, on the inside looking out. It had been a place she'd always felt safe, yet now, this house felt as though it were crumbling around her, falling down, just like the priory and, for a second, she considered opening the window and screaming for help. But then, fear filled her mind. She didn't know who would come, who was a friend, or a foe. Whether, inadvertently, she'd be alerting the killer and suddenly she felt another, more violent sob erupt from her throat.

'I'm to blame,' she whispered, 'by coming here. I brought the killer with me... I... I should never have come back.' Sobbing, Lexi knew that Maggie's death was one death too many. It was as though someone somewhere was determined to take every single person from her, to kill them all and, knowing that Isla couldn't see, she finally allowed herself to sink to her knees, where the pain of loss tore through her to leave her lying on the floor, next to the bed, with her arms wrapped tightly around her body, rocking herself back and forth.

'Mummy, are you crying?' Isla's voice came from behind her, from within the drawer. Her innocence brought Lexi back to reality; the need to protect her daughter rushed through her like a surge of explosive electricity that made her jump up from where she lay. Quickly she began to formulate a plan in her mind, knew she had to get them out of the house and wished for Isla to be a few years older, knowing how as a teenager she'd have quite easily shimmied up and down the tree outside, made her way in and out of the house via the window. She shook her head; Isla was much too small, the risk of her falling much too high, and, with her ear to the door, she listened, realising that her only escape would be to leave the safety of this room.

Closing her eyes, she suddenly heard the sound of footsteps trudging along the landing outside, Becca's inquisitive voice echoing along the corridor. 'Lexi, you up here?' The words were followed by a gut-wrenching scream and Lexi felt herself shrink to the floor beside the bed, one hand protectively on the drawer.

'Keep quiet, baby, don't make a sound.' She whispered the words, felt her mouth go dry and, with the urge to cough, she felt herself gag.

'Lexi, Lexi... please... for the love of God... You have to help me.

It's Maggie... I... I think she's dead.' The words were interspersed with sobs; there was a thundering of fists against her door and Lexi could see the frame vibrate, the key rattle in its lock until she thought it might fall out. 'Yes, yes, I need the police and... and an ambulance.' The words were screamed into a phone. 'I don't know. I think she's... she's dead but she might not be, so I need you to come. I need you to help her.' There was a pause. A few seconds of silence, then the door handle was violently rattled again. 'Lexi... are you in there?'

It was a moment of indecision. And Lexi stared at the door handle, waited for it to rattle again, for the door to breach and for Becca to burst in, for the police to follow.

'Yes, yes... I'm here,' Becca continued. 'I don't know, I think she's been murdered. There's a scarf, it's tied around her neck and she... she's all cold, blue.'

With her eyes squeezed tight, Lexi took sharp inward breaths. It was more than obvious that Becca was pacing up and down the hallway, and she looked at the lock, knew that it was the only thing that was keeping the killer out, but her protective nature and the thought of Becca being out there terrified and alone was tearing her in two. Keeping Isla safe had to come first but, indecisively, Lexi focused on the key, couldn't decide whether she should let Becca in or not. Keep her safe too. And realistically, she couldn't think of a reason why she shouldn't. After all, she was Harry's girlfriend, a woman who'd looked after her daughter, brought her home safely.

'No. I don't think they're still here. Why, do you think they're still in the house?' There was a shuffling, then panic followed by the kicking of doors. 'Right, I have a weapon. I just grabbed a golf club. It was in the spare room but... I really do think they've gone.'

Again, Becca went quiet, then dramatically a sob left her throat. 'No, there was just us in the house. Me and Lexi, oh, and Isla, Lexi's two-year-old little girl.' She paused. 'My sister, Vicki, she was here, but we had an argument, and she went home... please... you are coming, aren't you?' As the desperation in Becca's voice accelerated, Lexi lay on her stomach, tried to look through the small gap under the door, could see nothing but the shadow of Becca's feet as they paced back and forth.

Blowing out through puffed-up cheeks, Becca slid to the floor, sat in the hallway, carried on with the call. 'Sure. Let me think. Harry. Harry Miller, he was here, he came over to see her. But Harry wouldn't kill her, he's like a son, he loves Maggie.'

With her fingers on the lock, Lexi listened intently, couldn't believe for a minute that Harry was involved. That he'd ever hurt Maggie and, with a furrowed brow, she considered opening the door and letting Becca in, get her out of the hallway, away from any possible danger. 'If I let her in, we could all be together,' she whispered to herself, allowed her fingers to graze the key, heard it rattle against the lock.

'The only other person that's been here is Lexi,' Becca suddenly said. 'Maggie fostered her for years and... she turned up on the island a couple of days ago. She'd have been the last person to see her alive.' There was a moment of silence. 'Alexandra Graves. Is that her real name? I... I didn't know... oh my God, are you saying that was her father? He was the serial killer, wasn't he and yes... she's still in the house... I think.' She paused, yelped. 'Do you think she could be dangerous?'

Hearing those words, Lexi felt the panic course through her, the sudden realisation that Becca knew who she really was and now she thought she'd killed Maggie. It felt like a stake piercing her heart and she could imagine a thousand scenarios. Images of police kicking down the door, arresting her, dragging her out of the house, kicking and screaming, just as they'd done with her father, and then how no one would listen, how the world would blame her. She'd be considered a copycat; she'd be blamed for her mother's murder too and she'd be locked away in a tiny cell, forgotten by all who'd loved her. Instinctively, she reached for the drawer, for Isla, wondered if tonight would be their last night together and considered the idea that she might not see her, not until she was an adult, and just as she'd done, turning up at the prison, looking for answers.

'Becca, please... you, you have to believe me. I... I didn't hurt her. I'd never have hurt her.' She unlocked the door, saw Becca mournfully leaning against the wall, golf club in her hand, sobbing. 'She was already dead when I came up,' Lexi yelled. 'Isla had got into bed with her... she had a chess piece in her hand, a white queen and I... I'm so scared.' She looked frantically up and down the hallway, until her eyes became firmly fixed on Maggie's door. 'We have to escape, you and me, we have to leave the island, keep Isla safe.' She nodded desperately, turned, and looked directly into Becca's eyes, saw the sparkling tear-filled black onyx within. 'Please... Becca, please help me. I think they want to kill me too.' Her gaze fell on the stairs. 'Did you say Vicki went home?'

With her mind obviously in a daze, and with the phone still to her ear, Becca nodded slowly, sighed. Then she held the phone out in her hand, flicked at the screen. 'They're not coming, not till the causeway opens.'

Shaking her head in disbelief, Lexi realised that her worst nightmare had come true. That the killer was here, on the island. That the tide was in and even with the uncontrollable urge she had to run, she knew she couldn't. She was trapped by the tide. They were all trapped by the tide and the killer was trapped here with them.

With Becca leading the way, golf club at the ready, Lexi followed
her down the stairs, one at a time, with Isla held tightly in her arms.
As a teenager she'd quickly worked out which steps creaked, which
didn't, where to place her foot and how quickly she could go down
them, so as not to make a noise. It was something she'd never
forgotten and as she carefully placed each foot on a step, she
remembered the multiple times she and Harry would leave the
house in the dead of night, make their way to the beach where the
most riotous parties would be held, the way they'd always drink far
too much, giggle all the way home and up the stairs, where either
Maggie or Stanley would always be standing, arms crossed, wry
smiles on their faces. 'So long as you're both safe,' Maggie would
say. 'Now, off to bed with you both and, tomorrow, I hope you can
live with those hangovers, 'cause you more than deserve them.'
She'd spin on the spot and pretend to flounce up the hallway,
leaving her and Harry to crawl to their beds. It was a sight that Lexi
wished for, an image that would stay in her mind forever and something she'd give just about anything for, for it to happen again, for
Maggie to be standing there.

Placing Isla on the window seat, it was the sudden thought of Harry that made her stare out of the window and wistfully towards the pub. She wondered if he were there, whether it was easier to run to him, to ask for his help, but remembered what Becca had said, that Harry had been to visit Maggie, which meant he'd been the last person to see her alive, not her. It was a thought that whizzed around her mind on high speed, with one question after the other spinning around, each one with an answer that negated his guilt. Yes, he'd been here. Yes, he'd seen Maggie. But Maggie had been like a mother to him too. A stalwart figure who'd always stood in his corner. Someone who'd loved him when his own parents hadn't. *It just can't be Harry.* She stared out of the window, shook her head, knew it just didn't ring true. Also, if it had been Harry that had killed Maggie, it would mean that he'd killed her mother too and that... that just didn't add up. There would have been no reason for him to do that.

Watching the weather outside, Lexi tried to decide whether or not she should phone Harry but instead she concluded, as she always did, that it was easier to run away, to escape the island – to leave Harry behind. It was a painful reminder of the last time they'd been together, the passion they'd shared and the way she'd run from the island the very next morning to start a new life, a life on the mainland that hadn't included Harry.

'Where are we are going, Teddy?' Isla sat in the window where Lexi had put her. She spoke directly to her teddy bear, making it more than obvious she knew something was wrong, that once again they were on the move and, with the bear held tightly in her arms, she fixed her eyes on the window, where the rain continued to lash heavily against it.

'We're going in the car.' Lexi caught Becca's eye, wondered what she'd do. Whether she'd stay here, on the island with Harry, or go with them. Either way, she was likely to be in danger. Knew that until the killer was caught, everyone around her could quite easily become a victim. It wasn't something she wanted on her conscience and, while biting down on her bottom lip, she considered her options, tried to come up with yet another plan.

'Your daddy... he's missing us. So I thought we'd go and see him.' She gave Isla a fixed smile and watched the way her daughter bounced with delight.

'Is that where you're going? Back to Nate?' Becca stood nervously by the door, golf club still in her hand. She kept looking anxiously over her shoulder, checking the house for intruders. Stood between Lexi and the rest of the house.

Lexi took a breath and nodded. She thought of Nate, couldn't think of anyone else she'd rather be with. After the night before, after the love they'd shared, after all of his explanations, she knew it was the right thing to do and that as soon as he knew what had happened, here on the island, he'd be the best person to protect them both, to keep Isla safe. Even if that meant them all staying home, locking the doors, waiting for the killer to be caught and locked up forever.

Picking up the car keys along with her phone, Lexi scoured the room, watched as Becca continued to stand motionless, her whole body physically shaking. She held the golf club tightly in her hands; it was now balanced on one shoulder, ready to swing. Her gaze fixed on the kitchen door, waiting. Then suddenly, she screamed. 'I swear, if anyone comes near...' The club was brought down like a hatchet, to bounce heavily against the carpet. 'They'll wish they hadn't.' She took gulps of air, stared at the floor, at the club, then gave a sly, twisted smile, making Lexi catch her breath and take a step backwards.

'Mummy, my coat,' Isla squealed, jumped down from the window seat and jumped on the stairs.

'No... Isla, no... you don't go up there.'

'But...' Tears welled up in Isla's eyes, her bottom lip wobbled and, instantly, Lexi felt cruel for snapping.

'I'm sorry. Mummy's sorry.' She kneeled down, held Isla by the shoulders. 'But we have to go. We have to get in the car. Right now.' Leaning past Becca and across the settee, Lexi pulled at Maggie's knee blanket, held it to her face, breathed in its aroma. 'Here you go, we'll wrap this around you. It'll keep you warm, won't it?'

'But that's Maggie's...' Isla whispered, her fingers gently reaching forward to stroke the material. 'She needs it.'

Feeling a sob reach her throat, Lexi closed her eyes for a beat, puffed out her cheeks and blew out a long, meaningful breath. 'Maggie won't be needing it, baby girl, and... I really don't think she'd mind you taking it.' She didn't want to explain any further, knew that Isla wouldn't understand, couldn't bear the thought of saying the words out loud, acknowledging the fact that Maggie was gone.

'We need to get going,' Becca chipped in, uneasily pulled open the door, nervously looked outside. 'We should get in the car, drive into town, wait for the causeway to open.'

Looking at her watch, Lexi tried to work out the movement of the tide. Knew it would be another three hours until the causeway opened, until the police arrived.

With Becca pacing up and down the pavement in the pouring rain, Lexi ran Isla to the car, clicked open the door, strapped her into the car seat and, with tear-filled eyes, she wrapped Maggie's blanket tightly around her. 'There you go. That'll keep you warm.' Sighing, she looked back over her shoulder, fixed her eyes on the cottage, wondered if this would be the last time she'd ever see it, whether she'd ever come back, and shook her head, knowing she wouldn't. It was time to let go of the island, time to leave it behind, and if she ever wanted to make her life with Nate, she had to leave Harry behind too.

'Mummy, what about Agafa? Are we leaving Agafa behind, with Maggie?'

Spinning on the spot and without thinking, Lexi ran back into the house. Scooped up the smoky-grey kitten who'd been hiding beneath the Christmas tree playing with baubles and, with a sigh of relief, she tried to remember what they'd done with her basket but stopped in her tracks as she caught sight of a pair of feet lying prone on the kitchen floor. The unmistakable rainbow-coloured stockings that Vicki had been wearing, and the blood that pooled around her body and onto the white tiled floor.

Hesitating for just a second, Lexi tried to comprehend what she was looking at. The words 'Vicki went home' exploded in her mind, spiralled like a hurricane. She'd clearly heard Becca say that to the police. She'd asked her that exact question. But clearly – she'd lied. Which meant...

As the car engine turned, Lexi took a split second to realise what had happened and, immediately, she felt her skin turn clammy, her breathing altered without warning, she began to hyperventilate. Her mind zipped rapidly from one disturbing thought to another. A long, piercing scream left her throat and even though her feet felt as though they'd been welded to the floor, she dropped Agatha on the sofa, launched herself out of the house, towards the car and, with one hand on the door handle, she dragged it open, threw herself inside.

'Becca... Why... What did either of them do wrong to you?' Her thoughts spiralled out of control, and anxiously she spun around in her seat, saw Harry coming out of the pub, striding towards the cottage. Immediately, she banged on the window, realised he couldn't hear and frantically wound the window down and screamed, 'Harry! Help me... Harry... please. You have to help me.'

'Oh, he isn't going to help you now. No one is.'

Becca's voice had gone from being nervous but friendly to low and monotone, without depth or feeling. It was a terrifying change, a complete switch in personality, and while Lexi still hammered against the window, still trying to get Harry's attention, she began to viciously berate herself. She knew how stupid she'd been. Knew she'd made a thousand mistakes, and that she shouldn't have trusted anyone, especially with Isla. Terrified, she tried to decide what to do. Jumping from the car wasn't an option, not with Isla. Her only chance was to talk Becca down, to try and get her to stop the car, allow them the chance to escape.

'Becca, please, I don't understand. Why would you have done this to my family, to the people I loved?' She spoke between sobs, stopped banging on the window, resigned herself to the fact that Harry could no longer hear.

'What did you do? Your father, he killed my sister. His last victim. He took her away from us. Buried her in an unmarked grave, and now Vicki's dead too. She got too close; I kept warning her not to, told her so many times to stay away from me, to leave me alone. But she wouldn't. She thought she could stop me. But she couldn't and now... now you have to die too.'

'But he... he didn't kill Melissa. And yesterday, he told us exactly where to find her. They're looking for her, the police, they're searching right now.' Lexi rubbed her hands down her jeans, felt the panic within, continued to look over her shoulder, hoped that Harry had heard, that he'd realise what had happened, would follow, and save her.

Suddenly, the brakes on the car were hit. Becca turned in the driver's seat, glared over her shoulder. 'You're lying.'

'I swear to God. I'm not lying. My dad, he told me what happened; your sister, she was my sister too... my dad, he was her dad too.' She paused, swallowed, kept one eye on the rear-view mirror all the time looking for Harry, hoping for help. 'She went to see him. But he told her to go home. To leave the past behind. There was a terrible accident.'

'What accident?'

As she turned, Lexi saw Becca's eyes. They'd glazed over with fury and, disturbingly, she glared at Isla. The love and emotion she'd shown towards her earlier had gone; in its place was a vacant expression, a glazed inhuman stillness within her.

'They were in the street. They argued and she stormed off just as a car sped past. It clipped her arm, spun her around and my dad... her dad... he tried to catch her, but she fell. She hit her head on the pavement and died right there, in the street, in his arms. He knew the world would blame him, especially when they realised who he was, how many women he'd killed. So, he hid her in the woodland. Buried her, with a small stone to mark the spot. I remember him once taking me there. Which now I realise must have been within hours of it happening 'cause he was arrested right after her death. I remember him looking really sad and laying flowers by a tree and when I asked him why, he told me he was giving them back to nature.'

Becca shook her head furiously. 'It isn't true. You're lying. My mother, she'd have known, she'd have told me.'

'She did know. But your mother's husband, your dad, was violent. She was terrified of him finding out. Of him knowing she'd had an affair, that our sister hadn't been his. And my dad, he never told the truth, knew it wouldn't be good for her if he did. Which is why he didn't speak up, not while she was alive.' Lexi paused, inched closer to Isla, waited for Becca to turn away, to look at the road before cautiously sliding her hand towards the child seat, to the clip she knew Isla couldn't open. 'Becca, I swear, he tried to do the right thing; he thought it was best for your mum.'

'I killed them all, all of them because of him...' A sudden, unexpected sob left Becca's throat. 'I'd had dark thoughts for years, knew deep down how dangerous I could be. How dangerous I wanted to be.'

Lexi's whole body turned rigid. Becca had said she'd killed them all; she knew that that probably meant Maggie and Vicki, but the word 'all' indicated that she'd killed more than two and Lexi's inquisitive reporter's mind couldn't stop the questions forming in her mind. 'Becca... who did you kill?' She couldn't resist the question, knew that like the letters full of questions she hadn't posted, she'd always wish she had.

'All of them. Your mother, mine. Vicki, Maggie.' She shook her head, continued to stare at Isla.

'Your own mother, what did she do?' Lexi was now trying to taunt her, to get her to turn away, to stop looking at Isla, to give her the chance to unclip the car seat, to jump from the car – while it stood still.

'I was so sick of her sitting in that chair, rocking back and forth, watching those stupid newsreels over and over. I thought she was looking for clues, looking for my sister. But instead, she was looking for him, worrying herself to death in case he confessed, told them the truth. And in the end, she just lay there. Staring into space and, I swear, her eyes pleaded with me to do it. To take away her pain.' She laughed. 'You see, she was the one I killed first, and somehow I got away with it. It was so, so easy.'

Slowly, Lexi reached for Isla's hand. Felt the warmth beneath the blanket, tried to press the button below. 'And Vicki... what did she do?'

Turning, Becca revved the car. 'I don't have to tell you anything. All you need to know is it's your turn to go.' She began to laugh, loud, hysterically.

'Becca, please... We're family, we shared a sister that I didn't even know about and Vicki, she might not be gone. We could go back. Save her. It isn't right for us to leave her there, to die alone. You could lose her too.'

'She wouldn't stop shouting and I wanted her to stop. My mind was exploding. There was noise coming at me from every direction.' Blinking, a tear slowly rolled down Becca's cheek. 'I told her to stop but she kept on going and when I picked up the knife, she laughed, thought I was joking. Said I wouldn't do it.'

In an attempt to regain control, Lexi reached out, placed a hand gently on Becca's shoulder. Held her breath, hoped Becca would see sense but, without warning, she felt the shrug of Becca's shoulder, the reach of her arm, the car pushed into gear.

'It's too late. I'll be locked up. In one of those tiny little cells and... what about Harry. I won't have Harry.' She gulped, took a deep inward breath. 'Although, it was always you he loved. He never hid that fact.' She pressed her foot down on the accelerator, continued the drive through town, past the car park. 'I can't live in a cell, in a prison, I just can't...' She began to bang her hands wildly against the steering wheel.

'Becca, the causeway – it's closed. Take me with you if that's what you want but please, for the love of God, let Isla go. Let her out of the car.' Again, she reached forward, tried to grab Becca's arm, felt the car jerk to one side as she shrugged her off. 'Becca, please, I saw the way you look at her, the way you looked after her last night. You were kind, you were loving. You don't want to hurt her.' It was all she could think to say, knew that Becca was heading for the causeway, that the winter tides would have flooded it completely and that right now, the only place for the car left to go was into the sea.

Terrified, Lexi scrambled to unclip Isla's car seat, changed her mind and, without thought for her own safety, she shielded Isla's body with her own, held on to the chair. Waited for the impact that she knew would come.

As the car left the road, Lexi held her breath for what seemed like an eternity, felt the jolt as they hit the water, felt the pain shoot through her body, then the way her lungs deflated as sea water partially flooded the car and the coldness hit. Wave after wave rolled in through the window, leaving just a small void free of water near the roof and, with no time to think, she dragged Isla out of the seat, pushed her above the waterline, saw her baby's face full of fear. Screaming, Lexi could see the car rock back and forth to one side, knew that if the car tipped completely the open window would fall against the seabed and, as quickly as she could, she pushed Isla through the tiny space that was left, and while holding tightly to Isla's leg, she squeezed her way through, felt the full force of the tide. Salt water filled her mouth, her nose, her body was being dragged down beneath the water but as each wave hit, the thought of Isla drowning was too much, her fight too strong, and suddenly she kicked for the surface, pulled her daughter with her.

'Let her go.' Harry's voice bellowed above the sound of the waves. His body thrashed around in the water beside her. 'Lexi, I've got her. Let her go.' Feeling Isla torn from her arms, Lexi once again saw an invisible thread forming a line between them. It was a long sliver of light that had always bound them together but now it began to fade, to dissipate, and with a long, blood-curdling scream, Lexi saw it disappear and snap before her eyes as she swam towards the shoreline, where Harry was leaning over the child, blowing slow, measured breaths into her mouth.

43

With the sea surrounding my body, I push myself upwards, feel the shock of the cold as the waves rush in. A violent shivering overtakes my body and I know that these moments could be my last, as I desperately try to take in my final breaths of air.

Staring through the open window, I consider following Lexi through it and saving myself. But I quickly consider the life I will lead, the long, drawn-out existence prison days would become. It's something I've always known. Something I dreaded, and on so many occasions I wished I hadn't killed, wished I could stop. But the more lives I took, the easier it became, and I swiftly conclude that if I lose my life now, the world will be a better place without me in it.

Watching, I frown at the way Harry tries to save them both, just as I knew he would and, in doing so, I realise that he's left me behind, how little I must have meant to him. How he and Lexi should have been together from the beginning and, in a devastating thought, I realise that by doing what I did, I've pushed them both together. I've given them the exact opportunity Harry wanted.

As the breaths tear rapidly through my body, I feel the hyperventilation begin. Involuntarily, I gasp at the air, try to stop myself from swal-

lowing the water, from it surrounding me, and in a moment's panic, a sudden moment of wanting to live, I release the seat belt, push myself out of the car's window and, as I've been told so many times before, I float on my back, scull at the water, head for the island until I feel the sand beneath my back and, slowly, I turn onto my side, pull myself ashore, drag myself to hide within the sand dunes. Through half-closed eyes, and as the darkness descends, I feel tears spring to my eyes as I watch Harry work on saving the child, and with him knowing that I was in the car, I wonder how long it will be before he tries to save me too.

44

Closing the cottage door behind her, Lexi leaned against it, took in a deep breath of fresh air, and felt thankful for the warmth of summer, for days when the sunrise was early, when the birds happily sang their chorus and where seals could be seen bobbing up and down in the distance, looking for food.

Luckily, today was a day when the tide had come in early and would stay in until after lunch. Which meant that for most of the day, the roads would be deserted and all the people she loved were already here, with her, on the island.

Lifting the bouquet of flowers to her face, Lexi breathed in their aroma, picked up the skirts of her wedding dress, and with excitement building within her, she began to walk the short distance between the cottage and Saint Mary's church, only stopping for a short while beside Maggie's grave, where she smiled at the mass of flowers that had appeared by the headstone and knew that quite a few of her many foster brothers or sisters would have called on their way into the church to leave blooms for the woman they'd all loved. Pulling a rose from her bouquet, Lexi placed it by the stone, read the words before her and felt the tears spring to her eyes.

Margaret Jakes
Loving wife to Stanley, mother to Henry
and foster mother to fifty-two children,
all of whom loved her.
Born 6th June 1953
Taken from us 12th December 2021

A lot had happened since Maggie had been murdered. The woman who'd been considered her father's final victim had been found and laid to rest and after learning that her father had just weeks left to live, Lexi had taken the time to go back to Frankland, made one more visit and, even though she despised what he'd done, he was still her father and she placed her hand against the grille, met his touch and looked into his eyes, asked all the questions she'd always wanted the answers to and felt a sense of morbid pleasure in his responses, knowing that once answered, she'd be able to put them far behind her and never have to wonder about them again. Becca had been found and jailed for life and even though Lexi hated her with a vengeance for what she'd done to Maggie, she went to visit her too and, as an act of solidarity, she took Vicki with her, helped her face the woman, her own sister who'd tried to kill her and, in doing so, they both tried to put the past behind them. It was a way of feeling confident and safe in the future and although Lexi hadn't felt confident enough to let Isla go alone, she'd agreed to take her to nursery. Slowly at first, and with Vicki still recovering from her injuries, Lexi had offered to help her plan the following year's nativity, angel wings and all.

'Hey, I thought I'd find you out here.' Harry's voice rang out, just as the bells on the church began to toll. His hand went upwards, pointed to the bell tower. 'And that means the service is about to start; are you ready?' He smiled, placed a small bunch of flowers on

Maggie's grave, then rested a hand on Lexi's shoulder. 'So, today's the big day?'

Nodding pensively, Lexi looked past him, fully expecting Isla to burst out of the church, where she could imagine her daughter prancing up and down, practising her bridesmaid walk. 'I had one very excited three-year-old in the cottage this morning, one who is going to be a bridesmaid for the very first time. She's even practising her speech.' Lexi rolled her eyes, winked, poked him in the ribs. 'Someone apparently told her it was her job to do one.'

Laughing, Harry tipped his head to one side, ran a hand through his overgrown hair and ruffled it. 'Well, uncles do that kind of thing, don't they?'

'Well, thanks to you, she's ready to go. So I hope you're ready for it because I'm sure she has your name in that speech somewhere.' Searching his eyes with hers, she gave him a genuine smile. Thought about her words before she said them. 'I never did thank you properly, for saving her.'

He hooked his arm through hers, walked towards the door of the church. 'There are no words. You know I'd never have let her go, not without a fight.'

For a moment, Lexi wondered which fight he meant. Realised that from that day to this he'd never again mentioned Isla's parentage, and for this she felt thankful. He knew how many secrets had torn their lives apart and had quickly and without question taken on the role of becoming Isla's mischievous uncle, and, after saving her life, it had been a role that Nate had happily allowed him to fill. A role that Lexi hoped he'd continue.

'First foster child arrives tomorrow,' she announced. 'A young boy, ten years old and full of angst. He's very misunderstood, reminds me of someone I used to know, all angry with the world but so full of life; I just want to protect him.' She reached up, kissed

Harry on the cheek. 'I hope you'll have a chat with him, you know, when he gets here.'

Taking a step back, Harry nodded thoughtfully. 'So you're definitely carrying on where Maggie left off.' He gave her an appreciative smile. 'She'd be so proud of you.'

Nodding, Lexi thought of the way they'd renovated the cottage, got it ready for children with a room she'd prepared containing a bed, desk, television and bookshelf. Everything a young boy would want, in a home full of all the love she could give and a place he could find the sanctuary he desperately needed.

'Hey, you two.' Nate's voice suddenly echoed out from within the church, where sun poured in through stained-glass windows and Isla could be seen prancing up and down the aisle, hand in hand with the vicar. 'If you don't mind... I think it's time you walked my bride down this aisle.' Stepping forward, Nate kissed Lexi on the cheek, shook Harry's hand.

Shocked, Harry stepped back, put a hand to his chest. 'Me?' He looked from Lexi to Nate, the biggest grin crossing his face. 'Are you sure?'

Nate nodded knowingly, winked; once again, he took hold of Harry's hand. 'Of course I'm sure.' He looked at Lexi for approval, smiled. 'Besides, if you don't do it soon, I think our daughter will either burst with excitement or drive everyone just a little bit crazy.'

Taking a step through the door, Lexi caught Isla's eye, felt her heart burst with love as she skipped happily towards her. 'If she wants to drive everyone crazy, she's more than allowed.' Lexi looked from Harry to Nate, laughed. 'And neither of you should expect anything less... after all, she is her father's daughter.'

ACKNOWLEDGMENTS

I wrote this book with a genuine love for Lindisfarne and would like to thank the people who live there for the way they continually look after the island, keeping it perfect for all the visitors who go there year after year.

I would especially like to thank Ellie Hannah for her help and local knowledge and Danny Dagan who runs the Facebook page Holy Island of Lindisfarne, along with the beautiful Belvue Guesthouse, which is well worth a visit.

I've seriously never known anyone on the island who didn't give visitors the most amazing welcome. The Manor House Hotel is no exception. I've stayed there many times, always in room 10, which is the room described in the story. They have a fabulous atmosphere, which along with the best breakfasts, which makes it a great place to stay.

Meals at the Crown and Anchor, along with The Ship Inn are always good and well worth the money. We always try and have a meal in each during our visits and I'd strongly recommend the Holy Island Gin, which is perfectly distilled and sold at The Ship Inn.

Pilgrims Coffee Shop sells the best coffee and cakes, and visits to the distillery, the castle and the priory are a must while visiting the island.

As with all stories, some details have been changed to suit the story and tide times may have varied. However, I did try to keep this story as true to the island as I could and at the time of editing, I even tried to include some details of Storm Arwen, which would have happened during the timeline of the story, destroying many parts, including some of the essential causeway that links the island to the mainland. Barbeques on the beach, along with camping, are now forbidden, but again for the story content, I have included a scene where fire baskets and barbeques are used beside the lime kilns. In reality, this hasn't been allowed now for many years. So please, don't go to Lindisfarne to do this. It's a beautiful place and needs to stay that way for many years to come.

A very special mention goes to Christine Tootle, who during Children in Need joined in an online auction for a signed copy of my book and gave an amazing amount of money. And as it does every year, every penny of it went to the children. THANK YOU x

As always, I would like to thank my amazing husband, Haydn. He's my whole world, my absolute rock. We've been together now for thirty years and I have no idea what I'd do without him.

Also, to my brothers and sisters who keep me grounded on a daily basis. Stuart & Joanne Thompson, Alan & Jayne Stacey, you're all amazing.

Special thanks to the best friends in the world, Annemarie Brear, Kathy Kilner, Jean Fullerton, Jenny Woodall, Milly Johnson, Chrissie Bradshaw, Amanda James, Jane Lovering, Rachel Dove & Elaine Everest. Each one of you are very special to me, you all help me continually and I'm sending so much love to you all. xx

Many thanks to all the team at Boldwood Books. I'm not surprised you won Publisher of the Year at the recent RNA (Romantic Novelists' Association) awards. Without a doubt, you're a wonderful publisher and deserve every accolade.

And last but definitely not least, to my fabulous editor, Emily Ruston, who seems to keep me on track. She always knows exactly what the story needs to give it that perfect level of tension and I have no idea what I'd do without her. Thank you x

MORE FROM L.H. STACEY

We hope you enjoyed reading *The Serial Killer's Girl*. If you did, please leave a review.

If you'd like to gift a copy, this book is also available as an ebook, digital audio download and audiobook CD.

Sign up to L.H. Stacey's mailing list for news, competitions and updates on future books.

https://bit.ly/LyndaStaceyNewsletter

The Sisters Next Door, another gripping thriller from L.H. Stacey, is available now.

ABOUT THE AUTHOR

L.H. Stacey is the bestselling psychological suspense author of five novels. Alongside her writing she is a fulltime sales director for an office furniture company and has been a nurse, an emergency first response instructor and a PADI Staff Instructor. She lives near Doncaster with her husband.

Visit Lynda's website: http://www.lyndastacey.co.uk/

Follow Lynda on social media:

facebook.com/Lyndastaceyauthor

twitter.com/Lyndastacey

instagram.com/lynda.stacey

bookbub.com/authors/lynda-stacey

ABOUT BOLDWOOD BOOKS

Boldwood Books is a fiction publishing company seeking out the best stories from around the world.

Find out more at www.boldwoodbooks.com

Sign up to the Book and Tonic newsletter for news, offers and competitions from Boldwood Books!

http://www.bit.ly/bookandtonic

We'd love to hear from you, follow us on social media:

facebook.com/BookandTonic

twitter.com/BoldwoodBooks

instagram.com/BookandTonic